SUMMER
at HOPE
HAVEN

Books by Kristin Harper

Aunt Ivy's Cottage
A Letter from Nana Rose

SUMMER *at* HOPE HAVEN

KRISTIN HARPER

FOREVER

NEW YORK   BOSTON

Copyright © 2020 by Kristin Harper

Cover design by Brigid Pearson
Cover images © Shutterstock
Cover copyright © 2022 by Hachette Book Group, Inc.

Forever
Hachette Book Group
1290 Avenue of the Americas, New York, NY 10104
read-forever.com
twitter.com/readforeverpub

Originally published in 2020 by Bookouture in the United Kingdom
First US edition: October 2022

Forever is an imprint of Grand Central Publishing. The Forever name and logo are trademarks of Hachette Book Group, Inc.

The publisher is not responsible for websites (or their content) that are not owned by the publisher.

The Hachette Speakers Bureau provides a wide range of authors for speaking events. To find out more, go to www.hachettespeakersbureau.com or call (866) 376-6591.

ISBNs: 9781538724361 (mass market)

Printed in the United States of America

OPM

10 9 8 7 6 5 4 3 2 1

In memory of Peter S.

With thanks to my parents, for giving me the ocean

And to my editor, Ellen Gleeson, for her vision

CHAPTER ONE

Emily Vandemark came to Hope Haven to get away from people, but the place was teeming with them, like minnows. She didn't remember Dune Island being this crowded when she vacationed here with her family as a child. Cyclists and pedestrians flanked both sides of the road and nimble beachgoers darted in between cars as they made their way past the crowded stretch of sand known as Beach Plum Cove. Emily watched them through the window of the cab as if under water. She jiggled her leg and sighed.

"As soon as we pass this beach, we'll speed up," the driver said, glancing at her in his rearview mirror. "It's always mobbed on Memorial Day. Tomorrow it'll quiet down again until school gets out at the end of June. After that, the island's population swells to five or six times its usual size until Labor Day."

Just as he promised, traffic diminished within a few blocks. As they drove toward her destination, the roads narrowed and became curvier. During the last three miles, they didn't pass another vehicle, cyclist or runner. They climbed the final hill, gradual and long, and bordered on the right by woodlands of pitch pine and scrub oak. On the left, the trees thinned out, opening onto wide dunes bending with beachgrass, bayberry and sand heather. *I'm in an Edward*

Hopper painting, Emily thought. At the crest, the vantage revealed a spectacular ocean view and she gasped, in spite of herself. The shimmering azure waves were highlighted by whitecaps; otherwise she might not have known where the ocean ended and the sky began.

They descended the hill a couple hundred yards and turned left, winding their way down a sandy lane toward the sea. Beach rose shrubs—rosa rugosa—overtook the split rail fence running along both sides. At the end, the road branched into a shared driveway big enough for three or four vehicles. Emily assumed the little silver sedan was the car she'd use during her stay. Next to it was a dilapidated mustard-yellow van that she guessed must have belonged to a repairman or delivery person, although she didn't see anyone on the grounds.

Situated sideways on a slight incline to the right was a spacious, modern-style home with sliding glass doors, floor-to-ceiling windows and a multi-level deck. Despite its expansiveness, the house projected an earthy, weathered appearance and blended unobtrusively with the landscape—typical for homes on the island. Down a slope an acre or so to the left and angled perpendicular with the driveway a small, classical Cape-style cottage was tucked among a stand of red cedar and pitch pines.

"Here you are," the driver announced.

There she was, indeed.

She paid him, refusing help with her bags. As he pulled away, she paused, eyeing the view and inhaling the scent of ocean, roses and pine. In a single whiff, every childhood summer came rushing back and Emily could barely contain her tears. She turned toward the cottage. Glimpsing its faded trim and peeling turquoise shutters, she thought, *It looks a lot like I feel.*

Emily began tugging her luggage behind her. The long path from the driveway to the front doorstep was composed of crushed shells, which she realized would make the wheels of her suitcases twist and bump against her ankles. She decided to carry her luggage instead, but she could only manage one piece at a time. She took the bigger one first, leaving her carry-on bag behind.

Taped to the handle of the cottage's sturdy wooden front door, which was the same bleached turquoise color as the shutters, was an envelope with her name on it. Its contents jangled when she peeled it off. She unfolded the note and read:

Dear Emily,

   We hope you had a smooth trip. Here's your cottage key and a key to the car if you need to go out. We've left some goodies for you in the fridge. Can't wait to see you this evening!

   Love,

   Collette and Wilson

The note was legible, which meant Collette must have penned it—Wilson wrote with a stereotypical doctor's scrawl. Emily was grateful for their thoughtfulness, but she still fought the impulse to call the cab company and leave. No one knew she had arrived. She could have pretended she changed her mind at the last minute. She could have phoned Collette and Wilson and said that she canceled her cross-country flight and she wouldn't be following through with her plans after all.

But where would she have gone? Even if she returned to Seattle, what would she have done for the summer? The art history classes she taught at the university had ended until the fall semester and she was allowing two international students to stay in her apartment during the summer break. Squaring her shoulders, she grasped the heart-tipped, forged-iron door handle, turned the key in the lock and went inside.

The door opened onto a small foyer, with a staircase leading to the second floor of the cottage. Emily set down her suitcase. To the right of the entryway was an open-concept living room and dining area, which hosted sliders to a large deck. A breakfast bar separated the dining area from the kitchen around the corner.

Although the house was spick and span—Emily had arranged for it to be professionally cleaned before she arrived—the dark paneling on the walls, scratched hardwood floors and burnt maroon bricks of the fireplace were a gloomy contrast to the scenery outside. Emily hadn't paid much attention to the interior as a child, but suddenly she understood why her mother always tried to convince her grandmother the cottage would have benefitted from a little color. Emily's grandmother, a hoarder who resisted change at all costs, finally agreed to let Emily's mom paint the exterior trim white and the shutters and doors a bright turquoise green, but she hadn't allowed any interior redecorating.

At least Grandma's couch and chairs have been replaced, Emily noticed, recalling how her grandmother's flea-market furniture was even drabber than the walls surrounding it.

The house was so quiet she found herself tiptoeing down the hall, past the kitchen. She peeked into the room on the left, where her parents used to sleep, but she couldn't make herself cross the threshold yet, so she ducked into the bathroom opposite it.

She assumed it was Collette who had put soap near the sink and arranged the hand towels in scalloped folds. Emily glanced at herself in the mirror. Pale, willowy and without a dab of makeup, she wore a long, straight, sleeveless black cotton sundress. Her hair, the color of sand, was pulled into a severe bun at the nape of her neck and her usually vivid green eyes appeared as washed out as the shutters on the cottage. Another sigh escaped her lips.

As she returned to the kitchen, Emily remembered that she'd left her carry-on bag in the driveway. She exited through the sliding doors, stopping on the deck to survey the backyard. In the far corner, a tight path led through the rose hedges and honeysuckle and passed over the dunes toward a staircase to a private beach. Emily would take that path later; for now, she cut across the lawn. The yellow van had reversed from its spot and was idling with the driver's door wide open. Emily arrived just in time to see a man lifting her bag.

"Hey!" she yelled, suddenly enlivened. "What do you think you're doing with that?"

Startled, the man jumped back and dropped her suitcase. Dark and dripping, his hair curled in ringlets around his neck and temples. Beads of water spattered his tanned shoulders. He was wearing navy surf shorts and a sleeveless rash guard shirt. Emily felt a twinge of something—was it fear?—as she noticed the definition of his biceps.

"I'm moving it so I won't run it over." He straightened his posture. "Do you always leave your stuff strewn across the street?"

"It wasn't strewn and that's not a street," Emily snapped as she approached. She was woozy from heat and adrenaline, but she planted herself squarely in front of him. "It's a driveway. A *private* driveway. Which means there's no public beach access here, so I'm going to have to ask you to leave. Now."

An amused look crossed the man's face.

"Actually, I was *trying* to leave. But I do have permission to be here. I'm Lucas. I like to hit the beach to fish or surf and this is about the only spot on the island where I can do that alone this time of year. Wilson and Collette let me park over there."

He gestured toward his van, which was making an alarming rattling noise. When Emily didn't respond, he narrowed his blue eyes as if he was trying to place how he knew her.

"You must be Emily, the artist," he decided. "Wilson told me you were coming today. Sorry, I didn't mean to frighten you."

"You didn't frighten me," Emily said defiantly, although her legs were trembling.

She wondered what else Wilson had told Lucas about her. Before she arranged to come here, she had secured Wilson and Collette's word that they wouldn't tell anyone about... about what had happened. There were already too many people back in Seattle who knew. What happened occupied almost every waking thought she had. She didn't need it emphasized by people asking questions or feeling sorry for her, even if they only intended to be sympathetic. For the second time that day, she felt like bolting.

She grasped her suitcase handle. Lucas reached for it at the same time, his hand clasping hers. The warm pressure of his palm caused her to sway a little, but she didn't release her grip.

"Let me carry this in for you," he offered.

"Thanks, but I don't need any help." Emily jerked the bag away from him.

She turned on her heel and strode toward the cottage. Her arm strained under the weight of her carry-on bag, which primarily contained art textbooks and sketch pads, but she didn't slow her pace. She slid the screen slider open, sharply banged it into place behind her and stormed down the hall and into her parents' old room, where she unceremoniously dropped the luggage in the middle of the floor.

Emily returned to the kitchen to douse her face with cold water and then held her wrists under the faucet. She didn't know if she was more unnerved by the heat and humidity or by her reaction to Lucas. *What has gotten into me, to accost one of Collette and Wilson's friends like that?* She opened the fridge and basked in the icy draft. Collette and Wilson had stocked the shelves with cheese, fruit and yogurt. She couldn't remember when she last ate.

A year ago, Emily carried an extra twenty to twenty-five pounds on her thighs and hips, but now she was probably twenty to twenty-five pounds underweight. Once a compulsive eater and a frequent dieter, she always assumed that people who claimed they forgot to eat were either liars or show-offs. Now, she understood: ever since the day her life fell apart, food was the last thing on her mind and her meals were more often prompted by the clock than by hunger.

Frequently lethargic but unable to sleep, she took no pleasure in being so thin or in losing her appetite. Rationally, she understood that food provided energy. But in practice, fixing meals for herself was a futile chore, since she could rarely swallow more than a few bites. She removed a bowl of grapes and a pitcher of iced tea and set them on the table, as if that might stimulate her hunger.

When it didn't, she went back into the bedroom. Kneeling, she unzipped the carry-on bag, relieved that Lucas hadn't backed over it with his van. Secured in bubble wrap was her most precious possession: a framed photo of her with her mother, father and brother. Broad-shouldered and copper-haired, the men looked arresting in their suits, but Emily and her mother eclipsed them both with their prominent cheekbones, natural blondness and soft femininity. Although the occasion was formal, their smiles were relaxed. The four were gathered arm-in-arm in front of a large painting, *Tulips in April*, which had been part of Emily's first professional gallery exhibit. She placed the photo on her nightstand.

She fished deeper into the small suitcase until her fingertips brushed the soft velvet exterior of a little hexagonal box, which was jostled during the flight and rested near the bottom of her bag. She pulled it out and lifted the pearl-white lid. The three-stone emerald-cut diamond glinted as it caught the light. Emily removed the ring from its cushion to examine the script engraved on the inside of the platinum band: *Now & Forever*.

Not the most original sentiment, nor the most accurate, Emily mused wryly. *Although he got it half right; the "now" part*. She didn't doubt that Devon Richards had fully intended to marry her when he proposed with this ring last July. But so much had changed: the "now" had become "then," and there was no such thing as "forever." Emily replaced the ring and snapped the box shut. She almost regretted bringing it with her, but she knew it had cost a small fortune. Although she trusted the two students who were apartment-sitting for her, there had been break-ins in the complex lately. The ring would be the first thing a thief would steal. No, it was safer here with her, she rationalized.

Maybe after a few more months, she could convince Devon to take it back. She had always been bothered by his insistence that she keep it, as if it were a consolation prize. Suddenly, she wanted the ring out of her sight and she scanned the room for somewhere to stash it. Under her pillow seemed as good of a place as any; after all, this was Dune Island, not Seattle. "The only thing anyone ever steals on Dune Island is a quick nap in a hammock," her father used to joke, making everyone else groan.

Overcome by a wash of loneliness, Emily lay down on the bed and within minutes, the distant arrhythmia of waves against the shore had lulled her to sleep.

When she awoke almost three hours later, it took a few moments for Emily to recognize her surroundings. Her hair clung damply to her neck, reminding her where she was. She stretched, and then ambled into the living room for her other bag. After removing two small gifts—gourmet Seattle coffee for Wilson and a blown glass ornament for Collette—she placed the rest of her belongings in the dresser and closet. As she clicked the drawers shut, she realized that unpacking made staying here that much more definite. But before she could consider fleeing again, she heard wheels rolling down the lane: Wilson and Collette were home from work.

She smoothed her dress and flung open the front door just as Collette raised her hand to knock.

"Emily, welcome!" Collette extended her arms above her burgeoning belly. Her baby boy was due to be born the second week of September.

"Look at you!" Emily responded, hugging Collette back. "You're radiant."

"That's because I'm sweltering from the exertion of walking over here." Collette laughed. "But at this point, I'll take any compliment I can get."

"No, really, you're stunning," Emily reiterated truthfully, eyeing her sleek, inky hair and olive complexion.

Side by side with Collette, who was the picture of robust pregnancy, Emily felt haggard and wan. The concerned look in Wilson's deep brown eyes confirmed her perception of herself. She might have dismissed his worries about her during their phone conversations over the past nine months, but her appearance belied her claims that she had been faring all right.

"Emily." He cleared his throat but didn't say anything more.

Emily hesitated for a second and then dove into his arms. He gave her a gigantic bear hug, the way a brother would. The way *her* brother would. The association caused her throat to tighten and her eyes to brim.

"I brought you something," she announced quickly, feigning cheerfulness.

After making a fuss over their gifts, Wilson and Collette invited Emily to join them for dinner at their house. She tried to decline, but they wouldn't accept her refusal.

"We'll give you all the privacy you want as often as you want after this. But tonight is your first night here. You've got to come up to our place for dinner," Collette insisted. "Nothing elaborate, I'm tossing a salad together and we brought clam chowder home from the best seafood restaurant on the island, Captain Clark's. It's to-die-for and that's not just a craving talking."

Emily conceded and followed them out of the cottage and up the slope to their home. The three of them worked together companionably, chopping vegetables for the salad and setting the table. As they ate, Collette mentioned she'd tried to stock Emily's kitchen with all the essential cookware, dishes and cutlery but if she needed anything else during her stay, she was free to borrow it from Collette's kitchen. Emily thanked her, adding that she appreciated Collette making up the bed for her, too.

"You're welcome. It's new, by the way. Or fairly new. It's the one we moved out of our second guest room, since we're turning it into a nursery. I think I mentioned on the phone that the mattress set was too unwieldly for Wilson and his friend to bring upstairs, which is why they put it in the room on the first floor. I hope that's okay with you?"

Emily would have preferred not to sleep in her parents' old room, but she understood why that wasn't an option. "Sure, it's fine."

"It must have been weird to see the upstairs rooms so bare like that?"

"Mm." Emily hadn't actually been able to make herself go upstairs yet. She wasn't ready to face the rooms she and her brother had used during their blissful summer vacations.

"The rest of the furniture in the cottage is left over from the Johnsons. It's all the stuff that was too big to take with them."

Emily should have guessed as much. Her parents had inherited the cottage when Emily's maternal grandparents died ten years ago, but by that time, Emily's immediate family had long since moved from Connecticut to Chicago and their Dune Island summers had become a thing of the past. So, her parents had rented out the little house year-round to the Johnsons until the elderly couple needed to move into an assisted living facility. For the past three years, Wilson and Collette had kept an eye on the vacant cottage, which the Vandemarks invited them to use to host guests they couldn't accommodate in their own home.

Not that they needed the extra space; their house was huge. Originally, Wilson's grandparents, the Laurents, had owned a summer cottage just like the Vandemarks', but it had sustained extensive water damage in the aftermath of a particularly severe ice storm. When Wilson decided to move to the island permanently to work in the hospital here, he'd had the cottage razed and built the modern dwelling on the same site. *A building can be replaced—people can't*, Emily lamented silently.

"How long has it been since the last time you came to Dune Island?" Collette's question pulled Emily back to the present.

"Um . . . I was twelve, so I guess it's been close to eighteen years."

"A lot has changed since then," Wilson informed her. "For one thing, there's poison ivy growing near the staircase now. It's mixed in with the roses and honeysuckle, so you'll want to avoid picking those when they're in bloom."

"We've also had a couple of rip currents to the west of the beach stairs," Collette added.

"And we still don't get as much traffic out here as the rest of the island does, but it's definitely increased, so be careful when you're pulling out of the driveway," Wilson advised.

"Sure thing, *Mom and Dad*," Emily teased.

She meant it playfully, but suddenly the topic they'd all been tiptoeing around was out in the open. Their cheerful pretense shriveled like a stale party balloon.

"W-we didn't mean to sound like…" Collette faltered.

"No, of course not," Emily apologized. "I really didn't take it that way, either. I know you're just looking out for me."

Wilson hastily changed the subject to the unpredictability of island weather and they resumed eating. Emily forced herself to swallow a few spoonfuls of chowder, but if it was as delicious as Collette claimed, she hardly tasted it. She prattled on about the marvelous view from their house, the tasteful décor and especially Wilson and Collette's generosity in allowing her to use their second car for the summer.

"You're the one doing us a favor," Wilson said. "Everyone at the hospital is amazed such a talented artist is refusing any kind of compensation."

"It's a privilege to contribute to a good cause."

As Emily quoted her brother's life motto, Wilson winced. Even as a boy, Peter had demonstrated an unusual commitment to serving others. Just like Emily's parents, her brother would have gone to any extreme to help someone in need—especially children—in whatever capacity he could. That was part of the reason Emily had come to Dune Island: to carry on the family legacy by painting murals in the newly constructed pediatric wing of the hospital. Insisting she would only participate in the project on the condition that she could do it on a volunteer basis, she'd adamantly turned down the offer of a stipend.

The other condition of her presence here was far more personal. Emily had asked Wilson and Collette to promise they wouldn't tell anyone about the helicopter crash that killed her father, mother and brother nearly nine months ago, last August. It happened high in the Honduran mountains, where her parents—a retired special ed teacher and a school counselor—had relocated in order to teach schoolchildren through a newly established literacy program. Peter, a child welfare social worker, had visited them there during a vacation once, and he was so moved by the people he met that he arranged to return last summer to help out with a short-term disaster relief construction project.

After the accident, the school near Chicago where Emily's parents used to work sent her a copy of their campus publication featuring a tribute to her parents. It said: *While delivering medical aid, food and school supplies to a storm-ravaged village nearby, Janice and Frederick Vandemark, along with their son, Peter, paid the ultimate price for putting their beliefs into action...*

No doubt the reporter's homage to the Vandemarks was meant to convey admiration, but after reading it, Emily tore up the article, crying, "No matter how eloquently it's phrased, they're still dead, dead, dead."

By the time of the crash, Emily had been living in Seattle for several years, Peter was still in Chicago, and their parents resided several countries away. But they were close-knit and stayed in contact through weekly phone calls, email and texts. Emily's parents were almost forty by the time she was born, and her father had suffered ill health when she was in high school. Even so, losing one of her parents was a possibility Emily had hated to even imagine: losing both of them and Peter all at once was utterly unfathomable.

Since her mother and father didn't have any siblings and Peter was a bachelor, Wilson was the closest person to a living relative Emily had left. The Vandemarks had been his "second family" ever since his grandparents brought him to the cottage when he was around five. His mother had died the previous summer in an auto accident and his dad was out of the picture altogether. Since Wilson's grandfather had been partially immobilized by a stroke, Emily's father assumed the role of a substitute dad during the three-month summer breaks.

Only a few months younger than Wilson, Peter was his best friend and Emily adored them both, referring to them as "the twins." The connection between the Vandemark family and Wilson was so strong that he frequently visited them during the school year, too, and eventually Peter and Wilson ended up being undergrad roommates at the same university. If it hadn't been for Wilson, Emily didn't know how she would have gotten through her family's burial.

Propped up between Wilson and Devon in the front pew at the memorial service, she had been too incapacitated by trauma and sedatives to deliver the eulogies, but Wilson spoke for them both. Whatever he said completely escaped her addled memories of that day, but she'd never forget that when he took his place next to her again, she had burrowed her face into his shoulder, not her fiancé's, to conceal her tears.

The service was held in the Chicago suburb where Emily had spent her teen years and when they bid each other farewell at the airport, Wilson whispered into her ear, "We've still got each other and we have to stick together, okay?"

Six months later, when Devon broke up with Emily in February, Wilson intervened again. He told her about the art project at the hospital and unrelentingly pressured her to spend the summer on the island.

"Don't make me come out there and put you in a sleeper hold," he threatened with hyperbolic machismo. "You know I'll do it."

It was this reference to her brother's comical childhood taunt—Peter was so gentle he wouldn't hurt a fly—that finally won Emily over. In that moment, she felt as if she'd collapse if she couldn't be near the only other person who knew her family like she did. Now she fidgeted in her chair, questioning her decision. Not only had being back at the cottage and seeing Wilson stirred memories she'd rather suppress, but she suspected her presence there was unsettling for him, too. Pushing a potato around in her chowder, she avoided making eye contact until they'd finished supper.

Afterward, they stepped out onto the deck to gaze at the stars, but the cloud cover was too thick and the heavy evening air swarmed with mosquitoes. Recognizing Collette and Wilson were probably tired after a long day of work, Emily suggested she should go.

"I'll walk you to your door," Wilson offered.

"That's okay. I'll find my way back."

As Emily crept through the dark shadows, she realized she wasn't at all sure of her direction. Just like she wasn't sure whether she should have come to Dune Island or what good it would do anyone for her to be here. But since there was no turning around now, she continued moving forward, one step at a time.

CHAPTER TWO

A metallic breeze ruffled the curtains and thunder reverberated in the distance. Emily pulled the sheet over her shoulders. Because of the difference in time zones and the afternoon nap she took, she wasn't very sleepy. But, since her phone was out of range, there wasn't a television in the cottage and she'd deliberately left her laptop in Seattle, Emily changed into her nightgown, got into bed and turned out the light.

The smell of the salty air filled her with wistfulness. If only she'd come to Dune Island under different circumstances, like a vacation. Or a honeymoon. She dismissed the thought as soon as it came to mind. One thing Emily had learned that year was she couldn't live on *if only* or *what if*. She could only live on *what is*.

She reflected on how vivacious Collette appeared, but Wilson seemed preoccupied. Not quite himself. Given that he was still grieving, too, Emily supposed that was understandable, although it was odd that his chocolate-brown hair had become speckled with gray overnight. Then she realized it hadn't been overnight; it had been nine months since she'd seen Collette and Wilson at the funeral. At the funeral*s*. The plural form of that word caused Emily's heart to shudder within her chest.

As she rolled over, she felt a hard lump beneath her pillow. The ring box. She switched on the light and set the box on her nightstand next to the photo of her family and her. Looking at the two items side-by-side, she thought, *The photo was my past. The ring was my future. And now they're both gone.* Hot tears pattered down her cheeks.

In three months, it would be a year; wasn't that the traditional mourning period? And wasn't the world filled with people who were suffering far worse than she was? *I've got to get a grip*, she told herself for what felt like the millionth time. *I've got to think about something other than my loss. My losses. Starting work tomorrow should help with that.*

Collette, Wilson and the pediatric foundation officers might have thought she was being altruistic, and it was true that she wanted to use her talents to brighten someone else's experience if she could. But Emily was acutely aware that one of the main reasons she agreed to participate in the art project was because it would require her to focus on something different for a change.

It wouldn't be like in Seattle, where, after the accident, she had taught art history classes on autopilot. Here she'd have to concentrate. She'd have to exercise her creativity, which had lain dormant for so long that she'd begun to wonder if she could even call herself an artist anymore. Granted, painting murals in the children's wing of a hospital wasn't exactly high art, but it would be better than painting nothing.

Rather, it would be better than painting layer upon layer of gray on canvas after canvas, the way she'd done for weeks until Devon pointed out how uninspired she seemed. He was right, of course, but he hadn't understood the herculean effort it took just to go through the motions of normalcy. His observation squelched whatever minuscule glimmer of motivation she had left. After that, she stowed her brushes and canvases in the storage area in the basement of her apartment complex.

Once again, Emily shook her head and tried to focus on something positive. The best part about the project was that, with the exception of a few meetings with the board president, she'd be working completely independently. The pediatric wing wouldn't open until the end of the summer, when the last of the medical equipment would be installed, so she'd have the corridor mostly to herself.

In Seattle, Emily had taught large classes in a big lecture hall, which created a certain degree of distance between her and her students. Prior to the accident, she was always coming up with ways to bridge that gap, whether through hosting extracurricular art workshops, eating lunch in the Student Center or taking the students to local galleries.

But after her parents and brother died, she stopped trying to connect with her students—and with the faculty—on a personal level. For the first time in her teaching career, the evaluations her students submitted at the end of the semester were overwhelmingly negative and reflected her lack of engagement with them and with the subject material.

Not only did she isolate herself at the university, but she dropped out of her artists' group and stopped hanging out with her friends, too. Eventually, Devon was the only person she had any significant relationship with and he was traveling most of the time for work, anyway, until he broke up with her...

Emily redirected her thoughts, mentally reviewing the timeline for the project, and she began to relax. Over the past year, the days seemed to stretch on forever and she'd had too much time to think. She used to value the flexibility of her adjunct faculty teaching position, but right now having a clear purpose and a definite timeframe filled her with a sense of relief. Instead of focusing on the one-year anniversary of when Devon proposed or the one-year anniversary of the accident, she'd have a completely different deadline to consider.

"I can manage this," she said aloud as she turned out the light again.

*

For the first time since receiving the phone call about the accident, Emily slept more hours than she was awake during the night. In the morning, she buried the ring box back under her pillow, made the bed and then dallied in front of the closet, wondering what to wear.

Since she wouldn't start painting yet, she chose the most formal item of clothing she'd brought: a mid-calf, steel-gray sheath dress with cap sleeves. It was kind of prim, but after this she'd be wearing old tees and jeans, so she figured she might as well make an attempt to appear pulled together, even if she didn't feel that way. She slipped on a pair of low heels, grabbed a yogurt from the fridge and headed toward the car.

The lawn was wet from the night's rain and the air was fresh and crisp. A wild rabbit munching on the grass bounded away as she passed. When she noticed that Wilson and Collette's other car was gone, Emily snapped her fingers—she had forgotten to tell them about her interaction with Lucas yesterday. She wanted to extend her apologies for alienating him.

She'd also forgotten to ask them the shortest way to the hospital. When Emily was a child, her family infrequently ventured away from the cottage, except to go to the grocery store, since everything else they could ever want lay just beyond their back yard. But even if Emily had driven by the hospital as a young girl, she wouldn't have been paying attention to how to get there, the way she memorized how to get to other places, like the boardwalk or the drive-in theater her father took them to once every summer.

Oh well, I guess I'll take the scenic route, she thought. As she veered along the hills and bluffs beside the ocean, Emily recognized it was *all* the scenic route, no matter which roads she traveled.

Yesterday's driver was right: even on the main roads, traffic was much lighter today and a lone fisherman was the only figure at Beach Plum Cove. Along the primary thoroughfare, Emily followed the blue-and-white signs depicting the way to the hospital. Five towns, sometimes still referred to as villages or hamlets, collectively comprised Hope Haven, and she passed through three of them this morning. The hospital was centrally located in the most populated town, Port Newcomb.

Ready or not, she thought as the automatic doors parted and she walked through the hospital entrance.

Tim Donovan, the hospital's president of fundraising, was waiting for her inside the main lobby. Short, stout and talkative, he welcomed her warmly and thanked her profusely as he led her to a small conference room. There he told her all about the department's efforts to help develop the children's wing at Hope Haven Hospital.

"Wilson may have told you already, but our final fundraiser will be a silent art auction at the end of the summer. The event will feature new art by some of the island's most prominent artists and we've timed it to coincide with the opening of the children's wing."

"Yes, he mentioned that."

In fact, Wilson had also told Emily that Clive McGrath, a renowned New York City artist who now permanently secluded himself away somewhere on the island, was contributing a painting. Wilson had tried to cajole Emily into donating one, too, but she refused on the grounds she wasn't technically an island artist. In truth, she couldn't imagine painting anything new someone would want to buy; the mural was already going to be a stretch.

"It sounds like a wonderful way to wrap up the campaign and I'm sure the event will be very successful," she added.

Tim bobbed his head enthusiastically. "We're all very excited about it. We're thrilled about your murals, too. Can you tell me a little bit about your vision for the rooms?"

Emily swallowed, stalling. When Tim first contacted her by email, he'd provided general guidelines for what the Board hoped she'd paint. Animals, of course. And nature scenes. But nothing commercial or copyrighted, such as characters from books, movies or cartoons. It also was important for the murals to be gender-neutral and appropriate for toddlers as well as for teenagers. But so far the only idea she'd come up with was the most obvious one; she'd paint a seascape.

"I, uh, have some nature scenes in mind, but until I see the space, I hesitate to go into too much detail," she fudged.

"Ah, well, that makes sense. You're the expert, so whatever you create, we trust your taste. We've seen samples of your art. It's really gorgeous."

"Thank you," Emily said aloud. But she was thinking, *You might not be saying that if you could see the endless gray canvases in my basement.*

Tim slapped his hands against his knees and then rose from his chair. "Let's go get you a photo ID and key card so you'll have access to the wing and you can work whenever the muse strikes you."

By the time the security office had processed Emily's paperwork, it was almost noon.

"We're right on schedule for you to meet Dr. Socorro, the newest pediatric ER physician to join Hope Haven's staff," Tim said. "He's been a huge advocate for the project and he's going to give you a tour of the children's wing, since I've got to attend a home meeting with one of our major donors. But you'll like Dr. Socorro. He's got a great sense of what appeals to kids and he'll be your on-site go-to person if you need him for anything urgent. He'll treat you to lunch in the cafeteria, if you have time?"

Emily remembered the yogurt she left unopened in the car and she realized she hadn't eaten since last night.

"That would be wonderful. Thank you."

"No, thank *you*. We value what you're doing for Hope Haven. We know how rare it is for an artist of your caliber to donate her time and talent for a project of this scope."

"I'm happy to help," Emily automatically responded.

As she spoke the words aloud, she realized they weren't altogether untrue. *Happy* might not have been the best word to describe her emotional state, but everyone was so appreciative and the project seemed so meaningful that she momentarily felt *less sad* than she normally felt. Her discussion with Tim had at least sparked a sense of ambition, if not happiness. She was eager to meet Dr. Socorro to discuss ideas for the murals and other decorative touches, too.

"Ah, here's the good doctor now," said Tim as they approached a man who was studying the menu board outside the cafeteria. "Dr. Socorro, there's someone here I'd like you to meet."

The doctor turned around, grinning broadly, his hair an unruly mass of coils.

"Nice to see you again, Emily." He extended his hand. "But please, call me Lucas."

Dumbfounded, Emily hesitated before shaking his hand. Lucas seemed to hold her fingers in his a moment longer than necessary and she found herself disconcerted by his touch.

"You two know each other?" Tim questioned.

"Sure, we go way back," Lucas said, giving Emily a wink.

At exactly the same moment, she answered curtly, "No."

Tim looked puzzled, so Emily explained that they'd met briefly, but she hadn't realized he was a physician here.

"Well, then, I'll leave you two to get better acquainted. I wish I could stay for lunch, too, but I've got to run. If you need anything, just call," Tim said before loping off.

"This place serves the best hospital food on the island," Lucas joked, handing Emily a tray once they'd stepped up to the counter.

She twisted her lips into a semblance of a smile. As they were standing in line, a young boy maneuvered his way alongside them in a wheelchair. His parents trailed behind.

"Hey, buddy, no cuts," Lucas reprimanded him in an exaggeratedly gruff tone.

"Dr. Luke!" The boy gleefully exchanged a fist-bump with Lucas.

"We forgot his milk," his mother explained.

"Psst." Lucas leaned down and mock-whispered into the boy's ear, "There's chocolate milk in that other cooler."

"Good job, Socorro, encouraging your pedi patients to indulge in extra sugar," a woman's voice drawled flirtatiously from behind Emily after the parents and the boy passed by them.

"You know it," Lucas bantered back. "I just hope he leaves a couple of cartons for me."

Emily silently took it all in. Everyone seemed to want to talk to Lucas—no, to *Dr. Luke*. Especially the women. With his brawny physique, curly hair and affable smile, he exuded confidence. Because he didn't wear a wedding ring, she assumed he was single. Five or six more people stopped him to chat as he led Emily to a table for two, smack in the middle of the dining area. He unloaded his dishes from the tray, which he slid under his chair so there would be room for hers. The space was so tight that her knees knocked into his when she sat down.

"Cheers," he said, raising his carton of milk. Emily returned a small smile.

Struggling to cut her grilled chicken breast with a plastic knife, she took a bite of salad greens instead, while Lucas hungrily attacked his toasted cheese sandwich. *No wonder kids like him so much. He eats just like one.* She couldn't decide if it was endearing or unappetizing.

"Sorry," he mumbled when he noticed her watching him. "I'm starving."

Tongue-tied, she touched her napkin to her mouth and nodded.

After his sandwich was gone, Lucas leaned back and clasped his hands behind his head. "So, Emily, tell me a little bit about yourself.

Personally, I mean—I've already read your professional résumé and seen your paintings, which are amazing."

"There's not a lot to tell," she responded demurely and set down her fork. The cafeteria was so loud and cramped that she felt queasy—her body's recent response to crowded places. She continued, "But I'm very interested in hearing your thoughts on what kind of artwork you'd suggest for the wing. Tim said you have a lot of good insights about what might appeal to the kids you treat."

Lucas apparently was oblivious to her attempt to change the subject. "We'll get to that when I show you the wing. Right now I'm curious to hear what you like to do for fun when you're not painting. Or when you're not apprehending trespassers."

Emily cringed ever so slightly at the reference. What did she like to do for fun? It had been so long since she'd had fun that she drew a blank. She shrugged and took a sip of water.

"All right, maybe you could tell me about things you *don't* like, then," he prodded. "Other than the hospital's version of grilled chicken, obviously."

Emily tensed her jaw, embarrassed that he had drawn attention to her appetite. She couldn't tell from his dopey smile if he was goading her to get a reaction or if he was merely trying to break the ice. She didn't mean to be so uptight; it was just that seeing him here had thrown her completely off guard after the way she'd spoken to him and it seemed as if he was reveling in her uneasiness.

Determined to maintain a professional demeanor, she responded politely, "It looks really good, but I'm not very hungry right now. I'll pack it up to take it home and enjoy later."

Emily went to get a takeout container. When she returned, the auburn-haired woman who'd made the crack about the chocolate milk was standing over the table with her back to Emily, blocking her way as she chatted with Lucas.

"Was that the artist who was eating with you—or should I say, *not* eating with you?" the woman asked. Emily didn't hear Lucas's response before the woman continued. "She's awfully skinny. Does she have an eating disorder?"

"I don't know, but even if she does, it's none of our business," he replied.

Emily brusquely pushed past the woman and slapped the takeout container on the table. "I'm going to the ladies' room."

In her haste to get away, she nearly knocked into someone seated at the next table, but Emily didn't stop moving until she'd reached the women's room. Her legs felt spongy and she leaned against the sink, breathing rapidly as she recalled a conversation she'd overheard between a few of her students last semester. They were talking about how thin Emily had become and one of them suggested she was either a drug addict or she was anorexic. Emily wasn't abusing drugs, nor was she deliberately abstaining from food. She simply had no desire for it.

When Emily expressed concern about the issue, her doctor recommended that until her appetite returned, she should take a multi-vitamin and try eating according to the clock so that she'd still get adequate nutrition. She also suggested counseling or a bereavement support group, both of which Emily had already tried, but talking about her family only made her feel worse.

"You're going through a lot," the doctor had responded, touching Emily's arm. "Give yourself—and your body—time to recover."

The students hadn't been as compassionate. "Whether it's drugs or anorexia, she looks like a scarecrow," one of them said. "It's too bad—she was a lot prettier when she was fat."

Emily had retreated to the faculty lounge and peered into a mirror. By "scarecrow," she wasn't sure if the students were referring to her wardrobe, her hair or her weight. As she studied her reflection, she realized they'd probably meant all three. Her clothes hung from her shoulders as if from a hanger and her hair stuck out like straw. After that, she was careful to wear only dark or neutral-toned clothing and to tie her hair back, so as not to draw attention to herself. Apparently, however, there was no hiding her figure—or lack of one.

Thinking about it again, she shook her head and dampened a paper towel to cool her blazing cheeks. As appalled as she was that the woman in the cafeteria had made such a personal remark about her health, she was strangely disappointed to realize that Lucas probably thought she looked like a scarecrow, too.

After soothing her skin, Emily practiced deep breathing for several minutes until her emotions were soothed, too. Then she emerged from the women's room and collected her lunch. Lucas took her on a tour of the new wing, where a few electricians, carpenters and technicians were working on various tasks. Just as in the cafeteria, everyone seemed to know him. A couple of the men greeted him in a language Emily didn't recognize, but that Lucas seemed able to speak fluently.

"That's not Spanish," she commented conversationally. "But it sounds similar. You're bilingual?"

"It's Portuguese, but I wouldn't say I'm fluent in it. I spent some time in Portugal, working with a disaster relief organization."

The words *disaster relief* caused Emily's heart to palpitate and she dropped the subject. Lucas showed her the room where the brushes, special non-toxic paints and other supplies they had ordered on her behalf were being stored. He indicated he'd be stopping by from time to time to see how it was going, but otherwise, he'd leave the project in her capable hands. As they were exchanging cell phone numbers, in case there was anything she needed to discuss, Lucas was paged overhead and he apologetically excused himself.

No need to be sorry on my account, Emily thought as he dashed off. Emotionally enervated, she slowly meandered through the corridor one more time before leaving for the day.

On her way home, she stopped at a market in the town called Lucinda's Hamlet, or Lucy's Ham, as it was known to the islanders. *Awfully skinny? I'll show her!* she thought as she loaded her cart with food to spite the red-headed woman in the cafeteria.

Back at the cottage, she surveyed her purchases. Potato salad, cheese ravioli, a frozen chicken pot pie, bagels, cream cheese and two pints of ice cream were among the more fattening items she'd deliberately selected. Now, she regretted her choices, knowing she'd probably have to throw out half of the stuff uneaten.

Right then she would have liked nothing more than a bowl of her mother's homemade chicken soup. And she would have liked her mother to sit on the edge of her bed and talk to her while she was sipping spoonfuls. *But*, she lectured herself sternly, *I'm not a child and I'm not sick. And my mother isn't here to make everything all better again even if I were.*

Emily unzipped her dress and pulled on a pair of dark capri leggings and a sweatshirt. The day felt too chilly for a swim, but it was temperate enough for a walk. She paused at the bottom of the beach stairs, unable to tell from looking at the moist, flat sand bars whether the tide was on its way in or out. Emily remembered that a mile to the right the land was interrupted by a small inlet. It offered an idyllic place to swim, but it also made walking any farther impossible. To the left, there was nothing but wide open ocean, cliffs and sand for a good three or four miles, with only a few houses dotting the dunes until the beach rounded toward the mainland and eventually was cut off at the harbor. Emily walked in that direction.

The wind lashed against her face and she pulled her hood over her ears like a cocoon, as if to disappear within her own thoughts. Within seconds, it blew back down around her shoulders. Like it or not, the seascape intruded upon every one of her senses. An array of hues before her eyes. The commotion of waves against her ears. Beach-rose scent for her nose. Fine granules beneath her feet. Even the taste of briny air on her tongue. With each step, she felt a little more invigorated, as if sloughing off a lengthy hibernation.

By the time she returned and stomped the sand off her feet at the top of the landing, Emily not only felt hungry, she felt famished. She took a pint of ice cream from the freezer, a soup spoon from the drawer and settled into one of the chairs Collette and Wilson must have provided for her deck. A few minutes later, she noticed Collette filling a bird feeder up on the hill and she waved.

Collette padded over to where Emily was sitting. "Ooh, ice cream before dinner."

"Ice cream *instead* of dinner. Want some?"

"Does the pregnant woman want ice cream? Do you even need to ask?"

Emily chuckled and retrieved a spoon and the other pint from the freezer.

"Mmm," Collette hummed. "This is so creamy. Wilson can be such a worrywart about what I eat. He says it's because of the baby, but I think he's secretly concerned about my weight."

"No way," Emily declared. "I'm sure you're at a healthy pregnancy weight and you look fantastic."

"Tell that to my ankles." Collette propped her puffy feet up on the little glass table. "My ob/gyn says this amount of swelling isn't cause for concern, but it makes wearing shoes very uncomfortable. I know the phrase 'barefoot and pregnant' has a negative connotation, but taking off my shoes when I get home is the second best part of my day—taking off my maternity bra is the first."

Collette's unpretentious, easygoing attitude had a relaxing effect on Emily and she chuckled as Collette laughed at herself.

"Uh-oh, here comes the worrywart now," Collette whispered fondly when Wilson came trudging down the hill.

"Sorry to interrupt, but I brought Emily a flashlight. In case she needs to come over or walk to her car at night or something."

"That was thoughtful," Emily replied, but she wished he'd stop worrying about her. His face was lined with that same apprehensive expression today that she'd noticed the day before. Where was that infectious grin he used to wear? *Not that* I'm *one to judge* . . .

Wilson must have just spotted the carton Collette was holding because he asked, "Is that fudge brownie ice cream you're eating?"

Emily and Collette caught each other's eyes, before Collette said, "No. It's *chocolate* brownie," as if that clearly made it a healthier choice.

"You look more rested, Emily. Did you have a good sleep last night?"

"Yes." *But it doesn't seem like* you *did*, she thought. "Must be this ocean air. It's making me hungry, too."

"Yeah, that'll do it." Instead of sitting in either of the other two chairs, Wilson shifted from foot to foot as if he was eager to leave, but Collette kept chatting.

"How did your meeting go today?" she asked Emily.

"It went well. Tim Donovan was very informative and appreciative and I got to see the children's wing, too. It gave me a few more ideas for the mural." Actually, it had given Emily a few more *qualms* because she hadn't realized how big the patients' family room was. How would she ever fill its walls?

"You must have met Lucas, too?"

"Yeah," Emily answered offhandedly and tapped an ant off her shin. Lucas's conversation with that other staff member at lunch was so impertinent that she wasn't about to repeat it to Wilson and Collette. She'd feel self-conscious all over again.

"He's a real ladies' man," Collette announced in-between taking licks from her spoon. "At least, the women on staff all love him."

Really? I hadn't noticed, Emily thought.

"From what I've heard, he doesn't usually date women he works with. Not for long, anyway. I think there was one doctor he was seeing for a while when he first got here, but that's been over for ages. Rumor has it, she wasn't too happy about it ending, either."

Collette heaved her body from the low chair and handed Emily the spoon and half-empty carton. Without a hint of irony, she said, "I'd better go start supper now. Thanks for the decadence."

"Whenever you need the good stuff, you know where to find me," Emily said. Then, addressing Wilson, she added, "Pretend you didn't hear that. I don't want to be blamed for leading your wife astray."

Collette laughed but Wilson's smile looked more like a grimace. Was Collette right, was he truly concerned about her weight? Or was something more serious—something other than losing his best friend and Emily's parents—troubling him? For Wilson's sake, Emily hoped not. He'd already been through enough to last two lifetimes.

Within a few hours, Emily was snuggled in bed, pleasantly tired. She pictured the family room in the children's wing and tried to imagine what kind of images would make the best first impression on patients and visitors. Her thoughts jumped to the first impressions she and Lucas had made on each other.

She was struck by the realization that while Lucas and that other staff member might have assumed that she had an eating disorder, Emily had assumed that Lucas was a thief. She might not have called him one outright, but that was how she had treated him.

One of the qualities Emily had admired most in her father was that he never held a grudge against anyone, ever. One time she asked him how he could always be so forgiving, regardless of how severely he'd been offended or hurt.

"Because I've been forgiven for all sorts of offenses myself," was his simple reply.

It dawned on Emily that maybe she was wrong to interpret Lucas's comments at lunch as being taunting and his grin as being smug. After all, he'd seemed genuine when he'd complimented her art by calling it amazing. It was wholly possible that *she* had been hypersensitive because, well, because everything.

In either case, before falling asleep Emily decided she'd start anew with Lucas the next time she saw him.

CHAPTER THREE

Emily woke on Wednesday morning with a nasty stomachache. No matter how hungry she was or how desperately she wanted to gain weight, she vowed she'd never eat an entire pint of ice cream for dinner again.

Now that she had met with Tim and seen the children's wing in person, she figured there was no sense in going back to the hospital until she was actually ready to start the murals, and she couldn't do that until she had a better idea of what she'd paint. Since she was too nauseated to eat breakfast, Emily grabbed a sketch pad and pencil and stepped out onto the deck for some fresh air.

What kinds of things would I want to look at if I were sick or in pain? she asked herself. Because her stomach was cramping, the question didn't exactly require a stretch of the imagination. After settling into a chair, Emily pressed the tip of her pencil to the paper, but that was as far as she got. It was as if she literally couldn't move her wrist and after a few minutes, she let the sketch pad slip onto the deck. She pulled her legs up to her abdomen and wrapped her arms around them. The pressure felt good physically, but her mental block about what to paint was making her head fuzzy.

Facing the white walls at the hospital yesterday had reminded her of facing a blank canvas, except the walls were even more intimidating because they were bigger than any canvas she'd ever painted. She closed her eyes and chewed on the end of the pencil, hoping an idea would spring to mind. She supposed she could do a full seascape in the family room and individual details of marine life in each of the patients' rooms.

"No, too predictable," she muttered aloud.

"Eh-hem," someone coughed nearby a moment later.

Emily's eyes flew open. She expected to see Collette or Wilson, but it was Lucas who stood over her. Although he was wearing surf clothes, his hair was dry and he held a mug in each hand. She jumped up, embarrassed that he might have caught her talking to herself.

Lucas explained he'd come over at dawn to go fishing. He was next door bemoaning the fact he hadn't caught anything when he saw Emily on her deck. Since he'd had to dash off so abruptly the previous afternoon, he wanted to check in to ask if she had any follow-up questions or concerns about the children's wing.

"I think you covered everything for now," she said. Then, remembering her pledge to be more cordial to him, she added, "But thanks for asking. I appreciate it."

"Sure, no problem." A frown was creasing his forehead. "Are you okay? You look a little peaked."

"I'm fine. I was just gathering inspiration from the view."

"With your eyes closed?"

Emily giggled. "Yeah. No wonder I have artist's block, huh?"

"You have artist's block?"

Emily hesitated. She didn't want Lucas or the Board to lose confidence in her. "Yeah, but it's all part of the creative process. Don't worry, it will pass."

"I'm not worried," Lucas replied, holding her gaze as he held out a mug. "Here, maybe a little caffeine will wake up your artistic muse. It's piping hot—Collette just made it."

"Thanks, but I don't drink coffee."

Lucas's eyebrows shot up. "Is it possible to live in Seattle and not be a coffee drinker?"

"You mean because of the rain or because of all the coffee roasting companies headquartered there?"

"Both." Lucas chuckled, easing into a chair and setting one of the mugs on the glass table.

Since he appeared to be staying, Emily sat back down, too. He stretched one tanned leg straight and bent the other at the knee, resting his hand on top of it. Emily unexpectedly quavered when she remembered Lucas's handshake.

"Do you always come here so early in the morning?" she asked.

"I try to but it depends on the tide. And my shift." Lucas took a long pull from his mug before gesturing toward the sprawling dunes and beyond them, the radiant ocean. "Are you considering a nautical theme for the mural?"

"Maybe, for one of the rooms, anyway. Unless you think that's too much of a cliché for an island hospital?"

"Nah. Not if you come at it from a unique angle."

"Such as?" Emily studied Lucas's profile as he contemplated his answer. He had the kind of pronounced, rectangular jaw and straight-edged nose that was every silhouette artist's dream.

"Such as you'd start out painting the ocean, of course, but then maybe you'd include a pirate ship. And a captain who has a hook for a hand. You'll want to add somebody walking the plank, too, with a school of voracious sharks circling in the water below."

Sharks and pirates? Emily's mouth fell open. *Nothing like giving hospitalized kids nightmares on top of everything else they're already experiencing.* Then she realized Lucas was joking and she played along, tapping her chin thoughtfully.

"I like the shark idea, although it's a little trite. But definitely no pirate ship. And I've been instructed not to paint any characters from books or movies, so Captain Hook is out. How would you feel about a man-eating octopus instead?"

"Could you draw it holding a person in every arm?"

"All eight of them."

Lucas chuckled and then swilled down the last of his coffee. "See? I've helped you eliminate some of the worst ideas anyone could possibly suggest. Whatever you come up with now has to be an improvement."

"Thanks for that."

"Happy to help. I've got plenty more terrible ideas where those came from, so call me if you get stuck again." Lucas stood up and did a one-armed stretch before lifting the other mug from the table and bidding Emily goodbye.

Joking about the murals took the pressure off and Emily spent the day sketching seashells and sand dunes, lighthouses and sail boats, hermit crabs and beach grass. They weren't good sketches—

they reminded her of the kind of mural art found in seafood restaurants—but they were a start. And they helped her decide that although she definitely wanted to paint one room with a marine theme, she was going to create distinct landscapes in each of the other patient rooms. Somehow, she'd unify all the themes in the family room.

That's a problem for another day, she thought as she walked along the beach that evening. The surf, such a deep shade of blue it appeared black, was unusually still—only a narrow lip of white lapped the shore. It fascinated Emily how dramatically different the ocean could be from one tide to the next and for once, she experienced a glimmer of hope instead of a world of dread about what the next day might bring.

*

Unfortunately, what the next day brought were torrential downpours.

"This isn't a cottage—it's an ark," Emily's mother had complained during one particularly rainy summer that forced their family to spend more time indoors reading and doing jigsaw puzzles than they spent outdoors swimming or beachcombing. "Except the ark was probably better decorated."

Emily had always been so thrilled to be on vacation with her family that she never understood how the weather adversely affected her mother, but suddenly she felt like a caged animal herself. Having lived in Seattle for more than five years, she probably should have been used to the rain, but there was something about a "Dune Island deluge," as her mother referred to it, that made Emily want to climb the walls. Or maybe it was the *walls* that made her want to climb the walls. *Mom was right—that paneling is hideous*, she thought.

The rain continued and by Thursday afternoon, Emily was so stir-crazy she considered driving into town, but what would she do there? Shop? Go to the library? The hospital? She wasn't ready for that yet. She also considered going for a walk on the beach. She wouldn't have minded getting drenched, but every once in a while, she heard a rumble of thunder. Even if there wasn't lightning now, there was no guarantee a storm wouldn't come bowling across the sky any moment, and lightning had always made Emily nervous. So instead, she went upstairs to take a look at the ocean from the back windows, hoping it might inspire a few more mural ideas.

But the rain was pelting sideways against the panes, blurring her view. And seeing her and Peter's old bedrooms completely devoid of any furnishings made Emily feel lonelier than ever, as if their childhood never existed.

Grandma would have hated seeing the rooms like this, too, she thought.

According to family lore, long before either Peter or Emily were born, their grandmother started collecting what she referred to as "bric-a-brac" from yard sales, thrift stores, flea markets and the FREE bins that residents placed at the end of their driveways. When her shelves grew too crowded for the knickknacks, she remedied the problem by going "bargain hunting" for more shelves. Eventually, her hoarding habit included amassing furniture and appliances— not just at her home in Maryland, but here on Dune Island, too.

It got to the point when Emily's grandfather was so aggravated he insisted that for each new item her grandmother brought to the cottage, she had to put one item into the attic-like storage area behind the "knee wall." This low wall stretched across the entire second story beneath the slanted front roof and the triangular space behind it could be accessed by a little door in either bedroom. The back roof of the house had been expanded to include dormers, so there was no storage space on that side and Emily's grandfather used to bellyache that there was so much stuff stockpiled behind the knee wall that it was a marvel the cottage didn't tip over.

When Emily's parents cleared out the storage space before the Johnsons moved in, they donated or discarded most of what they found there. Only now did Emily remember her mother saying they had set aside "a surprise or two" for her and Peter.

"I wanted you each to have a keepsake to remember your grandma and your childhood summers by," her mother had said.

That was the day her parents also talked to her and Peter about their will, explaining they'd poured their savings and profits from selling their home into the literacy foundation and other charities. However, they bequeathed the summer cottage and the property—which was worth a mint—to Peter and Emily to sell, keep or hand down to their own children someday.

"Someday" won't ever come for Peter and it probably won't come for me, either, Emily thought.

Suppressing the impulse to weep, she retrieved the flashlight Wilson had loaned her and pried open the knee wall door in her old room first. Emily stooped down and tentatively swept the light back and forth across the storage space, hoping she wouldn't rouse any bats or mice. But the area was completely empty, so she pushed the door firmly into place and went to check Peter's end of the house.

Sure enough, she discovered several items immediately inside the door. The first was a desk with a wooden box atop of it. Since the doorway was narrow and the furniture was too cumbersome for her to lift by herself, she had to jiggle it through the threshold and then drag it across the floor.

Once she'd brought the desk into the open, Emily immediately recognized that the box sitting on top of it was the walnut antique chessboard Emily's father had taught Peter, Wilson and Emily to play chess on one rainy afternoon.

Using the hem of her shirt, she wiped the checkered surface clean and then opened each of the two side compartments, smiling when she saw the pieces lying there. They were made of glass, except the black queen Peter had dropped and broken; it had been substituted with a plastic piece. Her parents must have intended for him to receive the set, since Emily had never developed much of an interest in chess. But every year after her father taught Peter and Wilson to play, the three of them held a summer-long tournament.

Although she'd never seen the desk before, Emily guessed it was a valuable Georgian antique, something her grandmother had put into storage before Emily was old enough to remember—maybe even before she was born. Judging from the brownish-red wood she exposed by running a finger over a grimy edge, it was probably made of mahogany, with a tooled leather writing top. The desk had two narrow drawers side by side, each with two smooth mahogany knobs apiece. But when Emily tugged on them, she realized they were dummy drawers, a detail which would have intrigued her brother. Surely, her mother had intended the desk for him—she probably hoped he'd use it for studying or professional purposes.

Emily pushed the desk farther out of the way and then ducked back into the storage area. What appeared to be a stack of short poles was lying on the floor and even before she managed to angle them through the little doorway, she squealed. "An easel!"

Not just any easel, either; it was an adjustable antique Victorian painting easel. Emily's grandmother had stopped coming to the cottage long before Emily began painting and studying art, so the easel must have been an arbitrary acquisition. But Emily's mother had clearly set it aside because she knew her daughter would treasure the beautiful, functional gift. *Mom must have been ecstatic when she discovered this. She was my best fan—I think she had even bigger dreams for my art than I did.*

The thought made Emily's chest feel tight; she was on the verge of another emotional meltdown. *Inhale, two, three, four. Hold it… Exhale, two, three, four,* she instructed herself. *Again.* Twice more she repeated the breathing exercises until she felt calm enough to poke her head into the storage space one last time.

Off to the side she saw what looked like…a magazine rack? But no, when she pulled it forward she recognized it was the vintage cradle she used to put her stuffed animals in when she was a young girl. On rare occasions when Wilson wasn't home, Peter would play "zoo" with Emily and they'd use the cradle as a cage. In Peter's rendition of the game, the animals always escaped. He'd hide half of them in his room and Emily would hide the other half in hers, and then they'd switch rooms and try to find and round up the "runaways."

Only in hindsight did Emily realize what a sacrifice it was for a twelve-year-old boy to play a make-believe stuffed animal game with his seven-year-old sister. Even then, his kindness toward children was evident. Snuffling, Emily pushed the knee wall door shut with her bare heel, tromped downstairs to her room and dropped facedown onto the bed.

This place is a minefield of memories. Why did I ever think coming back to Dune Island would be a good idea? It wasn't helping her to be here and she doubted it would really help anyone else: Wilson looked as if he'd swallowed broken glass every time he glanced her way and she wasn't making any discernible progress on the mural for the kids who'd come to the hospital, either.

"You're the expert, so whatever you create, we trust your taste," Tim had said. But what if she wasn't? What if grief had robbed her of her talent and she couldn't finish the art project? What if she couldn't *start* it? She'd let everyone down at the hospital and Wilson would be even sorrier than he already seemed to be for inviting her here. Worst of all, Emily felt like she'd disgrace her family's memory and disappoint her mother, her most ardent supporter.

I don't deserve an easel like the one Mom saved for me. I'm a has-been, she thought. *No, it's worse than that. I'm a* never-will-be.

Her dejection was so paralyzing, Emily lay in bed for hours, alternately weeping, napping or staring at the ceiling, which was only marginally less depressing than staring at the dark paneling on the walls.

*

By Friday, when Emily finally rose at noon, the downpour had tapered to a steady rain and her doldrums had lifted a little, too. As she ate a bowl of yogurt, she cracked open the sliding glass door to listen for the roaring ocean, which in today's light was a bleak, gunmetal gray.

I still prefer that color to grandma's woodwork any day, she thought.

Emily simply couldn't comprehend why her grandmother would have prohibited her mother from redecorating the interior of the cottage, since it had meant so much to Janice and she was willing to do the work herself. *Maybe that's partly why Mom supported my artistic aspirations so firmly—it was because Grandma didn't foster her creativity.*

Suddenly it registered with Emily that there was nothing stopping her from making changes to the cottage now. Although Wilson and Collette had a spare guestroom up at their house, Emily had offered to let Collette's mother stay in the cottage when she came for six weeks after the baby was born, because she figured the adults might need a little breathing space from each other. After that, Emily didn't know whether she'd rent the cottage out or sell it, but painting the walls could only make the place more appealing to a prospective tenant. She would repaint the doors and shutters, too. Who knows, maybe she'd even whitewash the floors. *Redecorating the cottage will be like I'm supporting Mom's creative vision, the way she always did for me!* she thought.

Motivated, Emily quickly changed into her clothes. She assumed Collette and Wilson had drop cloths, rollers, brushes and a stepladder she could use, but she'd go purchase the paint and other supplies she'd need. She picked up her phone to research the nearest hardware stores online, but since she didn't get a signal, she decided to take a drive toward Port Newcomb. She could look up information about the stores when she got closer to town.

The shortcut took Emily through two of the hamlets she hadn't visited yet; Rockfield and Benjamin's Manor. She was amazed by how different the architecture and landscapes were in each of the island's five towns. As the most populated, Port Newcomb was also the most commercialized. Lucy's Ham was the second largest town and was known for its bayside boardwalk. Only a few houses—such as Collette and Wilson's—were scattered across Highland Hills, which faced the open Atlantic. Rockfield bordered Highland Hills. On the other side of Rockfield, Benjamin's Manor boasted some of the most picturesque whaling captain's houses on the eastern seaboard.

As Emily drove, she noticed that as different as the towns were individually, collectively they somehow seem to complement each other, like pieces of a puzzle. This was the exact effect she intended for her hospital murals to have, if she could only figure out a way to make it happen.

Finding her destinations, consulting with the staff and comparing products and prices between three different stores took longer than Emily expected. By the time she finally had what she needed, the rain had stopped completely, the sun was peeking through the clouds and it was after five o'clock. Emily couldn't wait to get back to the cottage to plan her renovations, but traffic had come to a complete standstill. She soon discovered the reason: a long stream of cars that had disembarked the ferry was merging onto the main road. Pre-season weekend traffic, a harbinger of summer on the island. *One more reason I'm glad I'm staying in Highland Hills*, Emily gratefully mused. *And once I redecorate the cottage, I'll be even more content to be there.*

As she continued crawling along the thoroughfare, she envisioned creating an environment that would complement the significance and beauty of the keepsakes her mother had preserved, especially the antique desk. *It deserves a place of prominence. I'll have to bring it downstairs to the living room*, she decided. She'd use the easel while she was here and then take it and the cradle back to Seattle with her. But what would she do with the chess set?

The answer was so obvious she said it aloud. "I'll give it to Wilson!"

She was so sure the chess set would mean as much to him as the easel meant to her that when she got home, Emily charged up the shell path, dropped her purchases inside the front door and bustled upstairs to fetch the wooden box. Once she'd cleaned it off, she slid it sideways into a canvas bag and trotted with it across the lawn.

Halfway to Wilson and Collette's house, she spied Wilson coming up the beach staircase, a fishing pole in his hand. He was wearing rumpled shorts and a T-shirt, his hair was windblown, his glasses were clouded and he had a line of sand stuck to his shin. He looked, as Emily's grandmother would have said, like something that had been washed ashore. Her father used to call the boys "Flotsam and Jetsam" and Emily jokingly greeted Wilson the same way.

"Hi, Flotsam."

He looked momentarily bewildered before he returned her greeting and remarked, "We didn't see your lights on yesterday evening. Are you all right?"

"Yeah, the jet lag caught up to me so I went to bed early." It wasn't exactly a lie; she had been tired. Noticing the dark circles beneath Wilson's eyes, Emily asked, "How have *you* been?"

"Good. Didn't get any nibbles, though." He wiggled his fishing pole.

"That's because the fish have been staying underwater where it's nice and dry."

Wilson cocked his head quizzically. Then he seemed to understand her reference. "Yeah, it's been raining pretty hard, hasn't it?"

He was never this spacey; something was definitely disturbing him. Emily could hardly wait to give him the chess set—that should cheer him up a bit.

"I have a surprise for you. I'll carry it to the house since your hands are full." She wanted to see his reaction to the gift in person.

Wilson left his fishing equipment on the deck and as Emily followed him inside, he commented, "I hear water running. Collette must be showering. She should be out in a minute."

But Emily was too excited to wait for her. Besides, the chess set was something that was part of Wilson and Emily's childhood and she kind of wanted to share the moment with him alone.

"That's okay. This is specifically for you. Please open it now."

Emily handed him the bag and held her breath as Wilson gingerly removed the chess set. He set it on the table without saying a word.

"It's the chess set my grandma found at a yard sale. The one you and my dad and Peter used for your summer tournaments." Emily opened the compartments to trigger his memory. "Don't you recognize it?"

"Yes. I do." Wilson's tone and facial expression were unnaturally inscrutable, as if he were deliberately willing his features into stone.

"My-my mother was saving it behind the knee wall for Peter," she explained nervously. "Since you've always been like a brother to me—like a son to my mom and dad—I know they'd want you to have it."

At that, Wilson's eyes instantly brimmed, the exact opposite of what Emily intended to happen. "Thank you, but I-I can't accept this." Hanging his head, he put the chess set back into the canvas bag.

Emily's cheeks prickled with heat, but his reaction shouldn't have caught her by surprise, considering all the caterwauling *she'd* done after finding the items her mother bequeathed to her and Peter. She regretted not being more sensitive about Wilson's feelings.

"I'm sorry, Wilson. I didn't mean to make you sad or lonely for them. I thought the chess set might bring back good memories but I understand why you can't look at it right now. Why don't you put it away for a while and some summer, when you're ready and when your son is ready, you'll take it out and teach him how to play. My father would have loved knowing you were using this to carry on the tradition."

"It didn't belong to your father. It belonged to your mother—to your grandma first and then to your mom. She wanted her son to have it, not—" Wilson stopped mid-sentence and placed the bag in Emily's hands. "Thank you very much for the gesture, but you should keep this."

Emily didn't understand. What difference did it make if the chess set had once belonged to her mother or to her father? Both of them would have wanted Wilson to have it. Maybe he felt like if he took it, he'd somehow be usurping Peter's role in the family? That would have been irrational, since Peter wasn't alive to inherit the chess set, but from her own experience Emily appreciated that grief could turn a person's logic upside down.

"I hate chess and Peter would have wanted you to take the set, too," she said, hoping to convince Wilson it was all right to accept the keepsake.

"No! I *can't* take it." He thrust his hands in the air like a police officer halting traffic and Emily was so startled by his vehemence she teetered as she repositioned the bag in her arms.

"Hi, Emily." Collette came into the room just then, squeezing the ends of her hair with a towel. "What's up?"

Emily was too crushed by Wilson's rejection to explain about the chess set and she was certain he didn't want her to mention it, anyway, so she hedged, "I came to ask if you have a stepladder and a few drop cloths I can borrow. I'm starting a home improvement project."

"We must, in the basement somewhere. Wilson, you'll get them for her, won't you, honey?"

"Yeah. If you're going to be painting, I have a respirator you should use, too," Wilson told Emily without meeting her eyes.

She started to say that wouldn't be necessary; she'd be using low odor paint, she'd bought disposable masks and she'd open all the windows and doors, but she didn't want to agitate him any more than she clearly already had.

Suddenly as desperate to get away from Wilson as she'd been to see him, Emily said, "Thanks. Can I stop by to pick everything up when I get back? I'm—I'm going for a walk."

"Sure."

"You can come by our place anytime for any reason. No need to ask. You don't even need to knock, just come on in. We never lock up," Collette expounded on Wilson's answer. "Will you be painting the cottage on Sunday, too?"

When Emily shrugged, Collette said she was asking because she and Wilson were having a few people over for a cookout and they hoped Emily would join them.

"I appreciate the invitation. I just..."

Her voice trailed off. She didn't want them to know she still didn't trust herself to be in a group setting. That she was worried even the most benevolent inquiry about her background or her family might reduce her to tears, or else her bizarre social anxiety or whatever it was that happened when she was with more than one or two people would kick in, the way it had when she was in the crowded hospital cafeteria with Lucas. Emily couldn't risk exposing her volatile emotional state, especially not in front of people she hardly knew.

Collette let her off the hook. "It's okay. You don't have to explain. Just remember you're welcome to join us any time."

"Thanks." Emily skittered toward the door before Collette could question her about what was in the bag. "See you in a little while."

As eager as she'd been to get down to the beach, Emily's walk was hot and buggy and the waves were breaking so high on shore they created an uneven slope, which slowed her pace and made her cranky. But she was even more vexed by Wilson's reaction to her giving him the chess set. Even if the gift was ill-timed, it was odd that he had refused it so adamantly. Emily could have understood if the chess set had made him feel nostalgic, but he almost seemed... not angry, but, well, ashamed. Or maybe "guilty" was a better word.

Emily thought about him saying, "It belonged to your mom—to your grandma first and then to your mom. She wanted her son to have it." Was it possible Wilson felt guilty for not wanting the gift because it once belonged to Emily's grandmother, who was often ornery? Or perhaps his reaction had something to do with Emily's mother, or with Peter. Was he holding a grudge against one of them? That didn't seem like Wilson at all.

But it didn't seem like him to act as strangely as he'd been acting almost every time Emily crossed his path, either. It was as if he couldn't wait to get away from her. Emily had initially assumed it was because she reminded him of the people he'd lost, but after seeing his reaction to the chess set, she suspected something else was going on. She had no clue what it was and right now didn't seem like a good time to talk to him about it, for both of their sakes. But she needed and cared about an open relationship with Wilson too much to let anything come between them. *Somehow, I'm going to have to find a way to bring it up...*

It was dark when Emily returned and she nearly traipsed right past the beach staircase. *I guess Wilson's flashlight was a good idea after all*, she thought when she reached the top step and realized that without moonlight, she couldn't see the cottage. Fortunately, Collette and Wilson had enough lights on in their house for Emily to see to pick her way across their lawn.

Although she could hear voices inside, no one answered when she knocked. Sweating and itchy, she swatted at a gnat, wondering if she should go home and shower and catch up with Wilson in the morning. But then a light flicked on overhead and she blinked as her eyes adjusted to it, unable to see who was at the door.

"Emily, come on in," Collette beckoned. "We were giving Barbara a tour of the house. She's never been here before."

As Emily entered the kitchen, she noticed two figures behind Wilson. One was Lucas. The other was the woman she'd overheard talking about her in the hospital cafeteria.

Wilson stepped aside to make the introductions. "Emily Vandemark, this is Barbara Reed."

"Actually, it's *Doctor* Reed," the woman emphasized, without extending her hand. "I'm almost finished with my residency. But socially, you can call me Barbara."

The buxom, redheaded woman was wearing more eyeliner and bronzer than she wore on Tuesday and her hair wasn't pulled back as it was then. But there was no mistaking her. There was no mistaking her voice, either. She was definitely the one who made the remark about Emily not eating her lunch.

"Nice to meet you." Emily's manners were automatic, if not entirely authentic.

"Hi, Em," Lucas chimed in. "See any pirates down at the beach tonight?"

"Hello, Lucas." Emily was too flabbergasted by Barbara's presence to acknowledge his private joke. To Wilson, she stated quietly, "Sorry to interrupt—it was too dark to notice any cars in the driveway, so I didn't know you had company. I'll come back for the ladder tomorrow."

Lucas was all ears. "A ladder for what?"

"I'm, uh, painting my living room walls. The kitchen walls, too."

"Another mural?" he teased.

"Another color," Emily answered. She reiterated to Wilson, "I'll come back tomorrow morning. It's not as if I'm going to start the project tonight."

"Barbara and I are on call but we're going to grab an ice cream cone on the boardwalk over in Lucy's Ham. There's a concert on the common," Lucas interjected. "The three of you should join us."

"I won't say no to ice cream." Collette chided Wilson, "And if you know what's good for you, you won't say no, either."

"Great," Lucas said. "How about you, Em?"

She wished he'd stop calling her Em: it reminded her of Dorothy's aunt in *The Wizard of Oz*. "Thanks, but I'm going to have an early night."

"Aw, c'mon. You haven't lived until you've tried Bleecker's famous cranberry ice cream. It's straight from the bog, according to the advertisements."

"Lucas, does she look like a girl you can tempt with ice cream?" Barbara asked, giving Emily a once-over.

"Oh, she may be slender but I've seen her polish off nearly a pint in one sitting," Collette announced in defense of Emily. "Makes me envious."

"*I'm* not envious. I *like* my curves. And a lot of other people I know seem to like them, too."

Emily respected that Barbara was proud of her body—more power to her—but it was the sidelong glance she gave Lucas that grated on her nerves.

"I'll get the ladder tomorrow," she said for a third time as she backed out of the room. "Have fun, you guys."

She shot out the door and across the lawn before anyone could stop her or say another word. Sprinting blindly up the deck stairs in the dark, she tripped and landed so hard she saw stars. For a long moment, she just lay there, considering whether she had it in her to get back up and keep going.

CHAPTER FOUR

In the bathroom mirror, Emily examined her swollen, bleeding chin, dabbing it with a cloth. It looked worse than it felt: her knees and hands had absorbed most of the impact but she had a low tolerance for gore and the sight of it made her feel sick to her stomach.

"You're a mess," she told her reflection.

She peeled off her clothes and stepped into the shower. The island had strict water conservation guidelines, but tonight she took her time. She was too emotionally and physically fatigued to hurry.

"Just who does that woman think she is?" Emily asked aloud as the water washed over her.

Then she realized that she herself wondered who "that woman is." She was a medical resident, that much was clear. But was she Lucas's girlfriend? She had seemed dressed up in her sleeveless linen maxi and platform sandals, although Lucas was simply wearing faded jeans and a T-shirt. But Collette said Lucas didn't date women from work. And besides, they were only getting ice cream cones before a concert close to the hospital. Maybe that was the kind of fraternal thing doctors did together when they were both on call?

After she showered, Emily fixed a bagel and carried it to her bedroom so she could eat it in bed. A mosquito whined near her head as she picked up her cell phone. She held it at different heights until she finally managed to get a signal. Not that it mattered; she didn't have any texts or voicemail messages. *Who was I expecting would get in touch with me, anyway?*

One of the things that used to drive her nuts about her mother was that whenever Emily was traveling, her mom would say, "Call us when you get there, so we know you've arrived safely." It didn't matter whether Emily was going to Europe or merely embarking on a two-hour car trip; her mother always asked her to let her know when she got there.

It was so exasperating that one time Emily snapped, "Mom, I'm not a child! I swear it won't matter if I'm ninety-six years old. On the day I die and I'm on my way to heaven, you're going to say, 'Call me when you get there.'"

Her mother responded genuinely, "No I won't, honey, because I'll already be there, waiting for you. I'll know the exact moment you arrive."

The recollection moved Emily to tears. She curled into a ball and cried into her pillow, but doing that irritated the scrapes on her chin and knee. She stretched flat on her back, tears trickling into her ears. It was so humid that she couldn't even tolerate a sheet against her skin. The mosquito continued to drone so she sat back up and started randomly flailing her arms at the air above her head, which made her feel less like crying. In fact, she began to giggle and pretty soon, she was laughing outright at how ridiculous she must have looked.

After she lay back down again, she spoke into the dark as if she was leaving a voicemail message, "Hi, Mom. It's me, Emily. Just wanted to let you know I made it to the cottage safely. Gotta go. Love you, Mom. Bye."

Or maybe she just dreamed she said that, but either way, it made her feel a lot better.

*

Throughout the night, Emily had kept waking up, her head throbbing. So in the morning, when she heard a tap-tap-tap-tappety-tap within her skull, she ignored it. But when it continued, she opened her eyes and realized the noise was coming from outside her body. Outside the *house*. It took a moment for her to get her bearings and identify the sound as someone knocking on the front door.

She opened it to find Collette holding a folded drop cloth and respirator in one hand and balancing a stepladder upright with the other.

"Sorry, if I woke you. Wilson and I are going off-island this morning to do some furniture shopping for the nursery and—hey, what happened to your chin?"

"I tripped. It looks worse than it is." Emily took hold of the ladder and held the door open so Collette could pass through to the living room. "You carried this over here yourself? You really didn't have to do that."

"Oh, yes I did! I needed to talk to you. I could hardly sleep last night, I was so riled up about how Barbara treated you. She's such a snot."

"It was okay," Emily said. "Or it is now. I was pretty ticked off last night myself. But at least *I* got to go to bed—*you* had to spend the evening with her. How was that?"

"Painful. Very painful. You should hear the way she talks to Lucas and Wilson. Her voice is saccharine-sweet. But when she talks to women, her words are full of little hidden barbs—which is what all of us nurses call her. *Barbs*."

"You mean like when she oh-so-subtly insulted my figure? Or when she acted like she was better than I am because she's a doctor?"

"Exactly!" exclaimed Collette. "I'm surprised she didn't tell you she's one of two people who are competing for a cardiology fellowship at Hope Haven when their residency ends in September. She's so smug, she thinks she's got it made. I don't know what Lucas sees in her."

Emily's eye twitched. She raised a finger to pull her lid taut. "Lucas is in a relationship with her?"

"Hard to tell," said Collette. "There are plenty of lovely women in the hospital who are dying to get together with him, so I'd like to think he'd choose someone nicer than Barbs. Then again, he's charming to everyone, so maybe his taste isn't as discriminating as I think it is. Actually, I was surprised when they dropped by together. He usually only pops in when he comes here to surf or fish. He's never brought someone with him."

"Well, if he brings her by again, you're welcome to hide in the cottage," Emily offered. "Where was it you said you and Wilson are headed today?"

"Furniture shopping for the nursery."

"Oh, fun!"

"Not really. I don't know what's wrong with me but I have absolutely no nesting instinct. The baby's going to have to sleep in a dresser drawer if I don't order a crib pretty soon." Collette glanced toward the door. "I'd better get going. Do you need an adhesive bandage or antibacterial ointment for your chin? I've got some up at the house."

"Nope, I'm good." She didn't want Wilson to know she'd hurt herself. If he saw the condition her chin was in, he'd realize she couldn't wear a respirator and he'd probably try to convince her not to start her painting project yet.

"Okay. See you later."

Until coming to Dune Island, Emily had only met Collette briefly at the wedding and the funerals. As she stood on the deck watching her lumbering up the dewy hill, Emily understood why Peter had always spoken so highly of her, and she made a mental note to ask Wilson if anyone was planning a baby shower for her. She wanted to come up with a unique gift before then.

After gently cleaning her scrapes, Emily got dressed. She'd intended to wash and prep the walls, but her head hurt so much she felt nauseated, so she decided to go outside and sketch on the deck instead. After nearly three straight days of rain, the sun seemed abnormally bright but Emily felt too lazy to go back inside to get her sunglasses.

Instead, she opened her sketch pad and leafed through her drawings, trying to find something to salvage. When she couldn't, her mind wandered to her conversation with Collette. She was bothered that Lucas and Barbara might be in a relationship. She was even more bothered that it bothered her. Why should it matter? Barbara was the one who was deliberately being rude to her; Lucas wasn't. Maybe that was it. Maybe it was because she was just starting to trust him. Now, because of the company he kept, she was unsure whether he was as authentic as he seemed.

Her ex-fiancé Devon had been genuine and caring in the beginning, but look how that ended. He couldn't keep up the act. Deep down, Emily knew that wasn't a fair assessment. She knew she had played the larger part in their breakup. She had pushed him away. It wasn't intentional; it was that she had been so consumed by grief that there was nothing left over for love. She had tried—how she had tried—to stop mourning. Or at least not to be a complete emotional disaster. But no amount of wishing or willpower could make that happen. She didn't blame Devon for giving up on her; she blamed herself.

"Concentrate, Emily!" she hissed.

She pulled out a pencil and started to doodle instead, but the page seemed blurred. Probably from her headache. She unfastened the tight elastic band from her hair, which was still damp and ropy from last night's shower. She allowed her locks to fall to her shoulders and gently massaged her neck. She picked her pencil back up.

Before she fully realized it, Emily was drawing an ugly, unwieldy octopus. Instead of being anatomically correct, the blobby creature was wrapping one of its arms around a tiny person who looked a lot like herself. Another arm was choking Lucas. As Emily drew additional victims, the sketch struck her as so hilarious she started cracking up and she didn't notice Lucas approaching the deck until he was practically beside her. *How does he keep sneaking up on me like that?* More importantly, *why* did he keep sneaking up on her like that?

"Hi, Emily. What's so funny?"

Chagrined, Emily rushed to fold the picture in half, but it felt as if her hands were moving in slow motion and she fumbled with the paper. "Oh, it's...it's...hard to explain," she stammered.

Lucas plunked himself into a chair beside her and tipped his head. "What happened to you? That looks bad."

Emily combed her hair back into a bun with her fingers. "I know it does, that's why I never wear it down."

"I didn't mean your hair—your hair looks pretty that way. I meant what happened to your chin?"

Despite Lucas's compliment, Emily was irritated that he was peering at her intently, as if he were inspecting her. "I cut myself shaving," she retorted.

When Lucas didn't crack a smile, she admitted she'd tripped and then quickly changed the subject. "Have you been fishing this morning?"

"Yeah. Trying to, anyway. No success. I blame Wilson. He promised to let me try out his new rod and reel, but he's not home." Lucas tapped his hand over his mouth as he yawned. "I could sure go for a cup of coffee. Want to come with me?"

"I don't drink coffee, remember?"

"Breakfast, then."

"It's nearly eleven o'clock."

"Brunch? There's a place in Benjamin's Manor that makes killer omelets."

Emily's stomach cartwheeled at the word. After overhearing his conversation with Barbara in the hospital cafeteria, she didn't want to tell him once again that she wasn't hungry, so she told him the truth. "Thanks, but I've actually got a headache and it's making me nauseated."

Lucas twisted his mouth to the side before saying, "Listen, Em, I really think it's important for your health if you come with me—"

"What is it with you and food, anyway?" Emily heard herself interrupting him. "Just because I'm not hungry doesn't mean I have an eating disorder!"

"I know it doesn't," Lucas replied softly. "But I think you may have a concussion from taking a tumble."

"A concussion? That's ridiculous. I landed on my knees and bumped my chin, not my head," Emily protested.

"Sometimes when people fall, they're so focused on any injuries that are bleeding that they don't even realize they've also hit their head. But even if you didn't knock your head directly, if you landed hard enough, the jolt could have still caused a concussion," Lucas explained. "Did you pass out when you fell?"

"I don't think so."

"Did you see stars?"

Emily's hesitation was enough to confirm that she did. Lucas asked her more questions about her symptoms and after hearing her answers he tried again to coax her to go to the ER, but she was obstinately against it.

"I probably have delayed jet lag and the headache is a coincidence. I would've felt this crummy today even if I hadn't fallen. I'll take a nap. I'll be fine."

"Rest is a good idea. But I want to run a few tests first. I promise they won't hurt," Lucas said. "I'll even give you a lollipop when you're done."

Emily was in no mood for humor. "I do *not* need a doctor, especially not a pediatrician!"

"Okay, that's fine. You can see someone else. But you're showing focal neuro—you're showing symptoms that need to be evaluated by a neurologist."

"No." Emily didn't want everyone at the hospital knowing what a klutz she was.

Lucas rubbed a hand over his eyes as if he were the one with a headache. "If you really don't want to go to the hospital, I respect that. But Wilson and Collette will never forgive me if I leave you here alone, knowing you're injured. Let me give them a call and I'll keep you company until they return."

Great. Wilson would want to come back to the island early and he'd probably be annoyed at Collette for not telling him about Emily's tumble in the first place. Emily didn't see any reason to ruin their day, just because Lucas seemed determined to ruin hers.

"Okay, I'll go to the hospital with you—but you've got to stop shouting."

"Does it sound like I'm raising my voice? I'm not. Hyperacusis—sensitivity to sound—can be a concussive symptom, too."

"It can be a headache symptom, too," Emily grumbled. "I'll go get my purse."

She must have stood up too quickly because the deck began to spin but Lucas grasped her elbow and eased her back into the chair. He told her to stay put before going inside to grab her purse for her.

"I've got an idea," Lucas spoke quietly when he returned. "How about if I carry you to my van?"

"No way."

"Why not? I'm stronger than I look."

"And I'm heavier than *I* look."

"You're feistier than you look, too," he said. "Here. At least let me—"

He wrapped one arm around her shoulder and offered his other hand for support. As lousy as Emily felt, she was grateful for the masculine sturdiness of Lucas's grip and she allowed herself to lean on him. He encouraged her along the way, and when she stubbed her sneaker against the pavement he bolstered her upright, saying "I've got you."

When they arrived at the hospital, he took her through a side entrance to the ER and summoned a nurse.

Two examinations, one IV drip, a set of imaging, and innumerable questions later, Emily was finally given medication to alleviate her headache. The neurologist told her Lucas was right: she had a mild traumatic brain injury. He said he wanted to keep her in the hospital overnight for observation, a suggestion Emily flatly rejected.

It was bad enough that she hadn't started painting the murals yet; she didn't want the Board to find out that she'd tripped and given herself a concussion. They'd regret taking on such a flake. When she told the doctor that the IV rehydration and pain medication had been effective and insisted she'd be better off at home, he coughed and excused himself from the room.

Thirty seconds later, Lucas entered.

"You're looking a little better. How do you feel?"

"A *lot* better, thanks. And thanks for forcing me to see the doctor. You can say 'I told you so,' now. I've got it coming."

"Not so stupid for a pediatrician, huh?" he ribbed. "Oh, that reminds me—"

He reached into his pocket and produced a lollipop.

"Grape? I wanted cherry." Emily laughed.

"I'll bring you cherry in the morning," he promised.

"Great. You can bring it to me in the children's wing, where I'll be working. But I'm not staying here overnight. No way."

"Mm, that's what I heard," Lucas acknowledged. "I actually think you're making the wrong choice, but this is a hospital, not a prison, and as you pointed out, you're an adult, not a child. However, you don't have a car and my guess is you're not going to want to sit in the sun waiting for the shuttle three blocks from here. So here's the deal. With your permission, I can convince your doc to discharge you to my care. Which means I'll drive you home and I'll talk to Wilson and Collette about supervising your recovery. You can receive follow-up care with another doctor of your choice. But until you get the green light from her or him, you have to promise you won't come back to work. Agreed?"

"What was that part about me being an adult, not a child?"

"I'm serious, Emily."

Emily sullenly gave in. "Okay, *Dr. Luke*. Agreed."

He left and was gone for so long that she worried he'd changed his mind. Staring at the ceiling, she counted the tiles six or seven times, which exacerbated her restlessness. After the eighth time, she came up with an idea: she'd paint details on the ceilings in the children's wing, as well as on the walls. *At least my day hasn't been a total wash*, she consoled herself.

After her discharge paperwork had been completed, a nurse wheeled Emily to the ER exit, where Lucas was waiting in the van. He jumped out and helped her climb in. When she fumbled with the seat belt, he leaned over and clicked it into place, his hand cupping hers.

"Things don't always work well in a vehicle this old." He rambled on: "But I love it. It took me months to find it—they don't make 'em like this anymore. I bought it on the spot from a guy on the beach and it hadn't even been for sale. He said, "If I sell it to you, you'll have to give me a ride home." So I did, but he made me wait until he finished clamming first.

"I like it because it's big enough to slide my surfboard and fishing gear right in—I don't even need racks or straps. It's also great for hauling stuff, although that's a catch-22 because then all your friends and all your friends' friends ask you to help them move. In the fall, I put the back seats in so I can take city kids from Boston on camping trips. Plus, it's one of a kind. If anyone wants to find me, all they have to do is look for the yellow van. Or listen for it."

Emily rested her head against the seat and smiled. It amused her that Luke didn't mind being conspicuous, whereas she preferred anonymity. Maybe it was the relief of getting out of the hospital, or that she was medicated and well-hydrated again, but she began to relax, mesmerized by Lucas's deep, assuaging voice.

"You're an extrovert who likes to be alone on the beach to surf and fish," she commented. "That's an interesting contradiction."

"And you're apparently repelled by hospitals, yet you're volunteering in one," he countered. "But yeah, I like to be alone when I'm surfing or fishing. It's when I think. I mean, I'm always thinking, of course, but catching waves—and catching fish—involves a lot of sitting around and waiting. Two things I hardly ever get to do at work. I use the time to consider the big picture. To problem-solve. To appreciate nature, you know? How about you?"

Emily pretended she didn't know what he meant by his question. "I don't know how to surf and I've never been fishing."

Then, on second thought, she disclosed, "My contemplation time is whenever I walk—especially if I'm walking alone. Nature is an important part of that for me, too. But sometimes I wish I could just turn my brain off."

"Sounds like I need to take a break to think and you need to take a break from thinking. Either way, it's not an easy balance to find, is it?"

Surprised by her own disclosure as well as by Lucas's understanding response, she rolled the window down a crack and switched topics. "Which way do you usually go when you're at the beach at Collette and Wilson's, to the left or the right?"

"If I'm surfing, I'll head west—left—toward the sandbars. If I'm fishing, I'll go east, or right, toward the inlet."

"I haven't been down the beach to the right yet this year. I used to go a lot when I was a kid, but now I like knowing I can walk and keep walking and walking if I need to, so I've been going to the left."

"Yeah, but the inlet is really something. Absolute solitude and magnificent beauty—and it's a good place for flounder and blues, too. When you're better, I could take you fishing there sometime."

"What about what you just said about hanging out at the beach alone?" Emily questioned.

"Solitude is good in measured doses, but too much of it and it's no longer solitude. It's isolation. And isolation isn't healthy."

Once again, Lucas's insightfulness hit a nerve. That past year, Emily had craved solitude like never before, but that was an expected response to grief, wasn't it? *I haven't crossed over into the realm of isolation, have I?* She quickly wicked away a stray tear.

After a few minutes of silence, Lucas said, "I'm trying to take the curves slowly, but we're almost there. You okay?"

"Yep, I'm okay," she fibbed, not wanting to break it to him that the noise and jostling of his beloved van wasn't helping her headache and nausea any.

When they pulled into the driveway, Lucas immediately pointed out that Collette and Wilson's car still wasn't there. Telling Emily to sit tight, he hurtled up the hill and knocked on their door. When no one answered, he returned, opened Emily's door and held out his arm for her to grasp it for balance even though she was a lot steadier on her feet now. Emily intended to let go of him once she'd climbed down, but Lucas drew his arm closer to his body, cushioning her hand between his bicep and his chest as he guided her across the lawn.

"Aha, the scene of the crime." He pointed to a bloody spot when they reached the deck.

"Ew, disgusting. If I had noticed that this morning, I would've washed it off. I think it's dry, but don't step in it. Sorry about that."

Lucas chortled. "Em, I'm a doctor. I haven't put in an honest day's work unless at least one patient has bled or puked on me."

Emily scowled, her nausea intensifying.

Now it was Lucas's turn to apologize. "Sorry, I shouldn't have said that. What a clod. I usually have a better bedside manner."

He seemed so embarrassed that Emily rushed to contradict him. "Your bedside manner is wonderful. If I ever have another concussion, you're the doctor I want with me."

The words tumbled out of Emily's mouth before she realized Lucas might have thought she was being sarcastic, which she wasn't. Or flirtatious, which she also wasn't. Or was she? The concussion must have been dulling her sense of inhibition. She was coming out with all sorts of things she wouldn't ordinarily say.

To compensate, she asked in a formal tone, "May I offer you something to eat or drink?"

"Nope, you can't," Lucas answered sternly. "You can't do *anything* except relax. It's even okay if you fall asleep. I'll wake you if you're not up in a while."

"I appreciate your concern and the ride home, but I'm sure you've got better ways to spend your Saturday than sitting around here with me. Collette and Wilson will be back any second and I'll fill them in."

"Absolutely not going to happen. You promised, remember?"

"Okay, you can stay, but I'm not sleepy," Emily said as she sank into the couch.

"That's fine, but you should put your head back and close your eyes," Lucas insisted. "It's called brain rest—the nurse probably told you about it. Where's your bedroom? I'll get you a pillow."

Emily yawned and gestured down the hall. Lucas returned and arranged two pillows near the arm of the couch and despite saying she wasn't sleepy, Emily put her head down. It seemed no time had passed before she woke to the sound of car doors shutting. When the screen slider clicked into place as Lucas left to go speak to Collette and Wilson, Emily's eyes fluttered open momentarily.

Don't go, she thought dreamily. *I like having you here with me.*

CHAPTER FIVE

When Emily woke again, Collette was stretched out in the armchair, elevating her feet on the coffee table and flipping through a baby furniture catalog while she sipped a glass of iced green tea.

"Good morning—or afternoon. How are you feeling?"

"Okay," Emily answered hoarsely.

Collette reached over and held out a glass of water with a straw in it. "Wilson made me promise when you woke up, I'd ask you to say your full name."

"Why? Doesn't he remember me? Maybe he has a concussion, too."

"Ha!" Collette snorted. "I figured you were all right, but this really is one time when you can't be too careful."

Emily twisted her knuckles against her eyelids. "Have you just been sitting here, waiting for me to wake up? You must be going stir-crazy."

"Are you kidding? Wilson practically ordered me to keep an eye on you while he ran the rest of our Saturday errands. He's been cleaning the house and shopping for the cookout tomorrow. If we stall long enough, he'll prepare dinner tonight, too. I've never had it so good."

"Yeah, but I feel terrible for inconveniencing you guys like this on your day off, right before you have special company coming tomorrow."

"We're not having special company—it's just some people from cardiology. We rotate hosting cookouts on Sundays during the summer, although somehow most of them end up being held at our place." Collette set down her glass. "Besides, it's not your fault you have a concussion."

"Actually, it kind of *is* my fault. Wilson bought me a flashlight, remember? If I had been using it, I wouldn't have tripped, but I just dismissed him as being hypervigilant."

"Yeah, I suppose sometimes he does have good cause for concern," Collette begrudgingly conceded. "But I swear, my dear husband is going prematurely gray from all the worrying he does."

Emily hesitated. She didn't want to be disloyal to Wilson by talking about him behind his back, but maybe Collette could shed some light on his recent behavior that would help Emily understand him better. "Is Wilson . . . is he okay? I get the sense he's upset about something and I kind of wonder if it has anything to do with me being here."

"No, no. That's not it. That's not it at all." Collette shifted her feet off the table and moved onto the couch. Emily bent her legs to make room for her as the cushion sagged beneath her friend.

In a low voice Collette confided, "I wouldn't ever share this with anyone else, but you're like a sister to Wilson and you know about his background . . . He hasn't said it explicitly, but I think becoming a father for the first time brings up a lot of issues for him. You know, since his own father never wanted anything to do with him."

Emily's eyes smarted. It pained her to think of anyone—especially Wilson—being rejected as a child. "I suppose that's understandable."

"Yeah. Up until now, he's never had much of an interest in finding his father. There were times when he was curious, of course, but ultimately he told me he was so well-loved growing up—by his grandparents and his aunt and uncle and by your family, too—that he never felt compelled to look for the one person who *didn't* love him. Besides, he always accepted it that his mother had a really good reason for refusing to tell anyone anything about the guy, except that he was Italian."

Emily nodded, even though she actually remembered her mother mentioning Wilson's grandparents knew a little more than that. They knew his first name was Marco. And that Wilson's mother, Michelle, who held an executive position with a U.S. company, had met him while she was working at her employer's sister company in Italy. She desperately wanted to marry Marco, but he broke up with her when he learned she was pregnant. Beyond that, Michelle's secret regarding Wilson's father's identity died with her when she was killed in the auto accident when Wilson was four.

Collette continued, "A month or two ago, Wilson bought one of those DNA testing kits, hoping he can track him down. He claims he only wants to find out his father's family's medical history for our baby's sake. But I think he's hoping to, I don't know, confront his father or something. That is, if he's still alive."

Wow. No wonder Wilson seemed so far away lately. That might have been why he'd had such a negative reaction to the chess set, too. *Maybe seeing the keepsake from my family's lineage somehow underscored the fact he never even knew his dad?* Emily could only guess at Wilson's specific emotions, but even having an inkling of what he was going through filled her with empathy and took the sting out of how rejected she'd felt when he refused her gift.

"Then he hasn't found his father yet?"

"I'm not even sure he's gotten the results back yet—so please don't mention I told you about it."

"I won't say a word, I promise." *But I hope he talks to me about it eventually, so I can try to support him if he finds his father, just like he supported me after I lost mine.*

As Emily adjusted the pillow behind her neck, Collette remarked, "You know, it was a good thing Lucas happened to be here to take you to the hospital today. Did you have to flag him down on the beach or something?"

"No. He wandered over on his own. I think he must have spotted me from your deck when he went up to your place to borrow Wilson's new rod and reel. He was hungry, so he asked me to go to brunch with him."

"That's strange. We told him last night we wouldn't be home because we were going shopping this morn— Oh, so *that's* it. He knew we'd be gone and he was taking advantage of the opportunity to ask you to go out to eat with him alone. He's got a thing for you, Emily!"

The volume of her squeal pierced Emily's ears and she cringed reflexively.

Collette repeated in a hushed voice, "He's interested in you! I had a hunch he was hoping to spend time with you when he came by last evening, too."

"While he was out with another woman? That's absurd."

"Okay, so I don't have all of the logic worked out, but that's what my female intuition tells me."

Emily laughed. "And I'm the one who spent the afternoon having my head examined."

"Seriously though, would you go out with him if he asked you?"

Emily paused before answering. Lucas had definite appeal, despite what she considered his borderline brash exterior. But, considering how emotionally bereft she felt, as well as the fact that her nostrils were constantly peeling from blowing her nose, her eyes were ringed hollows and her bones seemed to protrude from her skin, it was difficult for her to imagine that he—or any man—would be attracted to her. Part of her was flattered by the possibility. Another part of her felt like it was irrelevant, because a romantic relationship—even a fling—was the last thing she could handle right now.

"I don't know," she answered truthfully. "I think it may be too soon after...after—"

"After breaking up with Devon," Collette finished the thought for her.

Actually, Emily was going to say, "after the accident," but she didn't make a point of clarifying. "Besides, Lucas isn't interested in me like that. Do you know that I overheard him and Barbs discussing whether or not I have an eating disorder?"

"Pah!" Collette choked.

Emily quavered, "It's not funny."

"I wasn't laughing, I was gasping," Collette assured her. "As intrusive as their conversation was, I doubt they meant to be insulting. Lucas didn't, anyway. In his mind, he was probably checking off a list of diagnostic possibilities. My husband thinks like that, too. It's how physicians are wired. If Wilson didn't already know you, he might have suggested an even more outlandish diagnosis. Like a parasite."

"I look that bad?" Emily wailed, swiping her cheek with her palm. "When people look at me—when *men* look at me—the first thing they think is *intestinal parasite*?"

"No, no, of course not. I didn't mean anything about *you* by that." Collette frowned. "I only meant that's an option some doctors would consider because they have to rule out the differentials. Please don't cry, it's really not good for you right now."

She left the room and returned with a roll of toilet paper, which she unwound and handed to Emily in a big wadded bouquet and plonked herself back down on the couch. Collette rubbed her belly as she spoke.

"You have a certain . . . a certain *presence*, inside and out. That's why I think Lucas is interested in you—because he recognizes that about you and he's drawn to it."

Emily blew her nose. "I don't know what's wrong with me. I'm such a crybaby. I'm sorry."

"Emily, you must stop apologizing," Collette scolded. "You're not a crybaby. Having a concussion can put you on an emotional rollercoaster even under the best of circumstances. It's not your fault. It's *my* fault. I shouldn't have brought up the subject of dating when you're already in a fragile state physically. I say the stupidest things—"

Emily was surprised when Collette broke into tears. She sat upright, scooted closer and placed a hand on her back. "You didn't say anything stupid. I love talking to you. You're so honest. You remind me of my mom—you're a lot younger, of course."

Collette bawled louder. "I'm going to be a terrible mother! I'm going to say all the wrong things to my child and make him cry."

Emily tried to keep a straight face, but her friend's fears seemed so ridiculously unfounded that she had to bite back a smile.

"Collette, you're going to make a terrific mother, not a terrible one. Eating ice cream shows you know how to enjoy simple pleasures in life. Not having the nursery perfectly arranged three months in advance is perfectly normal. And even if you say the wrong things to your child, he'll forgive you. He'll just be thankful you're the kind of mother who talks to him about things that matter. Like my mother was."

In her attempt to cheer Collette, Emily ended up weeping again. When Wilson entered the cottage a few minutes later, the two of them had ruddy, tear-streaked faces.

"What's wrong?" His tone was panicked.

"My pregnancy hormones are acting up again."

"So is my concussion," Emily kidded.

"It is? Have you been having unprovoked outbursts of emotion?" he questioned her. "Prolonged, uncontrollable crying?"

Only every day for the past nine months, she thought, but Wilson's disquieted expression kept her from expressing the thought aloud.

"It isn't a concussive symptom, Wilson," Collette answered for her. "The crying was provoked. We were talking about girl stuff, that's all."

"Oh. I see, I think," he said cautiously. "Are you two hungry? I made supper."

Although Emily was worried food might make her queasy again, the chicken soup Wilson made settled her stomach.

"Yum. This tastes like the soup my—"

"It is," Wilson confirmed before she finished her sentence.

"It is what?" asked Collette.

"It's soup like Emily's mother used to make."

"I wouldn't be able to tell the difference between hers and yours," Emily said. Then she told Collette about how her mother always made soup for her, Peter and Wilson whenever they were under the weather. Actually, she made it for anyone—the mail carrier, the furnace repairman, the school staff—who was sick.

Wilson reminisced, "When I graduated med school, I told Mrs. V. that her soup probably healed more people than I'd ever heal as a doctor. That's when she gave me the recipe."

"Really? I thought you were just improvising. My mom actually *gave* you her secret recipe? She wouldn't even give that to Peter or me. You always were her favorite child!" Emily pretended to rant at him before turning to address Collette. "It's true. Whenever my brother or I accused my mom of favoring the other person, she'd say, 'Neither one of you is my favorite—*Wilson* is.' And the fact she gave him the recipe just proves it!"

Emily was surprised to notice Wilson's cheeks turning bright red. She hoped he knew she wasn't serious about being mad about the recipe. Not dead serious, anyway.

"Look at it the way I do," Collette suggested. "If Wilson has the recipe and you don't, you get to enjoy eating it but you don't have to do the work of preparing it."

As she ladled second helpings into their bowls, someone rattled the door.

"Hey, Lucas," Wilson greeted him. "Why didn't I hear the van? Did you get a new set of wheels or just a new muffler?"

"Neither. I coasted in. I didn't want to disturb Emily's sleep if she was resting."

"You've never done that for me when *I've* been resting," Collette complained. She raised an eyebrow in Emily's direction but Emily ignored her and said hello to Lucas.

"You're just in time for soup." Collette set a place for him. "It's Emily's mom's recipe. Enjoy it while it's hot."

Wilson asked what Lucas had in the white paper bag he was holding.

"It's a sort of a get well present." He handed it to Emily.

"For me?" She stuck her hand in and pulled out a quart of hand-packed cranberry-chocolate ice cream from Bleecker's. The bag also contained a pink gel eye mask.

"It's so you'll remember to take time out for brain rest," Lucas said and then slurped a spoonful of soup.

"Thank you. That was very thoughtful."

Emily self-consciously folded the bag into a neat square and avoided looking at Collette, who got up to put the ice cream in the freezer. The soup was making Emily sweat and her cheeks flush. She set her spoon beside her bowl and listened as Lucas, Wilson and Collette engaged in a lively debate about whether the owner of Bleecker's Ice Cream was the uncle or the father of the woman who managed the Donut Shanty.

"Are you going to finish that?" Lucas asked Emily a few minutes later, gesturing with his chin toward her soup. "Because if you're not, I'll eat it."

Emily pushed the bowl toward him, recalling that when Wilson and Peter were teenagers, they had insatiable appetites, regardless of how much or how often they ate. After finishing their meals, they'd cajole Emily into sharing hers with them, until one day Emily's mother forbade them to ask for the food off of her plate.

"If she offers it to you, you can have it, but I don't want the two of you whimpering and begging for table scraps. You're young gentlemen, not overgrown house pets."

That Wilson and Peter were so eager to eat her leftovers was the ultimate sign of fraternal acceptance to Emily, who, at that time, still lived in the world of "boy germs" and "girl germs." It occurred to her in retrospect that Devon never once shared anything from her plate during their entire relationship.

"Does your mother live in Seattle, too?" Lucas asked Emily as he tipped his bowl to scoop up the last of the broth.

Taken aback, she stuttered, "N-no. She-she doesn't."

"Well, next time you talk to her, give her my compliments. That was fantastic," Lucas said, allowing his spoon to clatter into his empty bowl as he leaned back and patted his stomach.

"What about Wilson? He was the one who made it," Collette prompted.

"Yeah, good job, Wilson. I didn't think you knew how to cook anything you couldn't toss on a grill," Lucas razzed him.

"The only problem with eating soup is that it always makes my nose run," Emily commented insipidly. Even though she was holding a napkin on her lap, she excused herself to get a tissue.

In the bathroom, Emily balled her fingers into a fist and bit her knuckles, rocking her torso back and forth. She recognized the signs that she was on the brink of a crying jag and she didn't want it to happen in front of Lucas. Emotional lability. The nurse had said she shouldn't be surprised if her moods went up and down. *What would surprise me would be if my moods* didn't *fluctuate*, Emily thought wryly.

Suddenly a wave of nausea overcame her—she supposed it was an effect of the concussion—and she had to concentrate so hard on not getting sick that by the time the bilious feeling passed, she no longer felt like crying. Emily waited an extra minute before opening the door.

Wilson was pacing the hall but when he noticed her, he stopped and frantically whispered, "I'm sorry, Emily. Lucas didn't realize what he was saying. He wasn't living on the island yet when I took time off to go to the fu— To go to Chicago. You asked us not to talk about the accident with anyone who didn't already know, so we haven't. We haven't talked about it with anyone except each other."

"It's okay," Emily consoled him. "My mom would have been happy to hear he liked the soup. But don't go giving him her recipe or I *will* be really upset."

Wilson raised his hand and pledged, "Not even if he puts me in a sleeper hold."

Emily giggled; now *that* was more like the Wilson she remembered.

When they re-entered the kitchen, Lucas was loading the dishwasher and Collette was peering into the open freezer. "Are you two up for ice cream and a board game?"

"I'd like to, but my brain needs some rest and I'm eager to try out my new eye mask," Emily said, reaching for it.

To her relief, Wilson backed her up. "Yeah, that's probably a good idea. You should stay in our guest room. Collette, you can walk her over to the cottage to get what she needs for the night, right, babe?"

"Sure," Collette answered and put her arm through the crook of Emily's.

"Thanks again for all the help you gave me today, Lucas," Emily said.

"Sweet dreams, Em," he replied.

"Sweet dreams of *me*, Em," Collette imitated Lucas's voice as soon as they were out of earshot.

Emily nudged her gently. "Shush—or you're not getting any of the ice cream he brought for me to try."

"Too late. I already ate some while you were in the bathroom," Collette confessed and the two of them laughed the rest of the way to Emily's cottage.

Before Emily went to bed, Wilson asked if he could do a quick evaluation. Emily rolled her eyes, but she let him test her reflexes and shine a light in her pupils. She also allowed him to walk her up the stairs to the guest room, since Collette was taking a shower and it would have been futile for Emily to tell him she wasn't going to fall. *I can definitely see why his vigilance drives Collette crazy sometimes*, she thought. *But at least things feel a little more normal between us again.*

Wilson let go of her elbow at the doorway to the guest room. "Hang tough," he said.

It was a phrase Emily's father often used, by way of encouragement when she was sad or sick. To some it might have sounded callous, but to her, the phrase spoke volumes about her dad's understanding of how low she felt, and it spurred her onward.

"That's what my dad used to say."

A shadow crossed his face. "I remember," he acknowledged softly, before turning away.

"You hang tough, too, Wilson," Emily repeated back to him as he plodded down the hall.

Hang tough. What else could either of them do?

CHAPTER SIX

During the night, whenever Emily's dozing was interrupted by the occasional foghorn of a passing ship, her drowsy thoughts would drift from one snippet of the day to another.

She recalled how uncomfortable Wilson had seemed when she'd teased him about being her mother's favorite child. She'd meant it as a compliment. As an indication of how much her mother cherished him. But it occurred to Emily she ought to be more careful about making comments like that. Especially since Wilson couldn't even remember his own mother and he clearly hadn't been favored or cherished by his dad.

I hope eventually he feels comfortable enough to tell me about his DNA testing. Emily didn't know how exactly she could help, but she wanted to encourage Wilson as he searched for his father.

Then she thought about how glad she was to have the opportunity to get to know Collette better. Or about how her redecorating project had gotten completely sidelined for the day and she hoped she felt well enough to prep the walls for painting tomorrow.

Mostly, though, Emily reflected on her conversations with Lucas, especially the anecdote he told her about buying his van from a fisherman on the beach. Then she thought about his get well gifts and that he'd coasted up the driveway so he wouldn't wake her. Emily remembered how his arm hugged hers so snugly to him that she'd caught a whiff of his musky aftershave as he steered her to the cottage.

Following her family's accident, Emily's desire for any kind of physical closeness—just like her appetite for food—had simply and thoroughly vanished. Fortunately, at the time Devon had been extraordinarily patient and hadn't pushed the issue. On the contrary, he'd deliberately given her more space, and if he did draw her close, it was only for a brief, platonic hug or peck on the cheek. Not that she could blame him—she was aware that her appearance and behavior in the midst of her grief were far from alluring.

Emily imagined he must have believed—as she did—that eventually she'd snap out of it. But as the months passed without her experiencing so much as a flicker of desire, she vaguely wondered if there was something wrong with her physically, as well as emotionally. Her budding attraction to Lucas confirmed that she was healthy after all. But the question remained, was Collette right about Lucas being romantically interested in her, too?

*

In the morning, Emily padded downstairs. Since Collette and Wilson had been so attentive to her needs, she wanted to return the favor and she decided to make a crustless vegetable quiche for breakfast. While it was baking, she set the table and then went outside to clip a spray of tiger lilies and fern from the side garden to use as a centerpiece.

"Oh, what a luxury," Collette cooed when she and Wilson shuffled into the kitchen a few minutes later. "We never have anything except yogurt and fruit for breakfast. What pretty flowers, too."

"I hope you don't mind that I picked them from the side of the house?"

"No, of course not."

"When we were kids, my mom once commented how much she loved looking across the yard and seeing all the tiger lilies in bloom, so the next morning Wilson brought her a bouquet, remember, Wilson?" Emily asked, chuckling.

He nodded as Collette wrapped her arms around his waist and smooched his cheek. "Such a sweetie, even back then."

"Yeah, it was really sweet," Emily acknowledged. "Except what Wilson didn't know was that my mom was highly allergic to lilies, but she didn't have the heart to tell him she couldn't keep them in the house. So, long story short, she ended up in the ER that afternoon."

"Oh, no!" Collette exclaimed.

"Oh, yes," Emily answered, picking up a melon to slice it.

Wilson was scowling. "Here, I'll finish that for you," he suggested when he saw Emily leveraging a blade through the rind.

"He's a fanatic about cutting technique." Collette sounded apologetic. "Typical surgeon."

Wondering if her story had humiliated Wilson and feeling a bit humiliated by his brusqueness herself, Emily handed him the knife. "Be my guest."

When they sat down to eat, Emily realized the quiche was more appealing to her in theory than in reality and after a few bites, she pushed her plate aside. The flurry of morning activity had made her brain feel wooly and she wanted to take a couple acetaminophen tablets to keep her headache at bay. So, when Wilson offered to clear the table, she gratefully excused herself, saying she needed to go back to the cottage to shower and change.

"You're coming back for the cookout, right?" Collette asked.

"I don't know—"

"Like I've said, it's just people from cardiology and their significant others. Very low key."

"I'll think about it," was as close as Emily would come to committing. Even if she was able to dodge questions that might set her off emotionally, how would she convincingly skirt inquiries from physicians about what happened to her chin? She'd have to tell them the truth, which would be embarrassing.

Furthermore, it might get back to people on the Board. Emily accepted that they'd eventually find out about her concussion anyway. After all, the doctor had recommended Emily shouldn't drive for at least forty-eight hours and the way Emily was feeling right now, she couldn't imagine driving for another forty-eight hours after that. As a courtesy, she planned to touch base with Tim personally and explain her extended absence from the children's wing. But she wanted a day to recover, first. If she went to the cookout and had to explain her injuries, it was possible someone else might mention her concussion to Tim before she had the chance to do it herself.

I suppose I could call him this morning, she thought as she headed back to the cottage. But she didn't even feel ready to do that yet.

The sky was gray and a dense fog that mimicked Emily's headache had settled low over the ocean, but the morning air was warm enough for her to use the outdoor shower. She loved the luxury of contemplating the sky and treetops while lathering her hair and body within the quiet confines of the wooden stall. She didn't even mind sharing the soap dish, an oversized quahog shell, with a couple of ants, although she kept as much distance between herself and the daddy longlegs crawling up the side wall as possible.

The piney air, steaming water and medication relaxed her so much that afterward she blotted her hair dry with a towel, pulled on an extra-long T-shirt and reclined on the couch. She secured her pink eye mask into place for a spell of brain rest. It seemed that no time had passed before Collette was tugging at her sleeve.

"I'm still alive," she mumbled, slowly straightening into a sitting position.

"I sure hope so," a man's voice answered.

"Lucas?" She whipped off her eye mask. He was eyeing her bony legs.

"Wow, your knees really did take a hit the other day."

She tugged her T-shirt over her bare skin. "What are you doing here? This isn't a hospital, you know. Just because you're a doctor doesn't mean you can waltz into my bedroom anytime you feel like it."

"Technically, it's not a bedroom. And I don't have any clue about how to waltz."

She glowered at him. "What time is it?"

"It's quarter past one. That's why I finally had to wake you, Sleeping Beauty."

Even if Lucas was only kidding, Emily felt a stitch of pleasure at being called Sleeping Beauty. He explained that Collette was running a last-minute errand and Wilson had to pick someone up at the ferry dock. Lucas had arrived early, so he said he'd stay there to greet the other guests for the cookout. He indicated that he wouldn't have come into Emily's cottage, but Collette had mentioned she'd popped in on Emily earlier and was surprised to find her sleeping again.

"She asked you to check up on me?" Emily asked suspiciously.

Lucas chuckled. "Why do I feel like I'm getting the third degree? Collette or Wilson asked or I volunteered, I can't remember. They must be stuck in weekend traffic because they're not back yet. I waited for as long as I could before waking you up. Now that I can let them know you're okay, I'll leave. Are you coming up for the cookout? I'm grilling fish. It's so fresh it's practically still wiggling."

"Yeah, maybe," Emily agreed. She hadn't known Lucas would be at the cookout; she'd thought the guests were all from cardiology. Now that her headache had abated, she was feeling a little more stable emotionally, too. Besides, given the restrictions on her activities, hanging out with Lucas, Collette and Wilson and their colleagues was preferable to lazing around the rest of the afternoon by herself, even if it meant fielding questions about what happened to her face.

After Lucas left, Emily brushed her hair. She didn't want to show up looking like she just rolled out of bed, even if that was true. She deliberated about what to wear. Her jeans were too hot and stiff, and they irritated the scrapes on her kneecaps. Ditto for her capris. She decided on a long, straight, sleeveless cotton dress, identical to her black one, except that it was navy. She piled her hair loosely on top of her head, but that made her feel juvenile, as if she were going to the prom, so she plaited it into a side braid. A few tendrils framed her face. She hoped they would distract people from focusing on the oozy sore on her chin.

Barefoot, she exited through the back sliders and crossed the lawn toward Collette and Wilson's house. She barely glimpsed Lucas's white shirt through the patchy fog. He was standing on the deck in front of the grill, a silver spatula in his hand. The glass door slid open and someone stepped outside but Emily couldn't immediately identify who it was.

"This fog is thicker than honey, honey," a woman said coquettishly.

Emily halted in her tracks. It was clear neither Barbara nor Lucas had seen her coming, since they were turned to one side and she wasn't in their immediate range of vision. She considered coughing to make her presence known, but before she could, Barbara asked Lucas, "Are you going to start grilling the fish? I'm starving."

"I'm waiting until everyone gets here, first."

"Everyone *is* here."

"Emily's not."

"Seriously, Socorro? I can understand why Wilson had to invite her since they're neighbors or he grew up with her perfect little family or whatever, but *you're* under no obligation to give her special treatment just because she's decorating the pedi wing for free. This cookout is for cardiology staff, not for hospital volunteers."

"*I'm* not on cardiology staff."

"No, but you're here with me. That's different."

Of course: it made perfect sense. Collette had said that the cookout was for cardiology team members *and their significant others*. Barbara and Lucas were a couple. Emily couldn't believe she'd been so naïve to think Lucas had any romantic interest in her. She knew that her emotions might have been unstable from the concussion, but that didn't fully account for how deeply disappointed and ridiculously foolish she felt.

"Okay, I'll put the fish on. You win," Lucas said.

"I always do."

While Barbara tilted her head back and laughed a throaty laugh, Emily tiptoed back to the cottage. Since she didn't want to risk being seen on the deck or toward the front of the house, she entered through the side door she rarely used. As she sat on her bed unbraiding her hair, she realized it had been so long since she'd felt anything other than numbness that she must have misread Lucas's kindness and care.

He probably calls all of his little female patients Sleeping Beauty or Princess or some other patronizing nickname, like "Em." The connection she imagined existed between Lucas and herself was merely a demonstration of the same bedside manner that made him such a popular doctor.

Emily fashioned a slingshot with her elastic hair band. Wouldn't she like to snap Barbara with it, *ping*, right between the eyeballs. Or better yet, right on that perfectly rotund rump Barbs so proudly bragged about.

Yet as obnoxious as Barb was, she was right about one thing: Lucas *didn't* have a responsibility to give Emily special treatment. Not because he was the advising physician for the children's wing project, not because he'd taken her to the hospital when she had a concussion and not because he was pals with Wilson.

"I never asked for his help, so it's not like he's doing me any favors," she muttered indignantly. "I'm too busy to hang around with him anyway. I've got a mural to paint and a cottage to redecorate."

If there was one good thing about overhearing Lucas and Barbara talking about her—*again*—it was that Emily had gotten angry. And anger had a funny way of motivating her. Of making her feel more confident about her abilities and about carrying through with her summer goals.

"Feisty," Lucas had called her and he wasn't wrong. Emily would take "feisty" over "forlorn" any day.

*

On Monday morning, Emily walked up the hill and called Tim to tell him not to be surprised if he popped into the children's wing and saw the walls were still bare. Although she was still a little embarrassed to tell him about the tumble she'd taken, he was very sympathetic and asked if there was anything he or the board members could bring her.

"I have everything I need, thanks. I only wanted to let you know so you wouldn't worry about the mural. I've already been working on the sketches and design, so I'll continue to do that from home and next week I should be ready to replicate them on the walls."

"Your recovery is the first priority, so don't rush it," Tim urged her.

A few minutes later, Wilson and Collette stopped in at the cottage to remind her how important it was to rest before they went to work.

"The bed in the guest room is still made up so you're welcome to take a nap at our house, if your place gets too hot. Turn on the

A/C and help yourself to anything in the fridge," Collette said. "You should come by for supper tonight, too."

Recalling what Barbs implied about Wilson feeling obligated toward her, Emily was determined not to take advantage of their hospitality. "That's okay. I haven't eaten half of what you brought me yesterday evening, so I'll just pick at that. Besides, you two should enjoy your alone time before the baby gets here."

"There's a baby coming?" Collette asked, but her joke seemed lost on Wilson.

"You can use our landline if you need to call us," he told Emily. "Promise you'll have us paged if your headache worsens or you develop new symptoms."

"Will do," she replied, glad he hadn't tried to get her to promise she wouldn't work on her home improvement project, too. She wasn't going to overdo things, but she wasn't going to underdo them, either.

Emily waited until she heard their car pull away and then she went inside and assessed the walls. Washing them was the first step. Fortunately, the previous tenants had been meticulous and the cottage had been professionally cleaned a couple weeks ago anyway, so the walls were virtually dust and grime-free. Even so, Emily found the light cleaning process tiresome and she barely finished washing a quarter of the wall nearest the front door when she needed to take a break.

After a brief rest on the couch, Emily ambled down the stairs to the beach. The doctor had listed bodysurfing, contact sports and any motions that involved jumping as activities to avoid, but he had allowed for leisurely strolls.

It wasn't raining but the sky was whorled with gray clouds and a stiff breeze stung Emily's chin as it whistled past her ears. It wasn't long before she was fatigued, so she plopped down in the sand, hugging her arms around herself for warmth. She watched a sandpiper scurrying along the edge of the raucous surf, which burst with dynamic sprays of icy whiteness. *I'll have to include a few sandpipers in the nautical room.*

The problem was, she already had plenty of ideas for the marine-themed room; what she needed was inspiration for the rest of the landscapes. She had decided one of them would be a rainforest and another a desert, both of which were inspired by her parents' exotic travels. Emily had saved all the emails they'd sent during their trips over the years. But even if she'd had a decent connection to the internet, she knew she couldn't reopen their messages to view the attached photos without descending into another bout of melancholy. *Maybe Collette or Wilson will let me use one of their laptops and I can search online for desert and rainforest images.*

Standing, Emily twisted to brush the sand from the back of her pants and she noticed the roof of a small cottage pocketed within the high dunes, some twenty-five or thirty yards back from the cliff. Either it hadn't been built when Emily was a child or erosion and time had left it more exposed now than it was then, but Emily didn't recall ever seeing it before.

As she turned to face it straight on, she caught a flash of white near the edge of the cliff and she squinted to make out its form. At first, it appeared to be a human figure hiding behind a sign of some sort, her long white hair billowing around her head like a sail in the wind. Then Emily recognized it was a woman standing at an easel, painting. Delighted, she waved exaggeratedly, but the artist didn't wave back.

Remembering her own easel, Emily returned to the cottage and cleaned the antique with lemon oil she'd purchased at the hardware store. Because she was worried about the possibility of rain and she didn't want the wood to get warped, once she had finished, she carried the easel into her childhood bedroom and positioned it in front of the windows with an ocean view. *Mom would be happy to know I'm going to put this to good use.*

Then she returned to Peter's room to dust and polish the desk. After cleaning the top and two front legs, she walked around to the other side to wipe off the back legs. She was delighted to discover this was a two-sided desk; like the front, the so-called "back" of the desk had two knobs on each of its drawers, too, but instead of being dummy drawers, these were functional.

When Emily tugged on the knobs of the left-hand drawer, it slid out easily. Its contents included a scattering of thumbtacks, rusted paperclips, a pencil with its tip broken off and a Massachusetts road map. The right-hand drawer was jammed, whether from age or from the humidity, but Emily kept wiggling it until it finally opened. Inside was a stack of four or five nature magazines, which, according to their dates, were published the year before Peter was born. *These have got to be collector's items by now.*

Emily removed them from the drawer and as she shuffled through them, she found a pad of yellow legal-size paper sandwiched between the last two magazines. She brought it to the window for a better look. Although the blue ink was faded, Emily would have recognized her father's handwriting anywhere: when he printed, he used all capital letters and when he wrote in cursive, his penmanship slanted to the left.

On the top sheet of paper was a printed list:

ONION

TOMATOES—2 LRG

BASIL

GARLIC

CHIX BREAST

HALF-AND-HALF

PARM CHEESE

NEWSPAPER

LIGHTBULB—DECK

O-RING

ANT TRAPS

BOSTON CREAM DONUT

Emily smiled to herself; clearly her father had organized his shopping list according to destination. First the market, then the hardware store and last the Donut Shanty. He must have been planning to eat his treat on the sly, since Emily's mom didn't like Boston cream and he hadn't indicated what kind of donut she wanted.

She lifted the page to see if anything was written on the next sheet. It was blank, so she leafed through a few more sheets until

she came to some words written in cursive. She had to squint closely
because he'd crossed a line through them.

~~Janice, my one and only love,~~

The same with the next phrases, which read:

~~I need you to know~~
~~I love you more than~~
~~The depth of my love~~
~~There aren't enough words to say~~

There were several longer passages that were blocked out so
thoroughly Emily couldn't make out what they said.

She pressed her hand over her mouth, uncertain whether she
was about to sob or to giggle. She'd always known what a strong
marriage her parents had, but she hadn't realized her father was such
a romantic in his younger years and it moved her deeply. *It's not even
as if Dad wrote this for a special occasion—it's dated July 1 and Mom's
birthday was in January and their wedding anniversary was in March.*

Emily would have considered it an unthinkable invasion of
privacy to read her parents' correspondence if they were alive. But
as she sat in her brother's empty bedroom, she felt so alone. Reading
about her father's love for her mother in his own handwriting was
a way of bringing the past back. A way of bringing *them* back. She
couldn't seem to stop herself from lifting the page to see if he'd
written anything else on the next sheet. He had. And again, he'd
scratched lines through his words:

~~I wish I could~~
~~If only I could~~
~~I would do anything~~

Emily flipped through the rest of the notepad but it was blank. As touched as she was by her father's sentiments for her mother, she knew she had no right to be reading his scribblings; but she couldn't bring herself to discard the pad, either, so she set it atop of the magazines and she was about to place the entire stack into the drawer when she heard her phone ringing downstairs.

She spun toward the door but that made her dizzy and she had to stop and catch her balance. By the time she got to it, the phone apparently had lost its signal. Curious to find out who called, Emily headed toward the hill near Collette and Wilson's back deck. She was confounded to discover Devon's number in her call log. He hadn't left a message or a text. What could he have possibly wanted?

Emily deliberated about whether she ought to text or call him back. No, if he really wanted to speak to her, he'd try again. Besides, maybe he'd just dialed her number by accident. It would be awkward to make small talk after all this time. Especially since Devon didn't know she'd come to Dune Island and she saw no reason to share that information with him now that their relationship was over.

I really wanted to have a marriage that lasted the rest of my life, the way Mom and Dad's did, Emily thought ruefully as she headed back toward the cottage. *Devon and I didn't even make it to the altar.*

In another month, it would be July Fourth, one year since Devon proposed in candlelight on the deck of a private yacht he'd rented for the occasion. He had timed his question so that immediately after

Emily answered, the sky erupted with the annual fireworks display over Lake Union. As a marketing executive, Devon knew how to pull out all the stops and Emily had been so overwhelmed by the romantic gesture—and the ring—that she almost didn't answer. He later joked to his friends that if she hadn't said yes when she did, he was going to jump ship in embarrassment over being rejected.

While Emily appreciated all the care Devon had put into making the occasion special, it would have been just as meaningful if he had looked into her eyes and whispered, "I love you, Emily. Will you marry me?"

He never seemed to understand it was the sincere, quiet gestures that mattered most to me, she thought, going upstairs to continue cleaning the desk. *Devon never would have interrupted his Saturday chores to compose a love letter, agonizing over every word, the way Dad did for Mom. He would have considered that too ordinary. Too boring.*

As Emily picked up the pad of paper and absently skimmed her father's shopping list, two words jumped out at her. Onions? Garlic? Why hadn't she noticed them before? Her mother was allergic to onions and garlic—they were part of the lily family.

From the rest of the items on the list, Emily assumed her dad had been preparing to make chicken parmesan, something her mother couldn't eat. She couldn't even be in the kitchen while it was cooking. As a precaution, Emily's family had always banned garlic and onions from their house completely, so Emily assumed her mother must have gone somewhere else for supper that evening. But just as quickly, it occurred to her that maybe the reason there was only one donut on her father's list was because her mother hadn't been at the cottage that morning, either.

Wait a minute—why was Dad really writing Mom a letter when he could have told her in person how he felt? Emily had thought he was being especially romantic by expressing himself on paper, but now she concluded her mother must have gone off-island for more than a day. Which would have been strange, considering how much her mother relished being at Dune Island. *Maybe she had to go to Grandma and Grandpa's house in Maryland for some reason and Dad missed her so much he wanted to send her a love letter. It's still very romantic.*

Yet as she put the pad and magazines into the drawer, Emily felt more confused than comforted by what she'd discovered. Although her grandparents owned the cottage, they only came to Dune Island for the first two weeks in July, so Emily couldn't make sense of why her mother would have been visiting them in Maryland instead. Especially not without her father, who would have had to stay alone at the cottage.

Unable to quash the uneasy feeling that something just didn't add up, Emily pushed the desk drawer shut. She almost wished she'd hadn't been able to open it in the first place.

*

For the rest of the week, Emily established a pattern that included indolently roaming the beach, sketching, napping, painting the walls and visiting with Collette in the evenings. Sometimes with Wilson, too, although he seemed to be making himself scarce.

By Friday, not only did she feel stronger physically and emotionally, but she had assembled all the sketches she intended to replicate in three of the eight children's rooms at the hospital. She'd also finished painting the cottage living room and dining room walls, which was particularly fulfilling because she could imagine how elated her mother would have been by the changes.

It was so warm, Emily briefly considered donning her bathing suit before she hit the beach for a late afternoon stroll. But, given that she wasn't an accomplished swimmer even in the best of health, and she still wasn't sure how strong the currents were, she figured she shouldn't venture into the water while she was alone.

Plus, she was embarrassed by her shape. Not that the seagulls would have cared, but she felt insecure about the possibility of running into Collette and Wilson—or worse, Lucas—afterward. She didn't want them to see her bony legs and practically concave chest. Instead, she lounged on the couch, fanning herself with her sketch pad.

"Anyone home?" Collette called through the screen door of the slider.

Emily invited her in and instantly Collette raved about the walls. She hadn't seen them until now because the women usually chatted on the deck or next door, as a precaution against exposing Collette and the baby to any fumes.

"I feel like I walked into the wrong house. With the paneling painted white, it looks a lot more like a cottage than like a cabin now."

"You mean looks a lot more like a cottage than a *cave* now." Emily was so motivated about how much brighter and more open the downstairs appeared, she had decided to make other improvements, too. She pointed to the clunky wooden light hanging above the dining table. "Now, I've got to replace that thing."

"I thought wagon-wheel chandeliers were in right now."

"Yeah, the *style* is in. But I think that hideous thing is an actual wagon wheel. My grandma's grandma probably passed it down to her and she was running out of space to store it behind the knee wall so she hung it from the ceiling," Emily said with a chuckle. "You want some iced tea?"

"Only if I can swim in it." Collette waved her hand in front of her face. "I'm stinking hot. Want to come for a dip with me?"

"Is the tide in or out? I'm not a very strong swimmer."

Collette said that it was going out, which was why she wanted to swim at the inlet, where the water was calmer than in the open ocean. She reminded Emily that the current would gently carry them from behind the dunes around to the front beach, so they wouldn't have to swim a stroke; they'd just have to float.

"It's also ultra-private, which is a necessity for me at this stage in my pregnancy. The fact that I'm allowing you to see me in my bathing suit shows how much I trust you not to judge me."

"I'll make a deal with you. You don't judge how I look in my bathing suit and I won't judge how you look in yours."

"Ha! The deal should be that I won't *envy* how you look in your bathing suit and you won't judge how I look in mine."

"Listen, I've been overweight before—which is not the same as being pregnant, I might add—and the comments people have made about me being underweight have been just as hurtful as the comments they made when I was overweight. Surprisingly, most of them have come from women. Why do we do that to each other?"

"Why do we do it to ourselves?"

"Good point," Emily said and agreed to meet Collette at the top of the staircase to the beach after they'd changed.

Despite the conversation they'd just had, when Emily glanced in the mirror, she regretted not buying a new suit for the summer.

Spandex wasn't supposed to be baggy, but the elastic gaped around her legs and armpits. Her breasts were little nubs lost in a wrinkle of fabric. For years, she'd fantasized about how she'd flaunt it if she ever achieved her goal weight, but now she couldn't cover up fast enough. She seized a T-shirt from a hook and tied a towel around her waist.

As she and Collette waded through tidal pools on the way to the inlet, Emily dropped hints in an effort to find out if someone was planning a shower for her. But Collette didn't offer her any information and Emily didn't want to ask outright, in case the shower was supposed to be a surprise. So instead she asked if Wilson had gotten his DNA test results back yet.

"If he has, he hasn't mentioned it to me." Collette pointed to the water. "Lucas told me he saw three seals at this end of the beach the other day."

Emily felt a pang of discomfort at the mention of his name. She was surprised to hear he'd been to the beach, since she hadn't seen any trace of his van or of him the entire week. She supposed he'd decided Barbara was right; he didn't need to give Emily any "special treatment," so he hadn't stopped by her cottage to see how she was doing. Which was just as well for her.

"I never heard about seals being in this area when I was a kid. They won't bother us, will they?"

"Nah, they keep their distance. Some people are wary of swimming with them though, because sharks prey on seals, but what are the odds?"

Emily gasped. "Seriously?"

"I wouldn't worry about it. If a shark is going to mistake anyone for a seal, it's going to be me, not you."

Emily clucked her tongue. "Collette, what did we just say about criticizing our bodies?"

"I wasn't criticizing. I was merely pointing out my shape is more circular than yours, so to the eyes of a shark, I look more like a seal and I'd be a better snacking choice."

"If you're trying to make me feel better about swimming in the inlet, it isn't working."

All along their walk, the women had been bordered by the ocean to the left and dunes to the right, but up ahead, the sandy mounds dwindled where the ocean merged with the inlet. Emily could make out where the beach picked up again about two hundred yards across the pool of rolling currents, but the water was too deep to swim across. A cormorant skimmed the scintillating surface as it flew low on its way to the other side. The blond sands contrasted sharply with the cobalt waters and powder-blue sky, and Emily was humbled by the inherent artistry of the landscape.

"Ta-dah. There it is in all its resplendent glory," she announced. "Mermaids' Inlet."

"Mermaids' Inlet?"

"Yeah, that's what my mother used to call it. She'd walk down here almost every day to see the sunrise. A couple of times I got up early and went with her, but mostly it was something she did alone."

"That's the perfect name. I'm going to call it that from now on, too."

They meandered along the little peninsula jutting into the inlet, the air feeling cooler and drier than it had only a hundred yards back. Once they'd looped around behind the dunes, Collette stripped off her T-shirt, dumped it in a heap with her towel and then stepped into the water backward. The embankment sloped steeply; within two steps, she was up to her waist. She held her arms out and lowered herself into a back float.

"Ahh. I've been waiting all year for this," she called as she drifted toward the bend, her stomach bobbing above the surface like a beach ball. "Wait till you try it!"

Emily dropped her towel, but she kept her T-shirt on. She hovered on the ledge of sand, contemplating the water.

"One, two, three!" she counted and jumped forward. It was so deliciously cool it made every cell in her body tingle. She floated on her stomach, keeping her head above the water. "This is great!" she shrieked to Collette.

"It's heavenly," Collette echoed.

Emily felt a twinge of loneliness at the word "heavenly." It never ceased to amaze her how the most benign expressions could trigger thoughts of her family's death. She swiveled flat onto her back and beheld the cloudless sky. *I wish you three were here. You'd love this.*

"Look out!" Collette yelled when Emily caught up with her a moment later. "Traffic jam!"

The current had carried them to shallow waters and Collette had to roll onto her hands and knees in order to get into a standing position. Emily barreled straight toward her and narrowly missed a collision.

"Here, take my hand, I'll help you." Emily rose and held out her hand but she foundered backward.

Collette lunged for her, but the sand was too soft and she was too heavy so she couldn't gain any traction and Emily landed on her bottom with a big splash. Once she was upright again, she managed to help Collette to firmer ground. Although the water was only shin-high, the current was powerful and they both struggled to keep their balance. The harder they tried, the harder they laughed.

"Wanna go again?" Collette asked when they finally reached dry land.

"I'll beat you!" Emily raced back to the starting point, leaped over their clothes, and plunged into the water.

When she emerged, she somersaulted onto her back again. As she contemplated the sky once more, she had a new thought. *Since you can't be here, I'm going to enjoy this enough for all four of us.*

CHAPTER SEVEN

On Sunday morning, Emily woke to the sound of a long, low rumble. Not waves against the shore, but thunder bowling across the island. She pinched her eyelids shut and reminisced about the time Devon had taken her to a Mariners game because someone had given his marketing firm tickets for third-row seats behind home plate. As was often the case in Seattle, it was drizzling that night. During the bottom of the seventh inning, Emily noticed a few flashes of light, which at first she assumed were cameras going off, but then the stadium reverberated with thunder.

Having lived in the Chicago suburbs, where tornado sirens often blared throughout the summer, Emily had a deeply rooted fear of thunderstorms. It didn't matter that electrical storms in Seattle were literally a flash in the pan compared to thunderstorms in Illinois; at the baseball game, she retreated to the women's room, where she wouldn't have to see the sky flicker and fork with light. The so-called storm ended about five minutes after it began, but Emily wasn't taking any chances. Instead of rejoining Devon and fifteen thousand other fans who had remained in their seats, she stayed in the bathroom until the game ended.

By that time, Devon had been so panicked by her absence that he enlisted the help of nearby female fans to check the restrooms in three different sections of the stadium until they located her. Emily had felt terrible about worrying him, but he said he was just relieved she was okay.

"When it comes to lightning, I operate on the principle of what I can't see won't hurt me," she had explained as he enveloped her in his arms.

"You're crazy," he'd replied fondly, nuzzling her ear.

Emily closed her eyes at the memory. *Even before the accident, Devon was always tolerant of my quirks*, she thought, feeling guilty. *I suppose it wouldn't hurt for me to return his call, just in case he needs to tell me something important—I was really fond of his mom, so I hope she's okay.* But she couldn't get a signal, which was probably for the best anyway; Emily had forgotten about the three-hour time difference and Devon might have been alarmed to receive an early morning phone call.

Instead, she got up and made honey-bran muffins, using the ingredients she'd picked up when Collette took her grocery shopping on Saturday. Since she'd finished painting the living room, she'd asked Wilson to come over to help her move the desk downstairs this morning, so she wanted to have something to offer him to eat. Emily was hoping he might take the opportunity to confide in her about his interest in finding his father.

"Your chin appears to be healing nicely," he commented as he wiped his shoes off on the mat near the back sliders. "How's the noggin? Any problems this week?"

"Not any that are worth mentioning."

"Meaning what? Blurred vision? Ringing in your ears? Muscle weakness?"

"None of the above, doc," Emily joked. "I had a dull headache last night. It's gone now."

Wilson frowned. "It could be you're not getting enough rest, although headaches can be symptoms of post-concussive syndrome. You may experience them for a few weeks. But if it worsens or you notice the other symptoms the doctor discussed with you, you should be checked out right away."

"I've got a follow-up appointment tomorrow, so I'll mention my headaches then," Emily informed him. "You know, Wilson, I appreciate your concern, but you've got to stop being such a Nervous Nellie. If Peter were here, he'd say, 'Lighten up, Wilson. Emily's tough, she'll shake it off.'"

"No. If Peter were here, he'd say, 'What happened to my sister? She looks like she lost a fight with a badger.'"

"Har-har," she jeered over her shoulder as Wilson trailed her into the upstairs bedroom. But inwardly she was pleased he seemed to be in good spirits, for once. She pointed to the desk. "Which end do you want to take?"

"I'll take this end, so you won't have to walk backward down the stairs. But let's remove the drawers so they don't fly open and fall out."

"The right-hand drawer sticks, so I don't think we need to take it out, but I'll put this one downstairs," Emily said, removing the left-hand drawer. "I'll be back in a sec."

When she returned, she discovered Wilson must have worked the drawer open because it was resting near his feet and he was holding the legal pad of paper. He looked as guilty as if he'd been caught red-handed robbing a bank. Immediately Emily realized he must have done the same thing she had done; he'd flipped through the notepad and happened upon her father's notes.

"I-I-I," he stammered, looking so mortified that she thought he might cry. So mortified that she thought *she* might cry on his behalf.

If it had been anyone other than Wilson who had read her father's private sentiments to her mother, Emily would have lit into them for overstepping their bounds. But Wilson reading them was like . . . it was like *Peter* reading them. Wilson was practically family and under the circumstances, that somehow made it permissible. She crossed the room and placed her hand on his shoulder.

"It's okay," she told him. "It's nothing to get so upset about."

But he blurted out, "Emily, I'm very sorry. I don't know what to say—"

"Really, it's all right. I actually don't think my father would have minded that we read what he wrote." Emily chuckled. "Knowing him, he would have been proud that his love for my mother was immortalized in print."

Wilson made a guttural noise and his cheeks and ears went crimson. Seeing his response, Emily thought, *That was insensitive of me to boast about my dad's love for my mom, considering Wilson's father ended it with his mother when he found out she was pregnant.* Emily left to bring Wilson a glass of water, which he drank slowly, as if he were stalling.

Finally he set the glass on the window sill. Bending to push the desk drawer farther out of the way, he asked, "So is that all you . . . all you found?"

Baffled, Emily scrunched up her forehead. She had told Collette and Wilson about the easel, which she frequently took outside to sketch the landscape and obviously he already knew about the chess set, too. "Well, my mother also left a vintage cradle for me behind the knee wall. It's in the other bedroom if you'd like to see it."

"No. I mean did you find anything else in the desk? Any other notes or...?"

"Only the nature magazines and some paper clips. Why? What else was I supposed to find?"

"Nothing. I was just curious. Sometimes people stash important documents in desks and forget all about them. But your parents were probably too organized to do something like that." Wilson's smile seemed forced when he jested, "Although the same couldn't be said for your grandmother!"

"Well, all that was in the desk were the magazines and that pad of paper," Emily reiterated.

Collette's voice sounded from the bottom of the stairwell. "Are you two up there?"

"Yep. We're coming down now. Clear the runway," Wilson joked, but Emily couldn't dismiss their peculiar conversation so quickly.

He acted as if I'm keeping something from him but he's *the one who seems to know something I don't know,* she thought as they carried the desk downstairs. *It's as if he expected me to find something else in the desk, like more letters.*

Then it occurred to her maybe Wilson was hoping her parents had left a memento for him, or at least a note. Maybe that's why he'd rejected the chess set, too; because he thought in time Emily would discover a keepsake designated specifically for him, instead of for Peter. That would explain why he'd hint at the subject instead of asking her about it outright.

If that's what it is, I really wish he'd reconsider accepting the chess set, Emily thought, but now that Collette was here, she didn't feel comfortable discussing it with him further. Besides, Wilson beat a path out the door as soon as they'd positioned the desk in front of the window in the living room.

"I shouldn't be eating again. I already had breakfast," Collette said when Emily served them both muffins with milk. "Pretty soon I won't fit into any of my clothes at all."

She lowered herself from the breakfast bar stool and motioned toward her black leggings and green and pink striped blouse.

"See this outfit? I look like a watermelon. But I'd rather wear this than the ridiculous maternity tops they sell in the shops around here. If I don't get off the island to go shopping pretty soon, instead of wearing a dress to my baby shower, I'll have to wrap a queen-sized sheet around me, like a toga."

"Oh, good, you're having a shower. Is there anything I can do? I'd love to help whoever is planning it."

"That's really sweet. It's going to be a Jack 'n' Jill party, so Wilson and his guy friends will be there, too. Some of the women at work are putting it together—they're having it at our house, though. Are you sure you want to help?"

"Definitely. I've wanted to ask if I could be involved but I didn't know if it was a secret or not."

"I'm really glad they decided not to surprise me. The last thing I need is to waddle home from a swim at the inlet and find fifty or sixty women *and men* gathered on my deck, yelling, 'Surprise!' "

Fifty guests? Emily gulped. On an island this size, she had assumed there would be fewer than twenty-five. She had also assumed all of them would be women. But it was too late to rescind her offer to help. After Collette gave Emily her friends' contact info and Emily said it was fine to share hers with them, too, she sauntered back up the hill to her house.

For the better part of the day, Emily moped around the cottage. She was so befuddled by her conversation with Wilson and over-whelmed by the idea of interacting with fifty strangers at a party that it required all of her energy just to close her eyes and give her brain a rest.

*

On Monday, Collette took half a day off so she could take Emily to an appointment with the neurologist Wilson had recommended, even though Emily insisted she would have been able to drive there herself.

After a thorough examination, the doctor said Emily appeared capable of driving safely and that her condition was improving, but cautioned her about taking on too much at once and told her to come into the office immediately if she experienced a worsening of her symptoms.

"As with any illness, you should get plenty of rest and plenty of fluids—except for alcohol. You'll want to avoid that for a while," the doctor said as she entered her report into Emily's electronic medical record.

Emily's father had been a teetotaler and her mother rarely drank, so alcohol hadn't been part of Emily's background growing up.

She'd never indulged in it when she got older, either, because most alcoholic beverages gave her a migraine, although she could tolerate the occasional celebratory glass of champagne.

"That won't be a problem."

"Good, because among other things, alcohol after a concussion can increase your risk of developing depression."

Trying to suppress a chuckle at the irony of the doctor's warning, Emily made a noise that sounded like a snore and the doctor looked up from her keyboard. Embarrassed, Emily repeated that she wouldn't drink and then she hightailed it out of the office.

Collette was waiting for her on a bench in the sunshine outside and when Emily came rushing toward her, she knitted her brows and asked what the doctor said.

"She said I'm as healthy as an ox."

"No, really, what did she say?"

"Really, she said I'm fine, *Wilson*," Emily teased. But Collette still looked skeptical so Emily elaborated, "Or that I will be fine if I keep doing what I'm doing. Getting rest, limiting my activities, blah, blah, blah."

"Blah, blah, blah? Those were her exact words?"

"Yep, they were. 'Blah, blah, blah.' Or maybe she said, 'Blah, blah, blah-dee, blah,' I'm not sure. She talked kind of fast," Emily retorted.

Collette stopped walking and clutched Emily's forearm, doubling over. For a second, Emily was afraid she was having contractions until Collette squealed, "Stop making me laugh or I'll wet my pants."

"You mean you'll lose control of your blah-blah-bladder?"

"Emily, stop it!" Collette gasped, digging her fingernails into Emily's arm.

Emily laughed so hard she had to press her legs together, too. And she kept laughing, even while people passed by, giving the two of them strange looks and a wide berth. She was cracking up so hard no sound was coming out of her mouth and tears were streaming down her cheeks, which was the most fun kind of crying.

If someone had told her yesterday that today she'd be standing on a public sidewalk, practically screaming with hilarity, she never would have believed them. But her friendship with Collette had that effect on her. *That's why I can't back out of helping to plan an amazing shower for her*, she decided. *And for Wilson, too.*

*

Over the next several weeks, Emily slowly increased her activity to include going to the hospital to work on the murals for a few hours in the mornings. In the afternoons she rested and then spent time painting the upstairs bedroom walls a washed-out, paler shade of the turquoise she'd bought for the shutters, before moving on to paint the sills, trim and molding with the same white paint she'd used downstairs.

In the evenings, she often visited with Collette and, less frequently, with Wilson, too. Emily had been so unsettled by his asking if she'd found anything else in the desk, she'd emptied its drawers a second time and then thoroughly checked behind the knee wall again at both ends of the house. Finding nothing, she decided she'd try harder to convince Wilson to accept the chess set, but either her timing was off or he was deliberately avoiding her, as it seemed whenever she came by he was either holed away in his study or he had an errand to run.

Once, after he suddenly decided to go fishing the moment Emily sat down in a chair on their deck, she remarked to Collette, "If I didn't know better, I'd think he doesn't want to be around me."

"Don't be silly. He's got a lot on his mind, that's all."

"Oh—did he get his DNA test results back?"

"I don't know. I gave up asking about that because he's been stressed out enough already. He doesn't need me nagging him. He'll tell me when he's ready."

She might have been wrong, but Emily interpreted Collette's answer to imply that *she* was nagging *Collette* about it, so she decided to back off the subject entirely until Collette or Wilson brought it up themselves.

Meanwhile, she had things on her mind, too, which was why she always made time to walk the beach. There was something about the movement of the ocean, coupled with her own gait, that triggered her imagination. She rarely returned without a new idea for the hospital or the cottage, or simply a new perspective about what Lucas referred to as "the big picture."

I can't believe how long it's been since I've seen his van here, Emily thought one afternoon in late June. *I haven't crossed paths with him at the hospital, either.* Not that she necessarily wanted to see him, but she sort of expected him to pop into the children's wing to check on her progress or ask if she needed anything, the way Tim had made a point of doing on several occasions.

Concerned something might have happened to him but uneasy about calling him herself, one evening Emily made up her mind to ask Collette if Lucas was all right. She had just painted her parents' bedroom and she needed to air it out before sleeping in it, so she arranged to spend the night at Wilson and Collette's house. Wilson had gone to meet with a colleague and Collette, whose "nesting instinct" had finally kicked in, was reorganizing her silverware drawer.

"I'm surprised I haven't seen Lucas around lately," Emily remarked nonchalantly as she sat at the breakfast bar, using Wilson's laptop to research images for a mountain mural.

"Why does my husband do this? It drives me nuts," Collette griped. She either hadn't heard Emily's comment or she was too distracted to answer.

"What drives you nuts?"

"He puts the dessert forks in the same compartment as the salad forks. Why?" Collette tipped the entire tray upside down on the countertop, making a terrible racket. "He's a surgeon, for Pete's sake! He can tell the difference between a dozen types of scalpels with his eyes closed, but he can't learn the difference between a dessert fork and a salad fork?"

Uh-oh. Emily had chosen the wrong night to stay at Wilson and Collette's house and the wrong moment to broach the subject of Lucas's whereabouts. She bit her lip and said nothing while Collette continued jangling utensils together as she tossed them one by one back into the tray.

She had just moved on to the cupboards—her husband apparently had no appreciation for the patterns and function of glassware, either—when Wilson walked through the door. Emily pretended not to notice that Collette lifted her shoulder, blocking him from kissing her cheek.

"What's new with you, Emily?" he asked, eyeing the laptop.

"Well, I've just put the finishing touches on my rainforest mural, so now I'm gathering ideas for a mountain setting. Don't ask me what I'll paint when I'm through with this one though."

"How about a jungle?"

Collette snickered. "That's too similar to a rainforest, Wilson."

Nervous that Collette was on the brink of lecturing her husband about the similarities and differences between various ecosystems, as well as between pieces of cutlery, Emily lowered the lid to the laptop and hopped to her feet.

"I need to go take care of something at the cottage. I'll be back in a few minutes."

The clouds were so heavy Emily feared she'd wind up with a second concussion if she tried to make it to her place in the pitch dark, so instead she blindly inched toward the staircase leading to the beach. She perched on the top step and faced the ocean. Although she couldn't see the waves, she could tell by their sound they were shattering against the shore hard and fast.

An "angry ocean," her mother would have called it. The discord of the surf and the tension between Collette and Wilson reminded Emily of a story her mother once shared after Emily had gotten into a terrible argument with her first true love, a college boyfriend. At the time, she was considering breaking up with him and she asked her mother for advice.

Instead of suggesting what she thought her daughter should do, Emily's mother had told her about a terrific argument she'd had with Emily's dad one summer evening. Afterward, Janice had sat on the staircase to the beach, watching and listening to the waves. The tide rolled out and the tide rolled in again and she'd just sat there, contemplating what their relationship meant to her and whether she had it in her to forgive him.

At first light, she wasn't any closer to an answer than she'd been at midnight, but she was tired, so she stood up to go back to the cottage and get some sleep. Because she'd sat in the same position for so long, her joints and muscles were stiff and she could hardly move. As she was stretching, the sun came up over the inlet and it saturated the sky with the most vibrant pink hue she'd ever seen. That's when she made up her mind.

"I decided the ocean of my anger wasn't more powerful than the sunrise of my love," was how she had expressed it, a faraway look in her eyes.

"That must have been one big fight," Emily had remarked.

"It was," her mother had answered, without divulging the specifics. "But it wasn't bigger than our relationship—our marriage. It wasn't bigger than our dream to start a family together."

As Emily recalled that conversation with her mother, it occurred to her that if there was any consolation whatsoever in her parents' dying, it was that they weren't alive to experience the death of one of their long-awaited children. A shudder made her shoulders convulse, so Emily stood up to go inside.

As she reached the back deck, Collette and Wilson's voices rained down from above. Apparently, they were arguing in their bedroom and they must have had their slider open because Emily could hear every word. In her haste to get into the kitchen so she could shut out their conversation, she knocked into the grill.

"Oof," she moaned, clutching her stomach and trying to catch her breath.

"I don't mind if Emily uses my laptop, but you should have checked with me first," Wilson barked. "I might have had something private on there I wouldn't want her to see."

"Like what? An email from your mistress?"

"That isn't even a little bit funny, Collette."

"It wasn't meant to be!" Collette's shouting was followed by the slamming of two doors in rapid succession.

Emily stood frozen in place for a good three minutes, afraid if she entered the house too soon, Collette and Wilson would know she'd been close enough to hear them bickering. She really just wanted to go back to the cottage. She could have slept on the couch. But her sudden disappearance also would have tipped Collette and Wilson off that she'd heard them fighting. She took a deep breath and went inside.

By then, Wilson was standing over the kitchen sink, gulping down a glass of water. Emily noticed his laptop was still on the table, but its lid was up and it wasn't where Emily had left it. *Was Wilson deleting a document? What is it he's so worried I'll find?*

"Did you take care of what you needed to do?" Wilson asked without turning around.

"Yeah. I'm all set."

The last couple of times Emily saw him, she thought Wilson looked rather gaunt, but now that she stood behind him, she could tell just how much weight he'd lost. His baggy clothes and slumped shoulders gave him an air of defeat. And it was no wonder—in addition to whatever else was troubling him, Collette had really let him have it tonight. Moved with empathy, Emily walked over and gave Wilson a sisterly hug.

"It will be okay," she said after letting him go. "My mom told me she and my dad had some huge arguments before Peter was born, too. But they got past it. It's normal for there to be some tension when people are becoming parents for the first time."

"Goes to show how much you know," Wilson muttered, shaking his head.

Emily smiled. "Okay. Maybe '*some* tension' is an understatement. But everything will be all right eventually, you'll see."

Wilson gave her a weak smile and then announced he was going to turn in for the night.

It wasn't until she was in bed herself that Emily realized maybe Wilson hadn't intended "Goes to show how much you know" the way she'd taken it. She speculated he could have meant the conflict between him and Collette had nothing to do with becoming first-time parents. *Maybe their fighting is related to whatever Wilson is hiding on the computer*, she thought.

Then an even more disturbing thought struck from out of the blue: What if he'd been referring to Emily's *parents'* conflict before *Peter* was born? What if he'd meant, "If you think they got past it, that goes to show how much you know"? Emily bolted upright in bed and hugged a pillow to her chest, as if to muffle the sound of her heart banging at her ribs. *Does Wilson know something about Mom and Dad's relationship I don't know? Is that why he was so curious about whether there were more notes in the desk?*

Of course, that was ridiculous. Emily's parents had the strongest marriage of any couple she'd ever met. *That might even be one of the reasons I'm not married yet—because none of my relationships lives up to what they modeled for me in theirs*, she comforted herself.

No, it was far more likely that when Wilson said, "Goes to show how much you know," he was responding to Emily's assurance that everything would be okay. It was probably an expression of his doubt, that's all.

Not entirely convinced but calmer now, Emily rearranged her bedding and leaned back against the pillow. It suddenly occurred to her that on top of everything else she was questioning, she still hadn't found out what was going on with Lucas. *That's a puzzle for another day*, she thought, before dropping off into a fitful sleep.

*

The next day, Emily was painting a pine cone in the mountain mural room at the hospital when she was startled by a woman's voice in the doorway.

"Excuse me. You're Emily, right?"

"Yes."

"I'm Gail Carson—Collette's friend," she said.

"Hello, Gail." Tired from waking up throughout the night and mulling over the argument she'd heard between Collette and Wilson, and pondering what Wilson might be hiding, Emily couldn't place how or why she should have known Gail.

"Collette told me you wanted to help us with the baby shower. We'd welcome your input." Gail said that she and two other women were having a planning session on Friday after work at Captain Clark's restaurant, which was within walking distance of the hospital.

"I'd love to join you," Emily agreed, although with everything else she'd had on her mind, she'd temporarily forgotten about the shower.

I'll have to reverse my schedule so I can work on the cottage in the morning and the murals in the afternoon, she realized as she headed to the market once she'd finished painting for the day.

The school year had ended and summer had officially begun, so the vacationers were out in full force. Traffic near the boardwalk in Lucy's Ham was bumper-to-bumper and the grocery store aisles were packed, too. Emily experienced a twinge of queasiness in the checkout line and at first she didn't know whether it was physically or emotionally triggered. But as she was loading her groceries into the car, she was gripped with the kind of familiar anxiety that had nothing to do with post-concussive syndrome.

What if Collette's co-workers ask me how I know her? She fretted. Wilson said he'd simply been telling people that Emily was an old family friend, a long-time summer neighbor. And he'd assured her only a select few people knew that he'd lost his best friend last year, but he was confident they wouldn't realize Emily was Peter's sister.

Emily wasn't convinced. They could put two and two together if they tried—anyone could, using the internet. *You're being ridiculous,* she told herself. *No one is that interested in your life. Your students never asked you about the accident and they had no inhibitions about asking all sorts of other questions. Collette's friends are going to be concentrating on planning her shower, not on quizzing you.*

Still, ever since finding her father's notes to her mother, Emily felt lonelier than usual and she was concerned she might be opening herself up to discussions she couldn't handle having with relative strangers. Even if Collette's friends didn't pry, Emily was fearful she'd become overwrought with emotion at the most innocuous of questions about her family background. But once she got home and took a long walk on the beach, she felt calmer about going to the planning meeting, especially when she reminded herself she'd be doing it for Wilson and Collette, the two dearest people left in her life.

*

The rest of the week seemed to elapse in a heartbeat as Emily worked on her renovation projects at home and the murals at the hospital. Although she'd decided not to bother asking Collette and Wilson about Lucas after all, she was still puzzled by why he never dropped by. But after a while, she stopped expecting him to, and that in itself was a kind of relief.

On Friday afternoon, she stepped into the dim interior of Captain Clark's for the baby shower meeting. A delicious aroma permeated the room, which was divided into various sections that were meant to resemble the inside of an old ship. Lanterns flickered as centerpieces, the windows were shaped like portholes and customers perched on wooden barrels instead of stools at the bar. In a funny way, it reminded Emily of her grandma's original décor, and she began to relax.

"Emily, over here." Gail beckoned her to a table in the bar.

She introduced Emily to another nurse, Sara, and a cardiologist named Liz. Emily didn't let on that she recognized Sara and Liz from seeing them at a distance at one of Collette and Wilson's cookouts.

"This place will be packed in about an hour so we ought to place our meal order now, while we're enjoying our drinks," Gail suggested. "Emily, the interior may look tacky, but it's got the best chowder and seafood on the island."

"That's what I keep hearing."

As the women discussed the plans for the party, they decided that they'd forgo the usual games played at baby showers.

"Nothing wrong with that type of entertainment," Gail said by way of clarification. "We played them at both of my baby showers and it was a blast. But somehow, I don't picture this crowd trying to guess what kind of candy bar we've smeared into a diaper."

"Definitely not." Liz shook her head. "The only reason my husband agreed to come to the shower is because I told him it would be like a bigger version of the Laurents' usual cookouts."

"Liz's husband is a cardiologist, too," Gail explained to Emily. "They both work with Wilson."

"I agree we need to make sure the shower appeals to the men, as well as to the women. And we can keep it loosely structured," Sara said. "But we need to have lots of unique touches that distinguish this from just another cookout. Collette and Wilson have hosted so many special occasions throughout the years. It's our turn to let them know how happy we are for them."

"You're right. And we don't want them to feel like they've got to be the hosts, just because the shower is at their house. They shouldn't have to do a thing. The four of us can manage the primary responsibilities on the day of the shower," Gail decided. "Meanwhile, I'll coordinate the food and beverages. I know all the guests will want to bring something to share. We can have a sign-up sheet online, so we don't end up with ten shrimp platters. Liz, maybe you can manage the decorations. And Sara and Emily can take care of sending the invitations."

"Ooh!" Emily exclaimed, getting into the spirit. "I'd love to design the invitations, too."

Gail was all for the idea. "Great!"

"That's right—Wilson mentioned you're an artist," Liz said. "How is it you know Collette and him again? Didn't you grow up with one of them?"

"Wilson and I vacationed next door as kids," Emily acknowledged, feeling almost traitorous for diminishing their relationship.

Fortunately, the server interrupted the conversation to take their orders. After he left, Gail said she'd email the guest list to Emily and Sara soon. "I forgot to mention the most important piece of information—the date. We all checked our schedules and although we haven't confirmed with Wilson and Collette yet, we looked to see when they're scheduled to work, too. The only Saturday we're all available is August twenty-second. So you've still got plenty of time to create the invitations, Emily."

Emily recoiled. August 22 was the day that— She could barely complete the thought in her own mind, much less, say it aloud to acquaintances. How was she supposed to throw a party celebrating a new life on the one-year anniversary of the day her mother, father and brother lost theirs?

She excused herself from the table and barely made it to the women's room before she threw up. Twice. As she leaned over the toilet wondering whether she'd vomit a third time, someone exited the stall next to her.

Emily waited until the other woman washed and dried her hands and left before she came out to splash tepid water against her cheeks. Cupping her hand, she repeatedly filled it with water to swish in her mouth but she couldn't get rid of the vile taste.

When she returned to the bar, the table was empty. Gail, Liz and Sara had moved to a large block of tables pushed together in the center of the next room. Several other people wearing scrubs or white coats had joined them.

"We saved you a place down here." Liz motioned to an empty spot. Seated directly across from the open space, Lucas and Barbara were handing their menus back to the server.

Emily cleared her throat and uttered, "I'm actually going to take off now. Someone else can enjoy my meal—I'll pay for it on my way out."

"Aw, don't go," Gail objected. "We want to get to know you better."

"Yeah, what's the hurry, Em?" Lucas asked, narrowing his eyes. "You have other plans?"

"Leave her alone." Barbara elbowed him in the ribs and for a fleeting second, Emily could have hugged her. Then, with a phony wink, she said, "She might have a tummy ache, right, Emily?"

Emily immediately understood: Barbs was the woman who had been using the stall next to hers. But instead of answering, Emily pretended she hadn't heard the question. She whirled around and left before anyone could stop her.

CHAPTER EIGHT

Even in her distraught state, Emily was aware she was experiencing a relapse, but what was less clear was whether it was grief or the concussion that was wreaking havoc on both her stomach and her emotions. Either way, her remedy was the same: when she got home, Emily crawled into bed and cried herself to sleep.

The next morning, she woke with puffy eyes and a swollen nose but that didn't stop her from weeping some more. *Between my concussion and finding Dad's notes and trying to figure out what's wrong with Wilson, it's been a hard enough summer already. But now I'm supposed to help throw a party for fifty people on the anniversary of the most devastating day of my life? That's asking too much. I can't do it. I just can't do it.*

Desperate, Emily decided to call the airline to book a flight off the island the week before the shower. She could stay in Boston until it was time for the students to vacate her apartment in Seattle. It was going to be deceptive to lie to everyone about it, but she could make up some reason why she had to leave earlier than planned. She'd have to rush to complete the murals, but she figured she could eliminate some of the finer details she had planned.

But when Emily tried to dial the airline, she couldn't get a signal. If she walked up the hill, Collette and Wilson might hear her and she didn't want to have to break the news to them already. Agitated, she tossed her phone aside.

The air was so viscous that her nightgown clung to her like plastic wrap. She stripped it off, wriggled into her bathing suit and then pulled her black cotton dress on over that. She clomped down the stairs and headed to the left. Dark clouds thickened across the water, which churned and smashed its way to shore. She was too grouchy to be skittish about being outdoors in the impending storm. *I'm pretty sure the worst that can happen to me has already happened*, she thought ruefully.

When she reached the sandbars near the little shack where the artist lived, she stopped walking and glared at the thrashing waves. She tore off her sundress and hurled it onto the dry sand above the tide line and then charged into the surf. The water was colder than usual and her skin prickled where it slapped against her stomach and chest. She plunged headlong into a breaking wave and emerged sputtering, her eyes tingling with salt water.

As she was trying to focus, another wave hit her straight on and knocked her off her feet. Water rushed into her mouth, nose and ears. She tried to balance and was pummeled by waves from the front and the side. She staggered and another swell toppled her. The surf rolled her violently and her arms and legs flailed like a rag doll's.

Emily could feel the drag of the undercurrent and the crash of the surface waves washing over her body simultaneously. Her lungs burned and she tried to surface but her sense of direction was obliterated and she couldn't tell which way was up. She reached out, hoping to brace herself but her fingers only closed around water. Kicking her legs as violently as she could drained the rest of her energy. She realized she was about to pass out, which, oddly, filled her with an intense sense of shame.

At that very moment, her face pushed into the sandy bottom and she used the last of her strength to position herself on her hands and knees. The ocean had deposited her near shore. As the water undulated and receded, she crawled toward dry land, too dizzy to rise. Sucking in deep breaths of air, she sprawled in the sand, her hair a snarled mop around her shoulders.

When thunder resounded in the distance, Emily writhed into her sundress and teetered back to the cottage. She rinsed off in the outdoor shower and then hustled inside. Incandescence illuminated the cottage as she was changing into fresh clothes. She stood in front of the sliders to the deck, watching the storm. For once, she didn't feel afraid. She felt...hungry. She mixed a large bowl of granola and yogurt.

As she licked the spoon, she marveled at what had happened at the beach. She had been tossed and spun like a towel in a washing machine. It struck her that the physical experience felt like a condensed version of her emotional experience over the past year. *If I can survive that*, she decided, *I can make it through August twenty-second.*

She retrieved her sketch book and began to doodle, trying to figure out how to decorate Collette's invitations. She wanted to hand-draw each one; they'd need to have a common theme but with individual variations, so the recipients would know that they were originals.

Emily racked her brain for an idea. What could she picture Collette doing with a child? Swimming in Mermaids' Inlet? Yes, but that would be better for a baby girl. Watching the rabbits that ran across their lawn? Too precious. Eating ice cream? Perfect! Emily sketched a silhouette of a mother holding a little boy's hand. His other hand encircled a melting ice cream cone, a few drips falling to the ground. She'd vary the flavor on each invitation for a unique effect.

Pleased she'd come up with a solution, Emily poured more granola into her bowl.

*

During Emily's morning beach walk on Sunday, the ocean was so flat and calm she could hardly believe it was the same body of water that chewed her up and spat her out the day before.

When she returned to her cottage, Wilson was standing on the deck, peering through the screen.

"Looking for me?"

"Hi, Emily." He seemed tired again. Tired *still*. Maybe he'd had another squabble with Collette?

"Have a seat." Emily wiped condensation off a chair with her towel. "What's up?"

"You're going to say I need to lighten up, but I heard you were ill the other night and I wanted to be sure you're all right."

"Who told you that?" *As if I have to ask.*

"Word travels fast on a small island," Wilson evasively replied. "If you're experiencing a worsening of—"

"I'm not experiencing a *worsening* of anything."

"So then, you're experiencing a *continuation* of . . . ?"

As frustrated as she sometimes was by Wilson's fretfulness, Emily was beginning to accept it showed how much he cared about her, so she confessed, "A continuation of sadness, mostly."

"Nothing physical?"

"Occasional vomiting if I get really upset," she reluctantly answered.

"And something really upset you on Friday night?"

Emily hadn't intended to tell him how she felt about the date of the shower, but Wilson's attitude toward her was so compassionate—it was like he was his old self again—that the words spilled out of her mouth.

"Yeah. I was upset the shower's going to be on August twenty-second. But it's okay—"

"August twenty-second! They want to have it on the twenty-second? I'm so sorry, Emily. They didn't check with us, first. We'll ask them to reschedule."

"That's the only date the majority of them can make it. It's okay. I'm fine with it now."

"I don't know if *I'll* be fine with it." Wilson shook his head, avoiding her eyes.

"I'm sorry, Wilson. I know you've been suffering even though you've been such a rock for me." Here was the opportunity Emily had hoped she'd have to talk to Wilson about whatever was bothering him. She prompted, "I want to support you, too, but I don't know how to unless you tell me what's on your mind."

Raking his hand through his hair, he looked toward the ocean. "This is going to sound terrible." He stole a glance at Emily and she nodded for him to continue, even though she felt as if her stomach had dropped to her knees. "I wish I could sleep straight through August twenty-second, so I wouldn't have to think about what happened a year ago on that date. Actually, I wish I could sleep through the twenty-third, too, since it was after midnight here when I got the call."

"That's not terrible, Wilson. It's completely understandable." Emily surreptitiously pinched the underside of her knee so she wouldn't cry. "You know, when I think back to that night, I wish I would have been the one to call you. I wish you didn't have to hear the news from a stranger. But I couldn't do it. I couldn't say the words, especially not to you. It was almost like if I didn't say it aloud, it wouldn't be true. So I just kept saying, 'no,' instead."

"I understood. And I'm glad you weren't the one to call me. Otherwise, I'd always associate a phone call from you with receiving news like that."

Wilson blew the air out of his cheeks. They both sat in silence a long time while goldfinches and tufted titmice sang from branches overhead.

Who-oo-oo-oo-oo, a nearby mourning dove cried.

"Peter's favorite bird call," Wilson said and from the droop of his mouth, Emily knew the irony wasn't lost on him, either.

"When do you miss him the most?"

"All the time." Wilson removed his glasses and breathed on the lenses before wiping them on his shirt. He balanced them on his knee and continued speaking. "It's as if I can't believe he's gone. I mean, rationally, I know he is, but sometimes I'll pick up the phone to get his input on a personal decision or just to shoot the breeze. When we found out Collette was pregnant, Pete was the first person I wanted to call. And then I remembered—he's not here."

"I purchased a postcard to send him the other day before I realized what I'd done," Emily admitted.

Even though it was painful to discuss their heartache, this was the closest she'd felt to Wilson since she came to Dune Island. She briefly considered segueing into a conversation about his search for his father—or about whatever else he might have been keeping from her—but she didn't want to risk spoiling their momentary connection. As Collette said, he'd talk about it when he was ready.

Instead, she suggested, "We can work something out with the shower. I don't know what excuse we'll give, but it's important that we choose a day when you can enjoy the party. It's meant to be a celebration for you as much as it is for Collette."

"No," Wilson insisted. "It's important to Collette that her closest friends from the hospital can attend. Let's keep the plan as it is and not mention a word about it to Collette, unless she brings it up. I'll be okay."

"We'll help each other through it," Emily promised. "Right?"

Wilson pressed his palms hard against his eyelids and then wiped them against his pants. "Right," he agreed.

*

July 3 was a Friday and because Collette had told her that some of the hospital staff members were taking Friday off from work and others were taking Monday as their holiday, Emily chose to take Monday off, too.

Which meant she needed to finish as much of the mountain mural as she could on Friday. Emily was so engrossed in perfecting the spray of a waterfall she had painted she didn't leave the hospital until nearly three o'clock. She had to stop for groceries on the way home, but she figured she still had plenty of time to beat the holiday traffic.

She figured wrong: the main road was more of a parking lot than the actual grocery store parking lot. When she detoured onto a side street she discovered the back roads were just as jammed. She hadn't seen anything like it before on the island and she hoped it wasn't going to be this congested for the rest of the summer.

It was after six o'clock when Emily finally got to the cottage. After sliding a chicken into the oven for roasting, she changed into her suit. She intended to zip next door to see if Collette wanted to join her for a quick ride at the inlet, but she noticed her friend was already waiting for her at the top of the beach stairs. Emily paused with her there to admire the panoramic view. The early evening's pastel light was softer but no less ravishing than at the height of afternoon and white scribbles interrupted the flat blue plane of the ocean. *I can't believe I considered leaving Dune Island early*, she thought.

Twenty minutes later as the two women were drifting with the current, Collette screamed, "Ack! Something just brushed against my leg!"

"Probably seaweed," Emily responded nonchalantly, having grown accustomed to Collette's theatrics in the water. She floated on her back, her long hair splayed around her head like a veil. "Or a seal. Everyone keeps claiming seals live here now but I have yet to see one."

Collette rolled onto her stomach, clapped her hands together like flippers and made a barking noise. Emily swallowed a mouthful of water as she laughed.

"You'll come to watch the fireworks at the cove with Wilson and me tomorrow, right?" Collette asked. "Gail, Liz and Sara will all be there. They're thrilled you're helping with the shower, by the way. Lucas will probably be there, too, although I haven't seen him around in ages. Have you?"

She's fishing to find out something about Lucas and me, Emily thought. "Nope, I've only seen him once in passing."

"I think he must be working double shifts or something."

Yeah, if by "or something" you mean spending all his spare time with Barbara. "Probably," Emily agreed. "Thanks for including me but I don't think I'll be up for hanging out with so many couples."

They waded out of the water to trek toward their starting point. They didn't even need to ask each other if they wanted to ride again; it was assumed they did.

"C'mon, Emily. It'll be fun," Collette pleaded before she bounded into the water. She slicked her hair back and continued, "It's not like we're really going as couples. Several people go alone. If anything, we split into male and female groups. You'll fit right in."

"That's not what I'm concerned about." Emily hesitated before confiding the significance of July 4 as the one-year anniversary of when Devon proposed. "I know it's maudlin, but I'm concerned the fireworks are going to evoke memories I'd rather forget."

Collette sympathized as they drifted around the bend. "I totally forgot about his Fourth of July proposal."

"Yeah. Now the holiday is ruined for me forever, unless Devon realizes he made a dreadful mistake by breaking up with me and he calls to beg my forgiveness," Emily said facetiously. "I'm kidding about that—I don't really want to get back together with him."

"Good, because if he was stupid enough to break up with you, that guy doesn't deserve your forgiveness."

"No one *deserves* forgiveness. It's a gift." Emily was quoting her mother.

"Hey, Wilson says that all the time, too. Except he always adds, 'And it's the best gift a person can ever give or receive.'"

Yeah, that's the rest of the saying Mom always used. "Hey, Collette, there's something I've been meaning to ask you, but I'm not sure if I should."

"I hope it's not about Wilson's DNA test results again because I don't know anything more about that than I did the last time you asked."

"Ouch. That's mean." Emily was only partly joking; she'd taken pride in not bringing up the subject lately, even though she really would have liked to know if there were any new developments. "But for your information, that wasn't what I was going to ask you."

Collette splashed a handful of water in Emily's direction. "Oh, c'mon, I was teasing. Ask me your question."

"Never mind now."

"I'm going to hold my breath until you ask me," Collette threatened.

Emily doggy paddled quickly until she caught up with her friend, whose bare belly protruded from her two-piece suit above the water.

"What I was going to ask is if you know how to balance a ball on your nose," she said in reference to Collette's seal imitation.

"Hey!" Collette kicking a torrent of water at her. "At least *I* can swim, *Lassie*!"

Whatever momentary tension there was between them dissipated and they laughed as they walked down the beach toward the place Emily was beginning to think of as "home."

*

Emily stared at a small beetle fixed in one spot on the ceiling. The Fourth of July. She tried to remember what her thoughts were when she woke exactly one year ago. She'd had no indication that Devon was about to propose that evening, so it wasn't as if she'd expected the day to become as memorable as it had.

Although they'd talked about the subject of marriage in general, she and Devon hadn't directly discussed the prospect of it for themselves prior to his proposal. Immediately after they got engaged, he was traveling so often it became problematic to discuss any qualms she had—and she *had* had them—about their relationship moving in that direction. Emily decided she'd wait until his schedule settled down after Labor Day to have a heart-to-heart discussion with him. Then the accident happened and her heart was elsewhere.

Despite her reservations about the engagement at the time, there was no doubt in her mind, even now, that she had truly loved Devon. Or at least, that she'd truly loved things *about* him: he was charismatic, generous and impulsive, unlike anyone she'd ever been in a relationship with. When she was with him, she felt reckless, effervescent, as if she didn't have to weigh every decision she made with such careful deliberation, the way she usually did. He, on the other hand, claimed she brought out the best in him, or at least made him want to be a better man.

And although Emily had had concerns about the novelty of their relationship wearing off, until the accident, it didn't. Whether that was because Devon traveled so often, or because their relationship really was that thrilling, she could no longer say. She had been so detached during the past year that it was hard to realistically evaluate that part of her life before her family's accident.

In her mind, she'd split her life into two time periods: before and after, like in photos of makeovers in women's magazine. Except that in her "before" timeframe, everything was ideal, beautiful. It was in the "after" snapshots that the flaws were obvious.

She knew this wasn't technically true—she certainly had experienced periods of mourning and discouragement in her personal life before the accident. Her father had suffered two heart attacks when she was in high school, and of course, she'd lost both sets of her grandparents. She also experienced the usual amount of breakups, disillusionment and injustice that were what her mother categorized as "all part of life." Likewise, she'd experienced slivers of joy and hope after the accident.

So it was wholly possible her perspective about her relationship with Devon wasn't accurate, either. Maybe there would have been other significant issues between them that would have surfaced even if her family's accident hadn't ever happened.

Emily got up and put on her bathrobe. Thinking about her relationship with Devon reminded her of the niggling misgivings she still had about her father's notes. She went into the living room, pulled out the pad of paper and sat down on the couch. Flipping past the shopping list, she read the phrases he'd written:

~~Janice, my one and only love.~~
~~I need you to know~~
~~I love you more than~~
~~The depth of my love~~
~~There aren't enough words to say~~

There was absolutely nothing on the first page of his draft to indicate any discord between her parents—on the contrary, there was only evidence of love—or to hint at why they might have been spending time apart.

Emily proceeded to study the next page:

~~I wish I could~~
~~If only I could~~
~~I would do anything~~

She supposed that the phrases on this page might be taken as sentiments of regret, but in the context of the rest of what her father had written, they sounded more like longing. For all Emily knew, he'd been about to write, "If only I could show you what's in my heart, you'd know how much I love you." Or "I would do anything to be holding you in my arms instead of writing to you across the miles." Or something along those lines.

What am I so worried about anyway? Even if Mom and Dad temporarily separated, it's not as if it affected their love for each other in the long run. They still had the strongest marriage of any couple I know.

Deciding she had been letting her imagination run away with her, Emily put the pad back into the desk. She was opening the fridge to see what she could make for breakfast when there was a knock at the door: it was Wilson, presenting her with a covered tray.

"Collette wanted you to have breakfast in bed, but she couldn't deliver this herself because she has to keep an eye on the waffle iron so ours don't burn."

He lifted the cover to reveal a plate heaped with waffles, sliced strawberries and a fat dollop of whipped cream.

"Wow, this is great. I thought you guys only ate fruit and yogurt in the morning."

"Special occasion." Wilson had his hand on the sliding door handle when he pivoted to comment, "I don't know if this will make you feel better, but for what it's worth, Peter called me a few days after you got engaged. He, ah, told me a little about your fiancé."

Emily set the plate on the table. "What did he say?"

"He said Devon made a great first impression."

"But?"

"But he said he couldn't get a sense of the substance behind Devon's polished exterior. Pete mentioned that he was going to wait to talk to you about it in person when you visited him in the fall, but then..."

Emily's eyes moistened.

"I'm sorry." Wilson shook his head. "I didn't mean to make you sad or to insult your taste in men. It was probably just Peter's protective, big brother perspective talking."

"It probably was." Emily sniffed. "That's what gets me."

After Wilson left, Emily lifted the napkin from the tray to blot her eyes. Beneath it was a note from Collette. "Sweets for the sweet, with extra calories so there's more of you to love—although we couldn't love you more than we already do!"

Emily blew her nose and carried the tray into her room so she could eat the waffles in bed, as Collette intended. She wasn't going to let any memory of Devon—or any doubts about her parents' past or anything else, for that matter—ruin her day.

When she finished eating, she busied herself with picking meat off the bones of last night's chicken to simmer for soup. She had played the guilt card on Wilson, cajoling, "You wouldn't deny me a culinary heirloom from my own mother, would you?" So he'd finally given her the recipe. She also intended to make chocolate chip cookies, her mother's other renowned comfort food, in celebration of the wedding that wasn't.

Next, she spent several hours on Collette's baby shower invitations. She needed forty-two of them; twenty-eight couples and sixteen singles would be invited, for a total of seventy-two people. Not everyone would be able to make it, but there would easily be fifty-some guests in attendance.

Emily puffed out her cheeks and then slowly released her breath. Excluding her university lecture hall series, where she didn't have to talk to any one student in particular, this would be the largest group of people she'd engaged in conversation with in months. The thought made her feel claustrophobic until she reminded herself there would be plenty of space outdoors to get some air if she needed it.

By late afternoon she felt antsy, so she borrowed Collette's bicycle. She wanted to explore the newly completed bike trail Collette had told her wound all the way around the island.

"Do you think you're up for that?" Wilson apparently was still on high alert about Emily's health, even though the Monday after she'd gotten sick at the restaurant, she'd made another appointment with the doctor, who agreed Emily's vomiting was more likely triggered by anxiety than by her brain injury.

"I'm only going a mile or two and I'll stay hydrated."

"Are you sure you don't want to come with us to the fireworks?" Collette asked. "We're going early so we can get a parking space. I packed a cooler. You wouldn't have to watch the display, but you could at least enjoy supper on the beach."

But Emily declined, saying she was still full from the wonderful breakfast Collette had made. A few minutes later, as she was coasting down the long hill toward the road crossing where she could access the bike trail, Emily noticed vehicles parked along both sides of the usually deserted road. *I bet they're all here to go biking*, she thought.

Sure enough, the trail was swarming with cyclists, skaters and an inordinate number of pedestrians pushing strollers or walking their dogs. As courteous as everyone tried to be about sharing the lanes, Emily quickly grew weary from dodging them and she turned around after only riding a mile. Her muscles were burning as she pedaled up the final hill toward the empty house and she decided to cool off with a swim before supper.

At the bottom of the stairs, she turned west. She hadn't submerged herself near those sandbars since the day she was battered by the waves and she felt it was necessary to swim there again before it became too much of a psychological obstacle.

Last year on this day, I said yes to "taking the plunge"—I might as well say yes again, she thought sardonically.

She strolled as far as the dune that housed the artist's cottage, but she didn't see the white-haired woman with the easel on the cliff. Emily imagined she was probably on her way to watch fireworks at Beach Plum Cove with the rest of the island that night.

She walked up to her waist in the surf, acclimating herself to its temperature. When a large wave crested in front of her, she ducked under it, safely escaping the surface turbulence. She emerged, utterly refreshed. When the next large wave swelled, she raced out to meet it so that she leaped weightlessly upward and allowed its power to lift her as it passed and then gently set her back down in place, as gracefully as a dancer. As with so many other things, she was learning that timing was crucial in how she responded to the waves that came her way.

Emily was so cool and relaxed that instead of walking up the stairs when she arrived at them, she continued on toward Mermaids' Inlet. She hummed as she strolled and searched the wet, silky sand for quahog shells to add to her collection.

Just as she was approaching the inlet, she spotted something dark, round and slick dive beneath the surface about ten or fifteen yards from shore. The animal was so corpulent at first she thought it was a whale, until it popped its head up again and she noticed its long, spiky whiskers. A seal! And then, another one. She hiked her dress to her knees and ran around the bend, to see if more of them were riding the current. She was so excited and focused on the water that she wasn't paying attention to the foreground. At the last second, she skidded to a halt so she wouldn't plow into a man standing at the back of the dunes, fishing.

"Whoa there." Lucas put out his hands to stop her.

"Seals!" she proclaimed, out of breath. "I saw seals! Did you see them?"

"Sure did. They're probably eating all my fish." Lucas's eyes were bloodshot and although his tone was cordial, his lips were drawn in a tight line.

"I'm probably not helping matters by yelling, either, but I've never seen seals in the wild before," Emily apologized. "I wouldn't have disturbed you if I'd known you were fishing—your van wasn't in the driveway when I came down to the beach. I was out walking toward the west."

"You're more entitled to be here than I am," Lucas responded, avoiding eye contact. "And the seals are even more entitled than either of us."

Emily could tell something was troubling him and she had a hunch it was something more significant than not catching any fish. But because it had been so long since they'd spoken, she was hesitant to ask him about it. "I'll let you have your space."

Lucas nodded and Emily began to turn back, but she just couldn't leave without asking if he was okay. It would have been like him leaving her alone at the cottage the morning he suspected she had a concussion.

"Is, um, something upsetting you? You seem a little down."

Lucas cast his line into the inlet, staring straight ahead as he reeled it back in. "You didn't hear about the accident yesterday?"

No matter how many times nor in how many situations, whenever Emily heard the words *the accident*, her heart dropped a beat.

"No, I didn't."

"It was on all the TV stations. Even made the national news. Traffic was stopped for miles in every direction," Lucas said, as if that might ring a bell.

Emily shrugged and shook her head, silently waiting for him to continue the story, which she knew did not end well, and which she knew was not merely a story but an event that had radically altered the course of someone's life forever.

"It was a head-on collision. Eight people were involved, two families of four each. One family was banged up pretty bad. The teenage daughter will probably lose her leg. The son fractured his skull. The mother and father are still recovering from surgeries for broken bones and internal bleeding. The driver of the other car and his seven-year-old boy died on impact. His four-year-old made it to the hospital. We worked on him for three hours, but—" Lucas shuddered, unable to say the words.

"Oh, Lucas," Emily whispered. She touched his shoulder and said the one thing she had resented hearing all of these months—not because it was unkind or insincere, but because the people who said it wanted to be comforting and there was simply nothing else they could offer. "I'm so sorry."

"The mother survived with a few broken ribs. Can you imagine? Can you fathom your entire family being gone, just like that?" Lucas snapped his fingers.

Emily stifled a gasp. Although Lucas had no idea, she *could* imagine. But this wasn't about her; Lucas needed to get this out.

"I've seen a lot of traumas in the ER, but this one—it's inexplicable. Witnesses said neither car was speeding. There weren't any drugs or alcohol involved. Just two families visiting the island for the holiday. Maybe it was the glare of the sun, maybe one of the kids distracted one of the drivers—but one car or the other came around the bend and crossed the line and . . . There was nothing we could do. Nothing *I* could do. I tried. I—" Lucas choked back a cough. Or maybe it was a sob.

"Don't do that to yourself, Lucas," Emily said firmly. "You did everything you could for him. I'd bet my life on that and so would any of your colleagues at Hope Haven."

He blinked rapidly, still staring out over the inlet. Emily waited. Eventually, he seemed to gather his composure. "I wouldn't be telling you anything about the exact nature of the patients' injuries, but they're in the paper. Some idiot reporter must have manipulated the friends or relatives into giving them the details or something but it's all public knowledge now. Everyone knows."

Wilson and Collette don't. They would have said something. Then Emily realized they might not have said anything because they wouldn't have wanted to bring her more bad news. She hoped that wasn't the case; she wanted to be there for them, just as they'd been there for her.

"I know this must be devastating for you and unthinkable for the families. Is there something I can do to help?"

Lucas opened his mouth as if to say more but he changed his mind and simply shook his head.

"Okay, I'll let you have your privacy." Emily started to back away, but then she drew near and enveloped him in a long, tight, sideways hug, as if to wring the sadness right out of him.

"Thanks," he mumbled after she let go.

When she reached the cottage, Emily picked up one of the blank cards for the shower, but instead of sketching a mother and child, she drew a man fishing alone in the rain. When she had bruised the sky with purple and blackened the waves, she opened the card and inscribed it with a quote by Van Gogh: "*The heart of a man is very much like the sea, it has its storms, it has its tides and in its depths it has its pearls, too.*"

She poured half of the chicken soup into a lidded glass pot and filled a container with a dozen cookies and then set both snugly in a cardboard box. She affixed the note to the outside, carried the package to Lucas's van and secured it with the seat belt on the passenger's seat.

After showering outdoors, Emily ladled soup into a bowl and when she'd finished that, she ate two cookies and sketched for a while, before going to bed early. And when she later woke to the distant explosions of midnight fireworks, Devon was the last person on her mind.

CHAPTER NINE

In the morning, Emily joined Collette and Wilson, who were sipping coffee on their deck.

"We missed you last night. How was your evening?" Collette wondered.

Emily could tell by their expressions that they'd heard about the accident on Thursday.

"It was all right, although I was sad to hear there was a fatal accident in town," she said. Since she didn't want to reveal that she'd heard it from Lucas, she added, "It was all over the internet."

"Wilson and I found out about that last night, too. Everyone's pretty shaken up. It's one of the worst traumas the hospital has seen."

Collette told Emily someone on the island was allowing the crash victims' extended families, who'd come to the island to comfort and care for their loved ones, to use two of their summer rental houses for free. But the hospital staff didn't want the families to have to worry about cooking or going out to crowded restaurants during such a stressful time, so they were getting together later that afternoon at Sara's place to make meals for them.

"Wow, people at hospitals actually do that for their patients' families?"

"People at Hope Haven do. It's one of the benefits of living in a small island community."

"Can I come?"

"We'd love it if you did."

Emily, Collette, Sara and half a dozen other staff members spent the better part of the day baking treats, cooking entrées, and washing and chopping vegetables that could easily be assembled into salads. To Emily's surprise, on her way to the hospital Barbara Reed dropped off two pans of zucchini lasagna she'd made early that morning.

As Collette was preparing it for freezing, Emily suggested she should divide it into individual or two-person servings, first. That way, whoever needed a meal could take as many or as few servings as they needed instead of eating the same thing for three days just because they had to defrost the entire pan at once.

"Smart thinking," Sara agreed. "And we should label them, so people can choose what they want to have instead of being at the mercy of a mystery meal."

"It sounds as if you've done this before," Emily commented, as Collette went to get a marker.

"I was on the receiving end when my husband died two years ago," Sara responded. "I appreciated it so much... But to this day, I can't smell chicken and broccoli casserole without crying because it reminds me of that period in my life."

Emily had no idea Sara had been married and widowed—she was so young. Not that that made any difference. Death didn't discriminate.

"For me, it's coffee cake that will always taste like tears," Emily confided quietly. "I'm sorry about your husband."

"Thank you. How long has it been since you lost your loved one?"

Emily appreciated it that Sara didn't ask her to say *who* had died. Even when she attended a bereavement support group, Emily hadn't been able to tell the other members she'd lost both of her parents and her brother. She'd merely said she'd lost a family member. That was partly because she couldn't admit it to herself. But, in an odd way, it was also that she didn't want anyone else to feel as shocked as she'd felt when she first heard the news her entire family was gone.

"It's been almost a year, but sometimes it feels as if it only happened last week."

"I know what you mean. I won't say it gets better after the first year, but it will change."

"And meanwhile?"

"Meanwhile, you hang on, however you can. Moment by moment, you keep hanging on."

"My father always said that, too. Actually, he always said, 'Hang tough.' My mother's advice was more along the lines of, 'Have some soup and a cookie and then go to bed. You'll see things differently in the morning.'"

"Sounds like a solid game plan to me." Sara laughed, reaching for the batch of cookies cooling on a rack nearby. "Want one?"

Emily held up her fingers. "Two, please."

*

After they arrived home, Emily invited Collette to go for a swim, but Collette said she needed to take a nap, so Emily set off for Mermaids' Inlet by herself. The tide was coming in instead of going out, so the current was the wrong direction for riding and the water was so frigid it took Emily's breath away. Shivering, she got out and pulled her leggings and T-shirt on over her suit. She settled on the sandy embankment for a while, wiggling her toes in the water. She hoped to spy the seals again but they were a no-show. She was about to hike back to the cottage when Lucas appeared from around the bend, toting a bucket and his fishing gear.

"Hi, Em."

"Lucas, how's it going?" she asked, even though his bright smile said it all.

"A lot better. Thanks for hearing me out yesterday. And for the note, that really meant a lot. I chowed down on the care package. Not a morsel left. The cookies were even tastier than the soup and that's really saying something."

"My pleasure," she said and motioned toward the inlet. "It's all yours. No seals anywhere around and I was just leaving, too."

"You were?" His shoulders drooped. "I thought we'd hang out. I haven't seen too much of you lately."

"Don't you need to be alone?"

"Not today," he replied. "I mean, no pressure, but you mentioned you'd never fished before and I thought I'd teach you how to cast. If you're lucky, you can catch dinner. Besides, I'd like your company."

Emily felt a surge of surprise at how much she liked it that he'd like her company. "Okay, but you'll have to put the worms on the hook."

"We'll be using sea clams, not worms, but sure, I'll bait the hook."

Lucas explained that he often fished for striped bass, or stripers, in the inlet. Once, he'd landed a good-sized blue fish, too, but he said he expected he'd have better luck with them when the blues ran at the end of August. In any case, today they were going to fish for summer flounder, which were known as flukes in this part of the country. He told her the trickiest part about catching flounder was setting the hook.

"Once you feel any weight on the line, you've got to give it a really hard tug to set the hook in the fluke's mouth. Sometimes, it takes two tugs."

Emily nodded as he spoke, taking in the information. His enthusiasm was contagious and although she was repulsed by the slimy, stringy pieces of raw sea clams he used for bait, she admired how deftly his fingers secured it onto the double-hook rig.

"So this is how you cast," he said, demonstrating. "Since there's plenty of room, you can pitch it overhead. Sidearm is fine, too. This button here releases the line. See? The sinker will take the bait to the bottom and you want to crank it back in nice and slow, but jiggle it as you're cranking."

He showed Emily two or three times, and then handed her the rod. She whipped the pole overhead but didn't press the button until the last moment. A few yards of line released and the sinker splashed into the shallow water immediately in front of them. She tried a second time and it sailed through the air and into the depths. Lucas cheered.

"You've already got the hang of it."

"Now what?"

"Now go ahead and practice cranking it in. Remember what I said about setting the line. Flukes have hard mouths and they're good fighters so you've got to give it a strong, fast tug or you'll lose him."

"What if a seal bites the hook instead? Will it hurt him?"

Lucas cracked up. "If a seal takes the bait, you're the only one who will get hurt. Or at least, you can kiss your fishing pole goodbye."

After Emily reeled the line back in, Lucas double-checked the bait and she cast again.

"Don't be discouraged if you come up empty-handed. It's actually better to fish in the morning than at this time of the day."

The words were barely out of his mouth when Emily exclaimed, "I've got something!" She jerked the rod once and then a second time, setting the hook just like Lucas had instructed. "I feel it! I caught something. Quick, I forgot what to do next. Tell me what to do. Quick, quick!"

"Reel it in, Em. Keep turning the— Here, let me—"

But Emily was so excited she hardly heard him. Determined not to lose the fish, she gripped the pole with all her might, her other hand locked on the reel handle, and started jogging backward in the sand. The pole bent as the fish struggled to get away, but she raised it higher and continued backing up until she smacked into Lucas, who had managed to dart around behind her.

He wrapped his arms around her waist and placed one hand over hers on the end of the pole and the other over her fingers on the reel. Together they began winding the handle until they could see the fish wriggling just below the surface.

"Steady," Lucas said into her ear. "Hold it right there until I get the net."

Once he was in position, she brought the fluke out of the water and he guided it into the net and unhooked it. The creature was flat and brown and dappled with lighter spots. It had a sideways head and fins all around the perimeter of its body.

"They call the really big ones 'doormats,'" explained Lucas. "This isn't a doormat, but it's close. Look at how fat its belly is. That'll make some nice fillets."

"What happens next?" she asked, holding the net out in front of her.

"You won't like this part since you're squeamish about the sight of blood."

Emily was surprised he remembered that about her. "You're not going to kill it, are you?"

Lucas chuckled. "How else are we going to grill it? You do eat fish, don't you?"

"Yes, but not fish I know," Emily declared.

Lucas struck his knee, laughing. "All right, all right, we'll let it go. And if I catch this same flounder again next week, I'll tell him you said 'hi.' But then I'm going to have him for dinner."

As they were walking back to the staircase, Lucas said, "Do you mind if I ask how the art project is coming along?"

"Of course I don't mind," Emily responded. "I'm pleased with my progress so far. Tim stopped by and he seemed to like it, too."

"Like it? He loves it. He told me he was blown away."

"That's encouraging to hear," Emily said. "I can't always be objective about my own art, so it helps to hear someone else's opinions, favorable or otherwise."

"I'm happy to give you my opinion, too, if you want. I'm dying to see what you've done. I got the sense you were avoiding me or I was crowding you or something, so I've tried to keep my distance."

"Really?" Even though he was partially right about her avoiding him, she wondered how she could have given him that impression, since she'd hardly seen him for the past month. "What made you think that?"

He shrugged. "I dunno. I guess because you didn't show up at the cookout after you said you would. And you beat a path out of the restaurant as soon as you saw me the other night..."

"That wasn't because of you. It was because of Barbara," Emily blurted out. She quickly back-pedaled. "I mean, I was the one who didn't want to crowd *you*. I didn't want you to feel like...like you're obligated to take care of me or something just because I'm working on the murals. Especially not when you're on a date with Barbara."

Lucas stopped short and pulled Emily to a halt, too. "I've never felt that way about you. And I've never been on a date with Barbara, either. She's a colleague, so sometimes we socialize together, but that's as far as it goes."

"Oh." Emily felt like skipping all the way back to the cottage. "Well, you're welcome to come by anytime. It's really quiet in that wing now that most of the electricians and carpenters have finished their work."

"Great. I'll stop in this week. I just hope that whatever you've been painting is better than your silly octopus illustrations."

Emily covered her face with her hand. "You saw that?" she asked, peeking through her fingers.

"Saw what? This?" Lucas made his eyes go wide as he pretended to strangle himself.

Emily dropped her hand and stuck her chin in the air. "Don't mock. That was a highly accomplished sketch for someone who had a concussion. And it was a very flattering likeness, too."

Lucas's mouth dropped open. "Hey! That's not very nice." He reached out to nudge her, but she took off across the sand.

Ten yards before Emily reached the staircase, Lucas outpaced her, even though he was carrying his fishing gear and bucket. He hurtled up the stairs, his feet leaving a wet trail. And just like that, Emily's impasse with the art project was solved: she'd connect the various rooms at the hospital with footprints.

It seems like every time I'm with Lucas, I get a new idea, she realized as Collette called to them from her deck.

"Hi, Emily. Hi, Lucas. Didn't you catch anything?"

"Emily caught dinner," Lucas answered as they clambered up the stairs to the house. "But she made me throw it back in the ocean."

"Then come share our pizza with us. We ordered delivery so we wouldn't have to drive into town. I've been a slouch; first an afternoon nap and now takeout for dinner. Wilson's in the kitchen, making a salad. C'mon, you two can wash up. Let's eat inside. The mosquitoes are bad tonight."

Collette strategically placed Emily next to Lucas at the table and then impishly commented, "With your hair down and your skin all sun-kissed, you look especially vibrant tonight, Emily. Doesn't she, guys?"

Emily shot Collette a look to silence her, as Lucas agreed, "She sure does."

Wilson, ever the worrier—or maybe it was just the physician in him—asked, "You probably weren't wearing sunscreen, were you? Just because it's after five o'clock doesn't mean you can't get sun-burned, especially because you inherited such fair Vandemark skin."

Now it was Collette who shot Wilson a silencing look. She steered the conversation in a different direction. "Any updates from the hospital, Lucas?"

Emily knew she was being deliberately vague to protect the patient's privacy, despite what had already been shared online and in the news.

"I heard surgery went well and things are looking good," Lucas answered, just as cryptically.

For the next several minutes, everyone was silent and somber until Wilson suggested, "Why don't you tell us the story of the one that got away, Emily."

For one horrifying instant, Emily thought Wilson was referring to Devon and she couldn't fathom why he'd want her to talk about him in front of Lucas. Her mouth went dry, so she sipped her water instead of speaking.

"It was a flounder," Lucas replied for her. "I'd say it was between seven and eight pounds."

Oh, he meant the fish! Emily was engulfed by relief. "It was so ugly, it was cute," she said, causing Wilson to smack the table.

"What are you laughing at?" she asked indignantly.

"I've never heard someone describe their catch as cute."

"And you've never seen anyone land a fish the way this one did, either," Lucas said, jabbing a thumb in the air in her direction. "She set the hook like a pro. Two tugs and she had him. But instead of cranking the reel to bring him in, she started hightailing it in reverse away from the water. It was like she was going to *drag* that flounder onto shore by brute force. If I hadn't stopped her, she would have walked backward all the way to your house with the flounder on her line like a kite on a string!"

Wilson whooped and banged the table again and the four of them laughed so hard Collette went into a coughing spasm and Lucas's face turned purple.

"In my defense, I've never been fishing before," Emily protested after their laughter died down.

"It sounds like you *still* haven't been fishing!" Collette gibed, which started everyone laughing again, especially Emily.

"Seriously, though, Emily was a force to be reckoned with, which didn't surprise me at all," Lucas said once they'd composed themselves. He palmed a few tears from the side of his cheek. "Did you know that on the first day I met her, she tried to kick me off your property? I was here surfing and she thought I was a luggage thief."

"Tattletale," Emily retorted, elbowing him in the ribs and hoping Collette wouldn't draw attention to her coloring again, because she was sure she was blushing from her smile right up to her scalp.

After everyone had finished the berries Collette served for dessert, Lucas said he had to get going since he was working the night shift.

"I'll see you next week, Em," he reminded her on his way out.

Emily offered to help Collette with the dishes but Wilson said he'd do them, since they'd been working in the kitchen at Sara's most of the afternoon.

"No, honey, you made the salad," Collette argued, nearly pushing him up the stairs. "You go relax; Emily will help me."

"That was subtle," Emily whispered once she and Collette were alone. "About as subtle as, 'Emily looks especially vibrant tonight, doesn't she?' You do realize that if you have to prompt someone, the compliment doesn't count, don't you?"

Collette waved her hand dismissively. "As if Lucas needed any help from me. What is going on between you guys? It's been so long since he's been around I thought maybe you had a fight with him, but clearly that's not the case. So c'mon, spill it."

It was useless to deny Collette's intuition. "First you have to promise, crisscross your heart, you won't tell Wilson what I'm about to say."

Collette raised her hand. "I hereby do solemnly swear I won't tell Wilson a single thing you're about to divulge. Now start divulging!"

"Nothing's going on between us. But Lucas made a point of telling me he's not seeing Barbara romantically."

"Oh, wow, I told you he likes you. Didn't I say that weeks ago? He's letting you know he's available."

"I'm not so sure. I mean, he's charming to everyone—you've said that yourself."

"Oh, please. The chemistry between you two was so palpable I was jealous! Wilson and I are practically newlyweds and even we don't flirt like that."

Emily gave a diffident little shrug.

"You're blushing right through your sunburn! You like him, don't you? And don't give me any of this 'as a friend' or 'as a doctor' business. You *like him* like him, don't you?"

Emily nodded. "Yes, I do," she admitted to herself, as much as to Collette. "I really do."

*

Since she'd taken the day off on Monday, Emily called Sara on the spur of the moment. "I finished making the last invitations yesterday. Any chance you want to come over and address them with me?"

"By hand? I figured we'd print labels."

"I suppose we could, but since the invitations are hand drawn, I thought we should address the envelopes by hand, too. Besides, I don't have easy access to a printer. If you can't make it, that's all right. But if you come over, I'll fix lunch."

"Can Liz come, too? I'm at her house right now. Her nutty husband is taking the kids to the boardwalk today, something about it being their summer tradition to pretend they're Fourth of July tourists. The two of us were going to hang out here enjoying the peace and quiet, but a girls' afternoon at your cottage sounds like more fun. We'll bring our suits."

Letting anyone other than Collette and Wilson—even a female doctor and a female nurse—see her in her bathing suit was a little more personal than Emily had bargained for, but she figured she could say she was cold and stay on shore while they swam.

By the time Liz and Sara arrived, Emily had prepared a platter of spinach and mushroom burritos and a bean salad.

To Emily's delight, as soon as she entered the house, Liz remarked, "What a darling cottage. It's a lot bigger inside than it looks from the outside."

"Yeah, and it's so bright and airy. My place is a dungeon compared to this," Sara added, picking up the stack of invitations on the coffee table. "Oh! They're beautiful."

"They're not too sentimental?" Emily wondered.

"There's no such thing as too sentimental when it comes to babies. Just wait until Collette sees these."

"Do we get one, too?" asked Liz. "I want to frame mine. I'll hang it in my four-year-old's room."

They had just finished eating and had begun addressing the envelopes at the dining room table when Collette tromped up the stairs to the deck.

"Is there a party going on in there? I brought ice cream, so you have to let me in."

"No! Don't open that door," warned Sara. "You'll see your shower invitations."

"She'll see them in a few days anyway," Liz pointed out.

Collette had already let herself in and she grabbed one of the cards from the pile. Her face screwed up and her eyes watered.

Emily was utterly deflated. "You don't like them?"

"They're beautiful," Collette whined. "That's why I'm crying. I cry at everything now. I'm literally a big blubbering whale."

"Collette, you've really got to stop saying derogatory things about your body. You are *not* a whale," Liz declared vehemently. "You're housing a baby."

"Yeah, with 'house' being the operative word," Collette complained, plunking herself down in a chair. When Liz opened her mouth to object again, Collette held up her hand. "Don't try to placate me, Liz. I'm every bit as much of a feminist as you are, so I already know all the reasons I shouldn't feel self-conscious about my...my *girth*. And believe me, as a nurse, I am plenty thankful I have a healthy body and a healthy baby and a smooth pregnancy, so far. But right now, I'm really hot and I'm tired and I'm hormonal. So please don't make me feel bad that I feel bad about my size. And don't stop me from cracking jokes about it, either. It's *my* body and I don't need to be told how to think or to feel about it."

"I'm sorry," Liz apologized while Sara picked up another envelope to address and Emily went to get Collette a glass of water. "I didn't mean to shut you down or make you feel bad. I meant it to be an encouragement."

"It's okay. I know you were trying to be helpful," Collette said, dabbing her eyes. "For the record, there are plenty of days when I love being pregnant so much I wish it wouldn't end for another year. Days when I feel like strutting down the corridor at work with a sign around my neck that says, 'Look at what my body is capable of doing. Isn't it awesome?' But today isn't one of those days."

"I remember the feeling," Liz said.

Collette was peering at one of the invitations when Emily came back to the table with her glass of water.

"I don't really eat ice cream all the time, do I?" she asked.

"I wouldn't say all the time, no. Definitely not," Emily answered, as Liz surreptitiously reached to hide the pint Collette had set in the middle of the table. But Collette caught her in the act.

"What can I say? My body craves calcium." She giggled at herself and Emily was glad the tension was resolved.

"You're inviting Barbara Reed?" Sara questioned as she turned to the second page of the guest list. "It's one thing for her to come to the cardiology cookouts, but to your shower?"

"It was Wilson's idea to invite her, not mine. He says it would be rude not to, but I think he's beguiled by her."

"Nah, I doubt that." Sara breezily dismissed Collette's concern before remarking, "I see you've got Lucas on the list, too. I've got to say, he and Barb are an unlikely couple. I was really surprised when he started showing up at our cookouts with her. I wonder if they'll come to the shower together, too."

"Doubtful," Collette muttered under her breath.

"What do you know that we don't know?"

Collette equivocated. "I heard he's interested in someone else, but it's just a rumor."

"Does anyone want to go for a swim?" Emily asked loudly, desperate to change the subject.

After they'd changed into their suits, the four women sauntered languorously along the water's edge, scouring the shallows for beach glass and shells. Emily planned to say she had cramps and couldn't go swimming, but she was so hot by the time they got to the inlet that she was the first one to drop her towel and jump into the exhilarating current, and the last to get out.

"Just one more ride," she promised the other three women, who watched her from shore as they warmed themselves in the sun.

"We're in no rush," one of them answered. "Take as many as you want."

If I did that, I might never get out, Emily thought. And she was looking forward to seeing Lucas again too much to do that.

*

Emily was penciling the markings for a penguin in the arctic room when Lucas showed up on Monday.

"Excuse me, Ms. This is private property and graffiti is strictly prohibited. I'm going to have to ask you to leave. Now."

Grinning, she turned to face him. "I'm never going to live that down, am I?" she asked about their first encounter.

"It's already forgotten," Lucas said. "Can I come in?"

"You can, but you're not going to see much in here. I just started and I try to keep the markings as light as possible. Let me show you another room."

She led him to the first room she had completed, the one with the nautical theme. Although the blinds were open, she switched on the light for a better view.

"Be honest."

Lucas entered and slowly rotated in a circle, perusing the walls. He let out a low whistle.

"You astonish me," he said. "These are—they're . . . I don't even know how to describe them."

Emily chuckled. "They're just murals. They're not the Sistine Chapel."

"Will you go out with me?" Lucas blurted out suddenly. "I mean, for lunch? Can I take you to lunch?"

"Now? It's only ten o'clock."

He slid his cell phone out of his pocket and lifted it up apologetically. It was vibrating. "At one-thirty. I'll meet you here. Please?"

"Yes, I'd like that."

As Lucas hurried down the corridor toward the ER wing, Emily could hear him say, "I'm on my way right now."

She beamed, looking around the room. *I astonish him*, she thought before turning off the light.

*

"Is Captain Clark's okay? It's the closest and the best." Lucas un-looped his stethoscope from his neck, removed his white coat and draped them both over the stepladder Emily had been using. "The lunch crowd should be gone and I've got the rest of the afternoon off. I've been working since five a.m."

"That's brutal," Emily replied. "Captain Clark's sounds great to me."

They cut across the parking lot. Blinking against the bright sunshine, Emily started off the curb as a cyclist turned the corner. Lucas touched her arm to warn her and the cyclist swerved out of her path. She felt a jolt of warmth where Lucas's fingertips had grazed her skin.

The host seated them at a table in the back, beneath a mounted jawbone of a shark. Emily scanned the menu. Her stomach was fidgety, but not because she was anxious or in a public place: these were first-date butterflies. *Is this a date?* she wondered, biting her lip.

"What's the matter?" Lucas asked. "Do you know all the fish on the menu?"

"No, just the one on the wall," Emily joked, and Lucas laughed. *He seems to laugh at all my jokes.*

"The chowder here is always a good starter," Lucas mentioned. "You can't beat their lobster ravioli, either. Ditto for their shrimp scampi. But I'll tell you a secret."

Emily waited expectantly. Lucas looked both ways and then leaned forward for dramatic effect. Emily leaned closer, too. Even though they were only kidding around, it was heady to be so close to him.

"Sometimes I order a burger and parmesan truffle fries instead of seafood. Don't tell anyone though."

"I won't. I'm good at keeping secrets."

"I've noticed that about you."

Emily felt her heart contract. What did he mean by that? The server interrupted before Lucas could say any more. After they'd both ordered burgers and fries, she asked, "Without violating patient confidentiality, can you tell me how the kids in the hospital are today?"

Lucas seemed to understand she was referring to the girl who'd almost lost her leg in the recent car accident. "Kids in the hospital are on the mend, generally speaking."

"How about you? How are you doing today?"

"I've had a few ups and downs, but today I couldn't be better."

They fell into easy conversation about the different hamlets on the island and Lucas described the area of Rockfield where he lived, saying it was even remoter than Highland Hills. He also told her he'd worked at a hospital in Philadelphia before moving to Dune Island last October. But when he asked Emily about her life in Seattle, she steered their conversation to the subject of the artists' silent auction at the end of the summer.

"Tim said Clive McGrath is donating a painting. I'm a huge fan of his art." Emily peeled the wrapper off her straw and rolled it between her fingertips. "I hope I get to meet him at the auction."

"Don't count on it," Lucas said. Then he told Emily that Clive was notoriously reclusive. According to island gossip, some fifteen years ago, he lost both his wife and his daughter in a rip current during a summer vacation. After that, he completely retreated from society. Apparently, his niece did all his cooking and cleaning and errands for him. It was only because of her help that the fundraising organization had secured one of his paintings.

A shiver ran up Emily's spine and wiggled her shoulders as she considered Clive McGrath's life, which was so similar to her own. Both were artists, both had lost their entire families in tragic accidents and both were living on Dune Island. *But grief hasn't made a hermit out of me*, she thought. *Not for good, anyway.* And she wasn't going to let it, either.

"Are you okay?" Lucas asked.

"Yeah. I was just thinking how fortunate I am," she said, before telling him how much fun she'd had swimming with Sara, Liz and Collette the day before.

By the time the waiter delivered their food, Emily was so relaxed and ravenous she gobbled down her meal and half of Lucas's fries as well. Afterward, they walked slowly back to the children's wing and Emily showed Lucas the desert and rainforest rooms, too.

"They're so lifelike. Were they inspired by places you've visited?"

"Yes. But I've also had help from the internet and from . . . other resources."

"Well, next time I feel stressed out at work, I'll come down here. It'll be like going on vacation," he said as they circled back to the seascape room.

"That's how the hospital should advertise the new wing. 'The next time one of your kids needs his appendix removed, bring him to Hope Haven. It'll be like going on vacation, a treat for the entire family.'"

Lucas shook his head, frowning. "No, no. I didn't mean it like that. I-I—"

"I know what you meant." Emily briefly touched his arm for emphasis. "And I'm pleased you feel that way. It's exactly the effect I was going for. Thank you."

The intense look in Lucas's eyes as he held Emily's gaze made her pulse thump in her ears. She was close enough to see the individual whiskers in the stubble above his lip and she realized he probably needed to get home to shower and shave and sleep, but she didn't want their afternoon together to end.

"You're welcome," Lucas said, his voice husky.

She was so torn between the impulse to say goodbye and step back and the desire to inch even closer that she was paralyzed, unable to so much as blink.

But then Lucas reached out and gently tilted her chin upward. "Almost all healed."

She knew he was referring to her skin but she thought, *Yes. I am almost all healed. I'm ready for this.* So when he slid his hand upward to caress her cheekbone with his thumb, she lowered her eyelids, savoring what was about to happen.

But Lucas's lips barely touched hers before he dropped his hand and pulled away.

"I am so sorry. I can't do this."

Emily's cheeks and forehead blazed with heat. *He's sorry? He's sorry? Why would he be sorry?* It took a moment to sink in. She knew the answer: he was more involved with Barbara than he had admitted. What a player. What a jerk. She should have known. She *did* know. She just didn't want to admit it to herself. She whirled around and tore down the wing and out the exit, weaving in and out of cars in the parking lot.

Lucas caught up to her beside her car and clutched her by the elbow. "Emily, wait."

She twirled around. "Don't touch me," she said, enunciating each word as harshly as she could. She yanked her arm away with such force that her knuckles hit the car's side view mirror and she winced. "Why would you jerk me around like that when you're seeing someone else? For your ego?"

"*Me?* I'm not the one jerking *you* around. You're the one who's engaged! You're the one who's playing games! *You* should be apologizing to *me!*"

Emily's head spun. She backed against the car window and then flinched away from its blistering heat. "What are you talking about? Who told you I'm engaged?"

"Nobody told me," Lucas admitted. "I found out by accident. I saw the ring. It was when you had the concussion. I was in your room, getting you a pillow and—"

Emily was aghast. "And you decided to search my private belongings?"

"It wasn't like that, I swear. The box fell off the bed and I wanted to be sure I hadn't broken anything. I peeked inside. When I saw what it was, I put it right back."

"So, then what? You decided you'd never tell me about it because you liked knowing something about me that I clearly wanted to keep to myself? What kind of power play is that?"

"It wasn't a power play. There just was never a good time to mention it. I hardly knew you when I saw the ring. Besides, what was I supposed to say? Whatever I said, you'd think the same thing that you think now. You'd think I was a creep. That I was being nosy. Which couldn't be further from the truth. I go out of my way not to offend you and not to intrude on your privacy. I have to be so careful around you that half the time I feel like I'm walking on eggshells!"

"Oh, so *you're* the wronged party here, is that it? I'm just being overly sensitive, right?" Emily shot back. "Listen, I'm fully aware of how popular you are around here, *Dr. Luke*. I can appreciate that you've probably gotten used to most people hanging on your every word, but did you ever consider perhaps you *should* be more careful about the things you say and do?"

Lucas shook his head and spoke slowly and that just ticked Emily off more—it was as if he was pacifying an uncooperative pediatric patient. "Listen, I didn't deliberately intend to look at the ring and I didn't intend to make a move on a woman who's engaged to someone else. I'm sorry about both of those things. I'm very sorry. I don't know what else to say."

The amount of humiliation Emily felt about Lucas apologizing for kissing her paled in comparison with the amount of disappointment she felt about him opening her engagement ring box. Unable to look at him, she folded her arms across her chest and focused on a lamppost in the distance.

"Talk to me, Emily. Don't clam up. Say something, anything, just don't shut me out."

"You want me to say something? What is it you want to hear?" she shouted, leaning forward. "You want to know about my fiancé? Okay, I'll tell you."

Even as she was screeching, she was aware that she was out of control, but she didn't censor herself. She flailed her hands as she yelled, "He broke up with me, Lucas. *That's* why the ring was under my pillow and not on my finger. Because he broke up with me. And do you want to know *why* he broke up with me? Because my parents and my brother died in a helicopter crash and I couldn't get over it. I couldn't stop grieving. I *still* can't stop grieving and it's nearly been a year. So I came here to escape. I came here to focus on something else for a change. I came here to get away from all the questions and the 'poor Emily' looks that make me feel raw with grief all over again. I came here for privacy. But, clearly, I'm not entitled to that. So what else do you want to know, Lucas? Do you want to read my diary? Do you want to rifle through my underwear drawer?"

Emily's shoulders heaved with sobs and Lucas moved toward her. "Oh Emily," he murmured softly. "Oh, Em."

Her posture stiffened and she pushed him away. "You are *not* allowed to pity me. You know my whole life story now. You got what you wanted. Now leave me alone. Just leave me alone."

She fumbled with the lock button on her car key before popping the door open. A blast of hot air enveloped her and when she got in she could feel the upholstery burning right through her clothes. She turned on the ignition and rolled down her window. Tears blurred her vision and she was so upset she nearly sideswiped a pedestrian who stepped out from between two nearby cars as she was pulling out of her parking space.

"Watch where you're going!" the woman barked.

There, inches from the hood of Emily's car, Barbara Reed planted her hands firmly on her hips and stood there long enough to give Emily the evil eye before sashaying away.

CHAPTER TEN

Although she blasted the air conditioner all the way back to the cottage and then took a cold shower outside, neither could quench Emily's temper.

Too hot to sit in the sun on the deck, she flopped on her bed and took the hexagonal box out of its hiding place to examine the ring. How could Lucas have snooped through her things? Even if he had innocently knocked the box to the floor, did he really believe he'd broken its contents or was he just being nosy? And why didn't he mention seeing the ring to her—didn't that just prove his guilt?

Suppose it didn't—suppose it was just an accident that he came across the ring and suppose it even might have been too awkward to tell her about it afterward. Suppose all of that was valid. What about the fact that he assumed she was engaged and yet he'd asked her out? He'd all but kissed her. What kind of man does that? What's more, he thought *she* was the kind of woman who would get involved with him even though she was supposedly engaged!

And now he knew about everything that happened, everything she'd been trying to keep to herself. The accident. Devon. All of it. Who knows who he'd tell. Tim? The Board? Liz and Sara? What if he told Barbara? Emily couldn't bear it if everyone knew. It wasn't that she imagined they'd be unkind; it was that it was *her* business. It was her heartache to share or not to share.

She had just begun to feel a tiny bit normal. But now her sorrow would define her again. She'd be known for what happened, not for who she was. Now people would start asking questions and she was going to have to relive the accident every time she answered them. She was going to have to endure people's concerned looks. Or convince them she was okay even when she wasn't at all sure she was.

Lucas said that he'd noticed she was good at keeping secrets—he must have been referring to the ring. He probably thought he was so clever, knowing something about her she didn't want him to find out. It was as if he'd been keeping a secret about *her* secret. *Whether it's Lucas or Wilson or Mom and Dad, I feel like everyone has been withholding information from me and it's absolutely maddening!* she silently fumed.

Emily groaned and sat upright. She needed to do something distracting—no, she needed to do something *destructive*—and she had the perfect idea. She'd start prying the baseboards off the wall in the bathroom, since she eventually planned to install new beadboard. She was searching for her putty knife when Collette came to the deck door.

"What's wrong?" she asked the second Emily invited her in.

Emily poured it all out, alternately weeping and raising her voice in anger and she ended by saying, "I should've known that anyone who'd hang out with Barbara Reed isn't a trustworthy person."

Collette tilted her head and lifted one shoulder in half a shrug. "I don't know about that, Emily. Lucas doesn't strike me as someone who would deliberately violate your privacy."

"How can you say that after everything I just told you about the ring?" Emily shrieked.

"I don't know Lucas really well, but I believe that if he said he saw the ring by accident, then that's what happened. Sometimes when we have a sensitive spot, we tend to question peoples' motives. But that has more to do with us than with them."

Emily stared out the sliding doors, fighting back tears. "So I'm just being paranoid, is that what you're saying?"

"I'm saying that I bet if you reconsider most of your interactions with Lucas, you'll recognize that he's got a lot of integrity. I understand how distressing it must have been to find out he knew about your engagement ring. But that doesn't change everything about his character. He's still the man you thought he was when you let him kiss you."

Emily couldn't believe Collette was saying these things.

"I'm not trying to hurt you, Emily," Collette continued, as if she'd read her mind. "You know why I came over here? To gripe about a fight Wilson and I got into on the way home from work. I had an ugly interaction with Barbara Reed this afternoon and I was so upset, I ended up lighting into Wilson for insisting she gets invited to the baby shower. I accused him of being blinded by her seductive ways."

When Emily didn't respond, Collette continued. "You've said it—and Wilson has said it, too—'forgiveness is a gift.' I agree. What I'm saying to you now is that trust is a choice. And I don't think Lucas has given you any real reason not to trust him. I think that maybe, when you have time to think about it, you might realize underneath it all, you're more upset about something else. That's up to you to figure out. And it's up to you whether you decide to trust Lucas or not. Anyway, I'll leave you to your thoughts. I've got to go apologize to my husband."

Collette gave Emily a quick hug and a kiss on the cheek and was out the door.

Still clammy from her shower, Emily felt as if she were literally stewing in her own juices as she tried to build a defense against what Collette had claimed about Lucas. But the more she considered her conversations with him, the more she realized how respectful Lucas was about her choices and her privacy.

Like when he supported her about leaving the hospital after her concussion. Or when he stopped coming to see her in the children's wing because he sensed she wanted to work alone. She remembered how careful he'd been to protect his patients' privacy, too, and how angry he was when details about their injuries appeared in the media. And even on that first day when Barbara suggested Emily had an eating disorder, Luke had told her it was none of their business.

But that was before he knew about the accident. And about Devon dumping her. Now that he knew, everything had changed— not because Emily necessarily thought Lucas would tell anyone else her secrets. But because *he* knew about her secrets himself.

Maybe that was it: maybe that was the issue "beneath it all," as Collette had hinted, that she was most worried about. Was it safe to be vulnerable with Lucas? Could she trust him? Could she trust herself? She had been numb for so many months, in so many ways. Was she ready for this, this coming back to life?

*

That evening as she pulled down her bedspread, Emily accidentally flipped the box from where she'd left it resting on the bed. When she picked it off the floor, she heard the ring rattling loosely inside, just as Lucas had said happened when he pulled the pillow from her bed. Emily was filled with shame. He hadn't been snooping around any more than she'd been deliberately eavesdropping on Collette and Wilson that night they had the argument about the laptop. And he definitely hadn't trespassed the way Emily had when she'd read her father's love notes.

Her father's words came to mind, "Because I've been forgiven for all sorts of offenses myself." Emily sprang from the bed and grabbed her phone. When it didn't immediately connect, she ran up the hill behind Collette and Wilson's house, not caring if they saw her roaming their yard in her nightgown.

She noticed she had a notification; of all the unlikely timing, she had received a call from Devon, the last person she wanted to talk to at that moment. Not bothering to check her voicemail, she scrolled through her contacts and tapped Lucas's number.

He didn't pick up so she left a voicemail. *There's something I need to say to you, Lucas. It's important. Please—* She lost the signal and ran farther up the hill but she couldn't connect again. She was so desperate, she would have asked to use Collette and Wilson's phone but their house was dark, so she went home.

Devon was a very tolerant person and he was engaged to me, but even he got fed up with my moods. Lucas hardly knows me—it would be that much easier for him to decide I'm not worth the trouble, she fretted as she returned to her room.

Emily retrieved the ring box from where she'd set it on the bed, but instead of placing it beneath her pillow, she put it in her nightstand drawer and then turned out the light.

*

Emily rose with the sun the next morning and she changed into her bathing suit, layered it with a T-shirt and wrapped her towel sarong-style around her waist. The weather was overcast but it was already oppressively humid. She might have gone in the water if the surf hadn't been breaking so close to shore, but at least it was easier to breathe on the beach.

Inhaling deeply, Emily stretched her arms toward the sky before slowly exhaling and bringing them down to her sides and walking to the west. She traveled so far that it was close to eight o'clock when she climbed back up the beach stairs. She figured Collette and Wilson would be up by now and if she hurried, she could use their landline before they left for work.

Her stomach tensed when she neared the top of the stairs and she spotted Lucas's van in the driveway. Was he having coffee with Wilson and Collette or had he walked to the east and she'd missed him? She decided to go get a drink of water before setting out to find him. But as she followed the path over the dunes and through the rosebush hedges, she spotted him sitting on her deck. He immediately stood up.

"Hello, Emily." He sounded so formal when he used her full name. "I called you back but you didn't pick up."

"There's something I want you to know, Lucas," she said, nervously securing her towel tighter around her waist. "I'm sorry I doubted you at first, but I believe you about the ring. I know you wouldn't deliberately snoop around in my room."

Lucas nodded and started to respond but Emily held up her hand.

"I also want you to know that even though this last year has been the most horrible period in my life, I'm not a victim and I don't want to be treated like one."

"A victim? Is that how you think people see you? Is that how you think *I* see you?" Lucas asked incredulously. "What do you even mean by the word *victim*? That I think you're weak? Emily Vandemark, you are one of the strongest, most independent people I know. I've thought that since the moment I met you and you practically arm-wrestled me for your suitcase."

She shook her head. "I'm not weak, but I'm not invincible, either. You don't know how hard it's been. You don't know all of the ways I've been shattered by grief."

"You're right; I don't know. That's because you haven't told me. Which is fine—I'm not saying you have to tell me, although if you want to, I'm here to listen. But there's a difference between being weak and being vulnerable. Do you see other people as victims when they cry or share their struggles? Did you see me as a victim when I told you I was having a rough time because I lost a patient?"

"Of course not."

"And that's not how I see you, either. Yesterday you said I wasn't allowed to pity you. Well, I don't pity you. I *like* you, Emily."

"You hardly know me."

"I know you enough to like you. Enough to want to get to know you more," Lucas argued. "I know that you're a highly gifted artist and a smart, generous, resilient woman. I know that beneath your guarded exterior, you're warm and sensitive and thoughtful."

"Do you want to know what I know about you?" Emily countered, not waiting for him to answer. "You're an exceptional pediatrician. You're compassionate and forgiving. You're insightful. And you've got a serious, loner side even though most of the time you relish being Mr. Popularity."

"Hey now!" Lucas objected. "That's just my Dr. Luke personality. It's for the benefit of my day job."

"Yeah, right," Emily teased and then grew serious. "You didn't tell anyone about those things I told you yesterday, did you?"

"Absolutely not," Lucas promised. "That's your business. But listen, here's the thing that worries me."

Emily prepared herself. *This is the part where he says he just wants to be friends. All that other stuff was leading up to this. "You're a terrific woman... but I don't think you're ready for a relationship." Isn't that the gist of what Devon said when he broke up with me?*

He continued cautiously. "I'm concerned that if I ask you about your family, you'll think I'm prying. Or you'll get upset because it's too painful to talk about. But if I don't ask you, it will seem like I don't care. I don't know what to do so that I don't hurt you either way."

Emily was quiet, allowing Lucas's concern to soak in. She replied, "I'm honestly not sure what to say. I hate it that you feel like you're walking on eggshells when you're talking to me. That can't be very comfortable for you. But when it comes to discussing my family— and even Devon—I can't predict how I'll react. Sometimes, I want to keep it all in; other times, I need to let it all out. I don't want to distance you, but I don't want to have a meltdown in front of you, either. It's not because of how I feel about you, personally, it's just that I'm learning how to handle this as I go."

"That's fair. How about if we agree to cut each other a lot of slack, knowing the other person isn't trying to hurt us?"

"I'm going to need to take things slowly. Very slowly."

"That's fine. You can set the pace, okay?"

Emily responded by saying, "There's something I want to share with you. I'll be right back."

She went inside and changed into her clothes and then brought her framed photo with her to the deck.

"Here's the reason I nearly ripped your arm off the day I thought you were stealing my luggage—this was inside. It was taken in front of one of the paintings at my first large gallery exhibit."

Lucas studied the picture. He pointed to her mother and said, "This must be the woman who taught you how to make such delicious cookies and soup. Was she an artist, too?"

"No. She was a special ed teacher. But she was very creative and she was the one who first encouraged me to paint."

"How about your brother and father?"

"My father was a school guidance counselor and my brother, Peter, was a child welfare social worker. They were both very tall, as you can tell."

True to his word, Lucas let Emily take the lead. Instead of peppering her with questions, he listened as she told him a little more about her family and then he told her a little about his family, too. They didn't exchange more than superficial information, the kinds of details one might mention to an acquaintance. But for Emily, talking about her family to Lucas without dissolving into tears was a huge step forward and he seemed grateful when he thanked her for sharing the photo with him, too.

After a few minutes, he said he had to go and they agreed to meet for breakfast the next morning at the hospital. Emily waved to him as his van rattled up the driveway and then went back inside with her photo. This time, instead of putting it on the nightstand in her bedroom, she carried into the living room and set it on the antique desk, out in the open, where it belonged.

After Lucas left, Emily went to Collette and Wilson's and lightly rapped on the door. An enticing aroma wafted from the kitchen; Collette mentioned she'd been having cravings for protein at breakfast lately. Emily had been too upset to eat supper the previous evening but now her mouth watered and her stomach growled.

"Something smells good," she said after Collette invited her in. "Is it bacon?"

"It's stir-fried chicken. You want some?" Collette offered, as if there was nothing unusual about eating stir-fried chicken for breakfast.

"Sure, why not?" Emily climbed onto one of the stools so she could talk to Collette while she prepared their breakfast. "I came to thank you for the things you said yesterday."

"You're welcome. I hope you know I was lecturing myself as much as I was addressing you. As I said, Wilson and I had a humdinger of an argument, which was ninety-nine percent my fault.

I was sniping at him about one thing, but it was really something else that was bothering me."

"It wasn't the silverware drawer, was it?" Emily teased.

Collette looked momentarily confused. "Oh, yeah. I kind of went off about that the other evening, didn't I? Sheesh. I must be a real peach to live with. But seriously, the salad forks have shorter tines and longer handles than the dessert forks. I'd get it if he had nothing to compare them to, but when they're laying right there, side by side, how hard can it be to see the difference?"

Emily held up her hands, laughing. "Forget I said anything about it!"

Collette laughed, too, before hinting, "I thought I saw Lucas's van parked outside when I got up."

"You did. We, uh, talked and he accepted my apology."

"And?"

"And . . . I was glad he did?"

"*And?*" Collette repeated pointedly.

"And we're sort of seeing each other, I guess," Emily admitted. "Collette, stop looking at me like that!"

"What did I say about women's intuition?" Collette bragged as Wilson entered the kitchen.

"Oh. Hi, Emily."

"Morning, Wilson."

"That tie has a little stain on it, honey," Collette told him.

Wilson looked down at his tie, scowled and then went back upstairs.

"I'll be back in a sec and then we can eat," Collette said over her shoulder as she edged toward the bathroom.

While she was in there, the landline rang and she shouted, "Can you get that for me, Emily?"

Emily grabbed the cordless receiver in the living room. "Hello?"

"Hi, Collette. This is Julia. How are you feeling?"

"This isn't Collette. This is her friend, Emily. Just one mom—"

"Emily Vandemark from the cottage next door?"

How did the caller know who she was? "Yes."

"Why, hello. This is Wilson's Aunt Jewel."

Until she said the nickname Wilson had used for her since he was a child, Emily hadn't recognized her voice. Julia and her husband didn't have any children and they only visited Wilson's grandparents on Dune Island for a week every August, but Emily remembered her well; she wore dramatic sun hats and ten or fifteen bangles on each wrist. Emily had seen her name on the invitation list for the shower and she'd meant to ask Wilson how she was doing.

"Hi, Mrs. Durand," Emily said, automatically reverting to the title she'd used to address Wilson's aunt when she was a kid. "What a pleasure to hear your voice."

"It's good to hear yours, too, but please, call me Julia," she insisted. Emily knew what was coming next. "I was so sorry to hear about your family, dear."

"Thank you. The condolences you sent meant a lot to me." Maybe it was because Julia had lost her sister in a sudden accident, too, but she had managed to convey a more meaningful sentiment with fewer words than anyone else who had sent Emily a card.

"Are you at the cottage for the entire summer?"

"Yes, I—"

"Can I have the phone, please?" Wilson barged in, holding out his hand.

Embarrassed to be cut off, Emily hastily said goodbye to Julia and handed the cordless phone to Wilson, who jogged up the stairs with it. *What is wrong with him, now?* she wondered. Collette had indicated they'd made up, so it wasn't that. Was he annoyed about his wife making chicken for breakfast? Or did he feel like Emily was wearing out her welcome? *I hope it's not that he contacted his father and the guy was a jerk to him.*

Collette returned to the room a moment later and as they were eating, she told Emily that the niece of a nurse at work was majoring in fashion design at college and she was going to create a dress for Collette to wear to her shower. "She's young and just starting out, but supposedly she's got an incredible sense of style."

"That's great," Emily said as Wilson re-entered the room, looking even grumpier than before. "How is your Aunt Jewel, Wilson?"

"Julia called? Is everything all right?" Collette asked.

"Yeah, she's fine. She was confirming she's coming to the shower."

"How did she know the date?" Collette pressed him. "Sara and Emily just finished addressing the invitations on Monday. Hers couldn't have reached New York City already."

It was clear to Emily that Wilson was hiding something from Collette. Maybe it involved a special baby gift Julia wanted to give her?

"It's possible Sara mailed a batch of them from her house earlier last week," she fibbed. *Emphasis on "possible."*

Wilson's back was turned to the women as he added milk to his coffee and Emily sensed that whatever he was hiding, it wasn't a gift.

*

Because Lucas was working an erratic schedule that week, for the next few days he and Emily only saw each other twice; once when he came to the children's wing with takeout from Captain Clark's and another time when they went for a walk on the beach.

"Sunday's the first day I have entirely free and I'd like to take you out on a real date," he told her.

"But Sunday's cookout day," Emily remembered. "I understand that you're a lot more social than I feel like being right now. I don't want to stop you from hanging out with your friends if that's something that you're looking forward to doing."

"I'm looking forward to spending time with *you*. Besides, those cookouts are a cardiology department thing."

"Yeah, but don't you usually go to them anyway?" Emily asked before she realized her mistake. "Or was that only because you were hanging out with Barbara?"

Beneath his tan, Lucas's ears were going pink. "I only went to them because I was hanging out with Barbara—"

Sorry she'd put him on the spot about his friendship with Barbara, Emily interrupted, "It doesn't matter, as long as it's not something you care about missing, sure, let's get together on Sunday."

"Wait, you didn't let me finish. I only went to the cookouts because I was hanging out with Barbara but I was only hanging out with Barbara because I wanted to go to the cookouts, especially the ones at Wilson and Collette's," Lucas explained, his cheeks reddening even brighter than his ears. "I was hoping you'd be there."

Emily's face felt aflame, too. *So, Collette was right.* "Okay, well, what do you want to do on Sunday?"

"There's a phenomenal Thai restaurant in Benjamin's Manor," he suggested. "You're probably thinking that Thai food in an old New England whaling village doesn't sound very enticing, but I promise you'll find it's as good as any Thai food you've eaten in Seattle. I also know a great Mexican restaurant in Rockfield."

"You're trying to fatten me up, aren't you?"

He looked crestfallen. "No, not at all. But you don't like crowds, so that eliminates most of the other places and events people go to when they're on a date on the Island. I've tried to think of somewhere relatively secluded I could take you, but all I've come up with is those two restaurants. They're both quiet and intimate—not at all like Captain Clark's."

"How about if we play it by ear for Sunday? We don't have to go on a formal date, do we? It's not as if you have to ask my father's permission to court me or something."

"Easy for you to say," Lucas grumbled. "You don't know how protective Wilson is of you. When it comes to you and Collette, that guy's a bulldog. Especially lately. It must be his paternal instincts are kicking in, in preparation for becoming a father."

At least that's better than not having any paternal instincts at all, like his dad, Emily thought.

*

"Tomorrow morning I'm going for an initial consultation with the student designer about my dress," Collette told Emily as they bobbed in the waves late Friday afternoon. Collette's thighs were painfully chafed from rubbing together the last time she walked down to the inlet, so the two women were taking a swim right in front of the staircase. "What are you up to?"

"Repainting the cottage doors."

"Do you have to take them down, first?"

"Yeah, I probably should. But you don't know how many tries it took my father to rehang the front door properly after my mother painted it the first time. No matter how long he worked on it, it wouldn't open easily or it wouldn't close entirely. He kept blaming the paint and my mother kept blaming the humidity. Eventually, he got it just right, so I'm not messing with it now." Emily added, "I'll take the window shutters down, though, if I have the right tools."

"I'm sure Wilson has what you need," Collette said. "Actually, he could take them down for you, if you want him to."

Instead of pointing out that ever since Wilson's phone call with Julia, he seemed to be distancing himself from Emily more than usual, Emily replied, "Nah, that's okay. I don't want to hit him up for a favor on his day off."

"You'd be doing *me* the favor. He's been really down and I think he needs a distraction."

Then Collette confided she had finally asked Wilson point-blank about his DNA testing results. Apparently he admitted he'd gotten them back some time ago, but beyond that, he refused to discuss what he'd learned. His secrecy made Collette suspect he'd been in touch with his father and it didn't go well. "I think he's been really upset about it but he doesn't want to upset me, too, so he's trying to process it on his own."

"I certainly hope that's not the case," Emily said, but judging from his mood and secrecy lately, she suspected Collette was right. The possibility made her simultaneously feel brokenhearted and outraged on Wilson's behalf. *I had a feeling his father would be a jerk to him.* "I'm glad to help cheer him up but there must be more pleasant distractions we can suggest than taking down my shutters."

"Like what? Fishing with Lucas? You know he can't do that—Dr. Fluke will be working."

"Dr. Fluke?" Emily chuckled. "Who came up with that?"

"I did, just now. Clever, isn't it?"

"Brilliant. It's right up there with *Barbs*."

"Speaking of Barbs..." Collette dropped back underwater and smoothed her hair flat against her head as she surfaced. "She just found out she didn't get the fellowship that starts in the fall—the other resident did."

"Oh, that's too bad." Emily meant it, too. As an artist, she'd applied for enough fellowships she wasn't awarded to know how discouraging it was to be rejected professionally. "Does she have a backup plan?"

"Yeah. Wilson said she's really skilled and smart and she has her pick of fellowships at about five different hospitals. She just wasn't the right fit for Hope Haven."

"How is she taking it?"

"Oddly, she's handling it very well. It's like the quiet before the storm, if you ask me," Collette said as they waded out of the water. "Hurricane Barbara, Category Five."

"She's not that bad."

"Trust me, she's going to take this out on somebody. I just hope it's not on Wilson, since he had a big role in deciding who'd get the fellowship."

"Maybe instead of helping me take down the shutters tomorrow, he should help me batten down the hatches," Emily kidded, trying to ease Collette's mind.

"I suppose I could ask him to take me to my consultation. He'll be bored to tears but at least I won't feel worried about him."

"No, you go to your appointment alone. I'll keep Wilson company." *He might not want me to, but I won't give him a choice,* Emily thought. *If nothing else, we can go for a walk on the beach—that's always good for whatever ails a person.*

CHAPTER ELEVEN

When Wilson answered the door, Emily's first thought was, *He looks so peaked I'm surprised Barbara hasn't started a rumor that* he *has an eating disorder.* But she greeted him with a cheery smile. "Good morning, Wilson."

"Hi, Emily. I'm afraid Collette isn't back from her appointment yet."

"That's good, because I brought cookies and she'd probably gobble them up in the blink of an eye." Emily stepped around him, into the kitchen, where she set the container on the breakfast bar. "Do you want milk with yours or are you having coffee?"

"I'm not hungry, thanks." He glanced at his watch.

"You have to at least try one. They're chocolate chip, your favorite."

"I'll have one later when I take a break. I've got a lot of research to do."

"But they're still warm. And you know what my mom always said about warm cookies." Emily was about to repeat another one of her mother's adages when she noticed Wilson's face blanch. "Oh, no, are you sick? Go sit in the living room. I'll get rid of these."

Assuming it was the aroma of the cookies that was turning his stomach, Emily put them on the picnic table outside and returned to bring Wilson a glass of ice water. He took a sip and gestured for her to sit down, too.

"What's wrong?" she asked.

Wilson took another sip and then set the glass on the coffee table. "There's, uh, something I've wanted to talk to you about for a while. I'm afraid you may find it very upsetting but I think it's time we discuss it."

I might find it very upsetting? Then that means it isn't about his father, so what else could it be? Emily's heart raced and her thoughts raced even faster. Had Wilson lost his medical license? Was Collette leaving him? Was Emily's brain injury really a lot worse than she thought?

"It's okay, you can tell me anything," she said, sinking into a chair. *I can take it—I hope.*

"I, uh, I've been concerned about the baby's health."

Emily gasped, but Wilson held up his hand.

"No, no, it's not like that. The baby's healthy. Collette is healthy," he assured her. Then he continued, telling her what Collette had already mentioned; he'd wanted to find his father in order to learn more about his medical history, for the baby's sake, so he'd taken a DNA test.

Since Collette had told her the same thing in confidence, Emily didn't want to let on she already knew, so she nodded thoughtfully. "That makes sense. Did you find him?"

"Yes. No. I mean, I found out he's deceased."

"Oh, I'm sorry to hear that." Emily was a little confused. She could understand why Wilson would be disappointed or saddened to discover his father had died, but she didn't understand why he thought this news would distress *her*. Had Wilson received foreboding medical information about his father's medical history? *Is Wilson going to inherit a terminal disease?*

"Yeah, so . . ." Wilson hesitated, clearly struggling. Emily was so anxious she felt like she might have to take him by the shoulders and shake the words out of him if he didn't stop hemming and hawing. "For one thing, I was quite surprised—shocked, really—to find out he wasn't Italian, like my grandparents and aunt always told me he was."

Emily nodded. According to the advertisements, people who took the tests were often surprised to find out their ancestral ethnicity wasn't what they'd always thought it was. "Do you think your grandparents just assumed he was Italian because your mother was living in Italy when she became pregnant?"

Wilson rubbed his temples. "No. They thought he was Italian because that's what my mother told them. It was the only piece of information she ever shared about him, other than his first name. But it wasn't true, he wasn't Italian."

"That seems an odd thing for her to lie about."

"Yeah, but it's possible she wasn't lying. It's possible she didn't know."

"She didn't know that her boyfriend wasn't Italian?" Emily was incredulous. "You'd think if he told her he was Italian, he lived in Italy and he was fluent in the language—"

Then it clicked. Wilson's mother had known her boyfriend was Italian. But what she might not have known was whether her Italian boyfriend was Wilson's father; he could have been fathered by someone else. Emily didn't know quite what to say, so she asked, "So if your father wasn't of Italian descent, what was his ethnicity?"

"It turns out he was, uh, he was Dutch."

Emily grinned. "Cool—maybe we're related."

She meant to lighten the mood but Wilson's frown lines deepened. "We are, Emily. I'm ninety-nine point nine percent sure we are, anyway."

Emily couldn't wipe the smile off her face. "Didn't Peter always say you were twins separated at birth? What are we, fourth or fifth cousins or—"

"No!" Wilson yapped and Emily drew back in surprise. His voice dropped half an octave as he said, "We're siblings. Half-siblings. Your father was my father. He was *our* father. Yours and Peter's and mine."

"Pffbt," Emily sputtered before the grin spread across her face again. It was a strange joke, but Wilson was never very good at making jokes. He had a great smile, but a lousy sense of humor. "No, really, be serious."

"I'm am being serious, Emily. I can show you the report. Several of my matches are Vandemarks. Even though neither you nor Peter nor Frederick are in the database, I'm as close to positive as I can be that we're related."

Emily couldn't believe Wilson actually thought they were siblings based on, what, a shared name? How could he possibly be that naïve? That unrealistic? Was it because he wanted it to be true? She'd read that sometimes men experienced emotional crises before becoming fathers for the first time. Maybe Wilson was clutching at straws about Emily's dad because he was overwhelmed about having a son and the association with Frederick made him feel more confident or something.

"Vandemark is a very common name in certain areas of the Netherlands. It's like having the surname Nelson and living in the Midwest. Don't get me wrong, Wilson. I'd love it if we were blood relatives, but I don't think having someone with the same last name in our lineage proves anything," Emily said, her voice soft as she tried to let him down gently. "Nothing will ever change the fact that in so many ways, you've been as much of a brother to me as Peter was."

Wilson was adamant. "I'm not basing my conclusion on the name alone. I'm basing it on the report, which is based on genetics. It's not wrong."

Emily took a deep breath and let it out, trying to quell the jitteriness inside. She was getting a little concerned for Wilson. His mindset wasn't healthy. "You, of all people, know that labs make mistakes. How many times have you ordered a second blood test after the first one came back off the charts because of assay interference, or whatever?"

Wilson shook his head again. "Let me show you the report."

"No!" Emily was struggling to keep her patience. The report was obviously wrong, so reviewing the results was only going to reinforce Wilson's flawed conclusion. She stretched her ponytail out to one side with one hand and held her other arm at a right angle in front of her. Even on a superficial level, statistics were in her favor. "If you told anyone on the street that one of us is Dutch and one is Italian, which would they guess you are?"

"I'm French, on my mother's side. Everyone in her family had dark hair and eyes and an olive complexion. I take after her." Wilson pointed to a photo on the bookshelf of a young, vivacious brunette holding a smiling, drooling baby with a mop of dark hair.

Next to it was a photo of Wilson with his grandparents and on the other side of that, a photo of him with all of the Vandemarks. That one was taken at his graduation from medical school and seeing it, Emily felt insulted on her father's behalf. How could Wilson keep insisting her dad was *his* dad? Her father wouldn't be unfaithful to her mother. Her father wouldn't abandon his child.

"My mother told me she never met your mother, because your mother never came to the cottage because she had a strained relationship with your grandfather."

"That's true, your mother probably didn't meet my mother—"

"There's no *probably* about it. If she said she didn't meet your mother, she didn't meet her. *My* mother wasn't a liar," Emily responded sharply. If she had to hurt Wilson's feelings in order to shatter his delusion, she would.

"Right. But the year before I was born, my mother came to Dune Island alone once, on a break from her job in Italy. My grandparents had just bought the cottage the previous winter, but they hadn't moved into it for the summer yet. Your father—*our* father—must have met her then because—"

Emily had had enough. "Stop it! Don't you hear yourself? How can you even suggest these things? You knew my dad, Wilson. You knew what kind of man he was."

"Yes, I did. He was a good man. A very good man. One of the best," Wilson acknowledged. "But he wasn't perfect."

"You don't have to tell me that—*I* lived with him for eighteen years," Emily snapped. "But there's a world of difference between being imperfect and being the kind of person who would cheat on his wife, have a baby with another woman and then essentially *disown* him except when he saw the kid in the summer. My father loved my mother too much to do something like that. He loved *you* too much to do something like that!"

"I don't think he knew I was his son. I honestly don't," Wilson insisted. "As I said, I don't even think my mother knew."

Emily inwardly screamed, *That's because you* weren't!

Collette's car rolled up the driveway and Emily and Wilson both swiveled their heads in the direction of the window. Emily stood, glad for the excuse to end this conversation.

"I know this is a lot to take in. I've had several weeks to mull it over and I still have a lot of questions. A lot of mixed emotions," Wilson said. "I haven't told anyone else about it, not even Collette. And I won't tell her until you've had a chance to wrap your head around it, too."

"There's nothing to wrap my head around, Wilson. If it puts your mind at ease, I'll take a sibling DNA test, but until I get the results back, I don't want to talk about this again."

Emily sped out the door, waving to Collette from a distance in the yard without slowing down. She tore down the stairs and across the beach to the west, passing the artist's cottage without even realizing how far she'd walked. Usually when she was this upset, she would have felt sick to her stomach; the fact that she wasn't either indicated she was getting stronger emotionally or it showed she was so far *beyond* upset she couldn't even get sick. She vacillated from feeling deep concern about Wilson's well-being to being really angry at him. Angry and hurt. Her father had committed his entire life to his wife and children, and his entire career to other people's children. Even when he retired, he was working side by side with

Emily's mom, helping kids learn to read. He couldn't have faked that kind of devotion.

Emily was startled by a rogue, unbidden thought: *What if Dad had an affair with Wilson's mother the summer Mom was away and those love notes I found in the desk were a cover-up for what he was doing with Michelle?*

No. She wouldn't allow herself to entertain the possibility. Wilson might not have any compunction about maligning her parents' marriage, but Emily wouldn't betray her father's memory by even thinking such a thought. She resented Wilson for planting such an erroneous—such an *egregious*—idea in her mind. It wasn't true; it just *couldn't* be. Emily was as sure of that as she was of her own name and once she took the DNA test and got the results back, Wilson would be sure of it, too. *Meanwhile, it's a waste of time for me to give his crazy theory another thought.*

Yet despite resolving not to dwell on her conversation with Wilson, Emily stayed up half the night regretting that she'd volunteered to take a sibling DNA test. Patient privacy laws might have prevented the medical staff on Dune Island from sharing her results with anyone else, but she didn't want Wilson's co-workers to know she was taking the test. *Even though I'm positive it will show I'm not related to Wilson, it doesn't reflect well on Dad that I'd take it in the first place*, she thought.

Finally, around 3 a.m., she decided she'd buy the same kind of DNA test kit Wilson bought. It would take a lot longer to get the results back and she wasn't sure if it would be as accurate as a sibling

DNA test taken in a lab on the island, but at least it would afford her more privacy. Which was important because no matter how far she'd come by opening up to Lucas about her family, this wasn't the kind of thing Emily would ever want him or anyone else to find out about.

*

As she got ready for her date with Lucas on Sunday, Emily stood in front of the closet, yawning and wishing she had brought more clothes from Seattle. Surely she'd gained a few pounds by now and some of the more colorful items she'd left behind would have fit her again. She considered wearing her gray sheath dress, but it seemed too stiff for an outside afternoon date, so she wore her black cotton dress and swept her hair loosely into a low pony.

Lucas smelled good and he looked even better: his sky-blue gingham Oxford shirt mirrored his eyes and enhanced his tan and dark, sun-lit curls. Once they'd buckled their seat belts in his van, he told her the plan for the afternoon. He said since she had tactfully but undeniably vetoed going to a restaurant, he had prepared a picnic lunch and was taking her to the bird sanctuary, which contained dozens of trails on acres of land.

"The sanctuary is considered one of the island's hidden gems."

"I remember. My grandma loved birding, so when she'd come to the cottage in July for two weeks, my family would go for a picnic at the sanctuary almost every other day."

"Oh. Will it, uh, bother you to be back there?"

"No. I can't wait to see it again."

There were only a dozen or so cars in the parking lot when they arrived, which made sense; it was such a gorgeous afternoon, most families were likely at the beach. Emily and Lucas decided to hike first and then return to the area where picnicking was permitted.

They cut across a wide open field to take the path that ran alongside the marsh, led to the ocean through a red cedar forest, and then looped back again. As they walked, Emily told Lucas about how Peter had been especially good at sighting birds. One time he'd claimed he'd spotted a cahow, or Bermuda petrel, in the waters off the sanctuary. Because the cahows had only been seen a handful of times in Massachusetts, no one believed him, Emily's grandmother least of all. But a week later, someone captured the bird in a photo, which was published in the island newspaper.

"After that, my grandma wanted Peter by her side whenever we came here. She even bought him his own pair of binoculars. The two of them were always lagging behind my parents, and Wilson and I would go running up ahead of them."

"Wilson went with you on your family hikes?"

"Yeah, he went with us everywhere. It was like having another brother."

But that doesn't mean he is *my brother.* Emily was still struggling to push intrusive thoughts about yesterday's conversation from her mind.

She pointed to a bend in the trail. "Around that corner is a gigantic oak tree. Wilson and I used to race to it and then he'd boost me up so I could climb it with him. When my parents came walking by, we'd jump down to startle them. My mother would scream every time."

Emily went quiet, recalling the afternoon she and Wilson must have waited ten minutes in the tree for her parents to stroll past, but when they didn't, the two kids jumped down to see what was taking everyone so long. They'd backtracked about a hundred yards when they spied her parents standing off to the side of the trail. Her mother had her hands clasped behind her father's neck and he had his on her waist. They were kissing.

My father loved my mother, Emily thought. *In addition to the hundreds of other ways he demonstrated his love for her every day, he was always physically affectionate, even after they'd been married well over a decade. He couldn't have kept a secret about an affair and about Wilson all those years. He was too honest. And Mom would have sensed it. She would have known.*

But what if she hadn't? What if Emily's mother had been as oblivious to her father's deception as she was to Wilson and Emily's childhood scheme to startle her by jumping out of the tree? Emily's stomach began doing gymnastics and her lungs felt like they were made of concrete when she tried taking a deep breath.

"You want to see if you can still climb it?" Lucas pointed as they approached the oak.

"No, I don't." Emily broke into a brisk stride. "I need to go. Please take me home."

In the car Emily rolled down the window, angling herself sideways so Lucas wouldn't see the tears bouncing down her cheeks. He quietly navigated the back roads toward the cottage. Halfway there, he began to whistle a tune she'd heard before, but couldn't place. It was so calming that by the time they arrived, Emily's breathing was steady. She sheepishly asked Lucas if they could have their picnic on the beach.

"Are you sure?"

"I'm positive."

She went inside to wash the smudges of mascara from her cheeks. When she got down to the bottom of the beach staircase, Lucas had spread out a blanket. On top of it, he'd arrayed dishes—actual china—of fruit, shrimp, salad and fresh bread and cheese. In the very center he'd placed a vase of yellow tulips, like the ones in the photo of her family. He handed her a cloth napkin and a goblet of sparking grape juice. *How did he pull all of this together after working the night shift?*

"Lunch was delicious," she said after she'd sampled a little of everything. "I'm glad I didn't miss out on eating it with you, although I wouldn't have blamed you if you didn't want to be around me after my little . . . *cloudburst* back at the sanctuary."

"It's all right. I can understand why being back there would make you lonely for your family."

For once, that's not what upset me. Emily couldn't tell Lucas what had really triggered her tears, so she said, "You can understand now, but it's going to get old. I should warn you what happened today could happen again at almost any moment, for almost any reason. It can wear on a person. I really put Devon—my ex-fiancé—through a lot with my moods."

"*You* put *him* through a lot? You're the one who lost her entire family."

"It's not that simple. I mean, I know I said he broke up with me because I couldn't stop grieving, but the truth is, I shut him out a lot of the time, too. I imagine that was hard on him."

"Maybe, but if ever there was a time to stick by you, it would have been when you needed him most," Lucas said. "It sounds to me like you're giving him the easy way out. Are you sure you're over him?"

"Are you kidding me? Of course, I'm over him. I only mentioned him because, well, because I don't want my moodiness—"

"Your grieving process."

"I don't want my grieving process to scare you off, too."

"You couldn't scare me off the first day you met me, remember?" A playful smirk danced across Lucas's lips. "And you can't scare me off now, either."

CHAPTER TWELVE

For the rest of the month, Lucas was assigned to work the night shift, so Emily grew accustomed to him visiting her in the children's wing in the morning with croissants or taking her out to breakfast before he went home to sleep. When their schedules allowed, they also met on the beach for early evening walks, or sometimes he'd help with her renovation projects. If either of them needed time alone, Lucas would fish or surf while Emily went for a walk or took her easel out on the dunes to paint *en plain air* with the acrylics she'd bought.

She tried, with varying levels of success, to keep thoughts about her conversation with Wilson from creeping into her mind. Except to discreetly tell him that she had ordered, taken and sent in her own DNA test, Emily hadn't said a word about the subject to him. In fact, because the topic was such a sore spot for her, Emily tried to avoid Wilson as often as possible and unfortunately, that sometimes meant sacrificing time with Collette, who was still worried about her husband's mood. Emily wished she could dismiss her concern, but that would have meant telling her what Wilson said about Emily's father, so instead she suggested Collette should try to help Wilson get more rest, if possible.

But Emily missed the warm rapport she had with her friends, especially Collette, and she was delighted when Collette invited her to accompany her to the boutique where the student designer worked. The fabric she'd chosen for her dress had been delivered and Collette needed to get her measurements taken.

As the two women sat in the fitting area waiting for Brandi to finish helping another customer, Collette asked Emily what she was planning to wear to the shower.

"Oh, probably a dress."

"The black one? The one you always wear over your swimsuit?"

"No, it's gray."

"Aren't you one of the hostesses? You can't wear a boring color like gray to a baby shower," Brandi interjected as she entered the room. "People will think they've come to a funeral, not a shower."

Emily was surprised by how quickly the irony of Brandi's statement caused her eyes to well. She fished through her purse for a tissue.

"Emily's got sympathy pregnancy mood swings," Collette jested by way of explanation to Brandi, who appeared to be on the verge of tears herself.

"I wasn't suggesting you'd look ugly in gray. You'd look good in almost any color except maybe orange," the young student ineloquently but earnestly apologized. "But here, see how this dress accentuates your figure and brings out your eyes? It's such a sunny, happy color, which is perfect for a baby shower."

She lifted a yellow maxi from a nearby rack and held it up in front of Emily. The Empire-waist dress was splashed with vibrant blooms of all colors and the front and back dipped in modest V-cuts.

Even before she tried it on and Collette gasped and told Emily how beautiful she looked, Emily had decided she was buying the dress.

Later, as they were walking toward the car, Collette confessed how guilty she'd felt when she realized the shower fell on the same day as the accident. She said she'd discussed it with Wilson, but he insisted that he and Emily had agreed it would be all right.

"We can still call it off. I mean that. I'd rather call it off right now than have it upset you."

"No way. I'll be fine—I've got my 'sunny, happy dress' to wear," she said, laughing as she imitated Brandi's chirpy tone.

Collette rolled her eyes. "If only it were that simple, right?"

"Well, she's got a point. I did feel happier when I tried on the dress."

"If you think it made you happy, I can't wait to see the smile on Lucas's face when he sees you in it."

Emily wouldn't admit it aloud, but she was secretly thinking the same thing.

*

One evening in early August, after not seeing him for two days in a row, Emily waited impatiently for Lucas at the top of the beach staircase. She'd brought her sketch pad with her to pass the time drawing, but she was too restless to concentrate. Instead, she recollected how Lucas had held her hand at the beach the other morning; or rather, how he'd linked his index finger around hers. Even the memory of that small amount of contact sent a shiver up her arm.

She picked up her pad and tried to draw his hands from memory, but she got the fingernails wrong, so she flipped the page over and tried again. She was so absorbed in what she was doing, she didn't hear his van coasting down the driveway, which was how he'd taken to arriving ever since Emily's accident.

"Whatcha drawing, Em?" he asked, peering over her shoulder before he sat down.

Flustered, Emily hoped he didn't recognize she'd been sketching his hands and closed the sketch book. "Hi Lucas. I'm really glad you're here."

"I'm really glad I'm here, too. I stopped by to see you this morning and you weren't home."

"I had a follow-up appointment. The doctor said it was my last one. You still owe me a cherry lollipop, by the way."

Lucas grinned. Emily loved making him grin. "I'll bring you one tomorrow morning at the hospital."

"Actually...I was wondering if I could ask you to stop coming into the children's wing for a while?"

Lucas pushed his hair off his forehead. Emily noticed his skin was freckled across his nose and cheeks—he looked more boyish than ever. "How could I be crowding you? I haven't seen you in, like, a month."

It had only been two days, but Emily was happy it felt as long to him as it had felt to her. She danced her fingers across his forearm. "You aren't crowding me. I definitely still want to see you in the mornings, just not in the children's wing. We can meet in the cafeteria or in the lobby. I want you to be surprised by what I paint from now until I'm finished, kind of like a grand unveiling."

The images in one of the rooms—the boys' bathroom, in fact— had actually been inspired by Lucas, but Emily intended to keep it a secret until he could see the mural in its entirety.

"Phew!" Lucas exclaimed. "You had me going there. But I'm glad you're being direct about what you want, because there's something I've been meaning to talk to you about, too."

Emily bit the inside of her cheek, apprehensive.

"You said you wanted to take things slowly and I've sensed that means physically, too. I've tried to respect that, really, I have. But there's something you've got to tell me. When are you going to let me kiss you?"

"I . . . I don't know."

Lucas groaned. "That is so *not* the answer I wanted to hear."

"I've wanted you to kiss me, but every time you try, I keep thinking, *What if Lucas says, 'I'm so sorry. I can't do this,' again?* Even though I understand why you said it the first time, I have this irrational fear you'll do it again. Telling a woman you regret kissing her has to be the worst possible thing you can say."

"I promise I'll never apologize for kissing you again. To be honest, I wasn't sorry the first time I said it. I apologized because of guilt, not truth."

"I know. I get that. But so much time has passed and the longer it's been since we first kissed, the more awkward it is to kiss again. And now we're blatantly talking about it, like two juveniles, which makes it even more embarrassing. I don't know; maybe we should just get our next kiss over with quickly so it doesn't feel so weird. What do you think?"

"Whoa!" Lucas rocked backward as if he'd been shoved in the chest. "Talk about the worst possible things you can say! You just came out with four or five of them. Juvenile. Embarrassing. Awkward. Weird. *Get it over with!*"

Emily giggled and Lucas began to chuckle, too. Before long, they were clutching their sides. When their laughter subsided, Emily wiped her eyes. Lucas pulled her hand away from her face and slowly kissed her fingers, which were curled around his.

"Does this count as our next kiss?" he asked in a low voice.

"Nope." She tittered.

He kissed her shoulder. "How about this?"

She shook her head, more serious now.

He smoothed her hair and then kissed her earlobe. "This?"

"Not even close," she whispered.

She moved her lips over his.

"Only this," she said. "And this, here. This definitely counts."

Lucas kissed her back for a long time. When they finally stopped, he exhaled heavily. For a while, they didn't say a word. They sat side by side holding hands, which was so much better than anything Emily could have replicated in a sketch.

*

Two weeks before the shower, Collette asked Emily to come with her to the boutique for her initial fitting. Emily was walking across the backyard on her way to the car when her cell phone rang. Assuming it was Lucas, she slid it from her pocket and answered without paying attention to the number.

"Good morning."

"Emily?" a man asked. It wasn't Lucas.

"Yes, this is Emily."

"It's me, Devon. Is this a good time to talk?"

Emily hadn't even recognized his voice. She waved to Collette, who was already in the car. "Sorry, but it's not. You'll have to try another time. Or you can text me."

As she crossed her lawn, the phone blinked in and out again. She wasn't sure if he heard, so she waited for him to respond. He must have been speaking because she could hear a lot of warbling noises, but she couldn't make out any individual words. She stopped walking, which helped a little, but his voice kept cutting in and out, "I'm going to be—soon. The—week or—next. Is—okay if I—so we can talk?"

Emily was losing patience with the tenuous phone connection and she was losing patience with Devon, too. She couldn't keep standing here in order to talk to him; Collette would be late for her appointment.

"Yes, fine. Call whenever you want. If I'm home, I'll pick up. If not, then you'll just have to try again some other time." Whatever he said next she couldn't hear, so she told him goodbye and hung up, determined to put him out of her mind so she could enjoy the day with her friend.

"Look at me!" Collette trilled as she twirled in front of the mirror forty minutes later. "This dress drapes and clings in all the right places."

With its aqua and teal ombre gradations, and its sparkling accents, the knot-front short sleeve maxi made Collette look exactly like a mermaid. For once, she didn't make a single crack about her weight.

Brandi indicated she'd make the final alterations a couple days before the shower.

"The baby might grow," she said diplomatically, causing Emily to wonder if the boutique owner had been coaching her on how to be more tactful. "If anyone asks where you bought your dress, please give them my card. Someone might want to commission me for another design and there's still a few weeks before I have to go back to school in Boston."

Emily cringed at the thought of the academic year starting. She supposed she ought to start perusing the books she'd brought with her to Dune Island and put a new syllabus together. She hated using the same material every semester, the way some of her colleagues did. But subconsciously, she had been pretending if she didn't prepare for her courses, summer wouldn't come to an end and she wouldn't have to leave the island.

On the way home, Collette reminded Emily that she and Wilson had both taken the following week off from work. Collette was going to Connecticut to visit her grandmother in a nursing home and Wilson was going to take care of a few household projects, including moving his stuff out of the nursery, and then join Collette in Connecticut. Before coming back to the island on Saturday, they'd take a trip up to Boston to pick up the furniture they'd ordered.

Since Emily knew Collette didn't want to expose herself or the baby to paint fumes, the timing was perfect for Emily to work on her surprise gift: she planned to paint a mural on the nursery wall. *I'll wait until Wilson leaves, too,* she thought. It saddened her to still be at odds with him, but it would have saddened her even more if he'd brought up the subject of his DNA testing results again.

*

Later that evening, as she was ambling hand in hand with Lucas along the cusp of Mermaids' Inlet, Emily was more reserved than usual. She kept thinking about how hard it was going to be to leave at the end of the summer.

"Are you okay?" Lucas asked. "Do you need some time alone?"

"No. There's plenty of time for that. I want as much time with you as I can get."

Lucas squeezed her hand and they continued in silence together until he spotted something in the sand.

"Open your hand," he directed and placed a narrow shard of beach glass on her palm. "When I first met you, the color of your eyes immediately reminded me of beach glass."

Emily made a fist around it and confessed, "It was your hands I noticed first about you. They were strong and masculine, but also gentle. A lot like your character."

"So *that's* why you drew a dozen sketches of hands! You were thinking of me." Lucas looked very pleased with himself—and with her.

"I was," she acknowledged. "Drawing your hands eight times over is the artist's rendition of doodling my initials next to yours."

"You never fail to astound me, Em," Lucas replied.

She recoiled ever so slightly, but he noticed and asked what was wrong. Emily tried to brush off his question, but he threatened to throw her in the water if she didn't come clean.

"When you call me 'Em,' it reminds me of Auntie Em in the *Wizard of Oz*. I'm not crazy about the association with an aunt. It's sort of matronly."

"Yeah, I can see why you wouldn't want that." After a thoughtful pause, he suggested, "How about if we change the meaning?"

Bemused, Emily tilted her head. "To what?"

"Well, when I met you, one of the first things I thought—apart from how intimidating you were, of course"—Emily lightheartedly swatted his arm—"is how mysterious you were." Lucas's voice grew more serious. "I felt like you were holding things back, but I wanted to find out everything about you. So when I call you Em, it can mean the letter *M*, for mystery. A mystery I'll always want to solve."

Emily's chest went warm and her legs felt as if they were made of rope.

"But I won't call you Em anymore if it bothers you," Lucas added.

"No, you can't stop calling me that now," Emily pleaded, fingering the sea glass.

After he brought her close for a kiss, she thought, *And don't stop doing this, either.*

*

Tim, the fundraising president, visited Emily in the children's wing the following Monday afternoon and he raved so enthusiastically about the murals that he temporarily forgot why he stopped by in the first place.

"Oh, yes. I have a favor to ask of you. Feel free to take time to think it over. Lucas warned me it might not be something you want to do, but he said I should go ahead and ask."

Emily was filled with appreciation for Lucas, knowing he was always on guard when it came to the board making additional requests of her.

Tim explained that prior to the ribbon-cutting ceremony for the opening of the new wing, the fundraising organization would be hosting a formal dinner in the hospital cafeteria. He said the emphasis would be on acknowledging the donors, sponsors and foundation that had made the project a reality. The artists would also be invited to the dinner on Saturday night, as a nod to their contributions and a way to garner any last-minute bids before the auction closed that evening at midnight.

What the Board was requesting from Emily was that she would say a few words explaining the inspiration and vision behind the murals. She wouldn't have to address the crowd during the dinner, Tim said, only at the ribbon-cutting ceremony. The dinner guests and the public would be invited to attend the ceremony, which would be followed by a small reception.

Because she understood the importance of such a presentation to the donors and the Board, Emily reluctantly agreed. But as soon as Tim left the room, she regretted her decision. It wasn't that Emily hadn't delivered hundreds of lectures to thousands of students and faculty members over the years. It was that, considering the source of inspiration behind many of the murals, she wasn't sure she could deliver a speech in front of a mirror, much less in front of a crowd. Overwhelmed, she went home early to walk on the beach and clear her mind.

A few seals were playing in the inlet and when Emily clapped, they flipped their tails as they dove underwater, showing off. It was too bad Lucas couldn't have been there to see them. He wouldn't be coming over later, either, since he had an important departmental meeting before his night shift began. Emily half-wished it was the next morning already so she could see him again, but at the same time, she didn't want the day to end because it would mean she was one day closer to leaving Dune Island.

When she returned to the cottage, she heated leftover chicken curry for supper and tried to figure out what other images she should include in the grassland mural. Collette had told Emily to feel free to use her laptop up at the house, but Emily didn't want to cross paths with Wilson. *I should have checked some nature books out of the library*, she thought, before remembering the magazines she'd seen in Peter's antique desk. *They're better than nothing.*

When she tried to wiggle the drawer open, it wouldn't budge, so Emily held the desk in place with one hand and yanked so hard on the knob that she pulled the drawer entirely free of the desk. Its contents spilled to the floor and she nearly dropped the heavy drawer on her foot. She bent to retrieve the magazines, as well as the legal-size pad of paper.

After scanning her father's shopping list, Emily briefly glanced at the phrases on the next two pages. "Janice, my one and only love." "I love you more than." "The depth of my love." *These hardly sound like phrases that could have been written by a man who was cheating on his wife*, she assured herself. *Especially not Dad. He didn't have it in him to be that duplicitous.*

She put the notepad back into the drawer and reached to pick up one last magazine that had slid across the floor, halfway under the armchair. As she lifted it by its spine, a folded sheet of yellow paper drifted to the floor.

Her fingers trembling, Emily opened it and smoothed it flat against the leather surface of the desk. It was written in her father's handwriting and this time, none of the words were crossed out:

Janice, you are my one and only love. You always have been and you always will be. I would do anything not to have to tell you what I'm about to say, but there is something I need you to know.

I was unfaithful to you and there aren't enough words in the world to express how sorry I am.

"No. No, no, no, no, no," Emily repeated, much like she had when the officers delivered news of the accident. Three fat tears stained the paper with wet circles as she leaned over the note. Emily blotted her eyes. She didn't want to keep reading but she was unable to stop herself.

It is no excuse to tell you I'd had too much to drink. It's no consolation to promise that it was one time and one time only. And it's futile to say I'd die if dying somehow meant I could undo what I've done.

So instead I'm begging your forgiveness.

Emily's knees buckled and she dropped to the floor, landing hard on her bottom. She reclined the rest of the way and covered her eyes with her arm, as if to shield herself from the truth. Then she bolted upright and read the note again, focusing on the line that said, "It's no excuse to tell you I'd had too much to drink."

Hope billowed within Emily's heart: her father never drank alcohol, so he couldn't have been the one to write this unsigned note! And almost instantly it struck her that the note held the reason why her father never drank. Why he never drank *again*. Disgusted, Emily shook her head. How could she have gotten it so wrong? Those other notes weren't the draft of a love letter—they were the draft of an apology. A confession.

But was this note also a draft of a longer letter or was this the final copy? It almost read like a speech. Emily realized her father might have been so nervous, he'd had to practice what he was going to say. But did he actually say it? Did he actually give or send or read her mother the note and *she'd* kept it in this drawer? Or was he so ashamed about being unfaithful that writing the apology was as far as he got? *Did Mom ever find out about the affair? About Wilson?*

Wilson. How was Emily going to apologize to him? She didn't wait to find the words before springing to her feet and barreling across the lawn. She charged into the house calling his name but he wasn't in any of the rooms. *The beach. He's fishing.*

She reached the top of the staircase just as Wilson reached the bottom. He was carrying his fishing gear and his eyes were downcast, watching where he stepped in the sand. When he glanced up, he did a double take and stopped in his tracks. Emily did, too.

"Wilson," she panted. "I'm so sorry."

Maybe it was the anguish in her voice but he immediately seemed to know what she meant. "You got the results already?"

"No. I found a letter." She raced down the stairs until her eyes were level with his. "I'm sorry for not believing you and I'm sorry for what my father did and I'm sorry you didn't get to live with us year-round. I'm sorry about all of it. Please forgive me, Wilson, please."

Wilson set down his gear and wrapped his arm around her shoulders from the side, lowering them both into a seated position. "There's no reason to apologize for anything. It's okay."

"It's not okay. None of this is okay. I feel like I don't know him at all. I feel like he just died all over again." Emily lamented, "How could he have cheated on my mother? How could he have denied you like that? Especially after your mother died. He should have—"

"I honestly don't believe he knew I was his child. Like I said, I don't even know if my mother knew."

"They must have known. They must have suspected. They could do the math."

"Well, as you pointed out, no one would ever mistake me for Hans Brinker," Wilson said with a laugh, but Emily wasn't anywhere near ready to joke about it. "As for the math, what I tried to tell you was that my mother was only here a short time while she was on vacation from her job in Italy. A week, maybe less. Maybe it was only a long weekend. So I can accept that she assumed her Italian boyfriend fathered me, especially since my aunt Jewel said she never wavered from that claim."

"Your aunt knows about…about who your father is?" That explained why Wilson had been so edgy when Jewel called the other day and Emily answered the phone.

"No. I've been asking her a lot of questions about my mother for the past couple of months, but I still haven't told her or anyone else, not even Collette, about the DNA test results yet."

"You should tell Collette."

"Are you sure?"

"Yeah, she's been really worried about you. You can tell your aunt, too. It's not fair to keep something like this from your family," Emily said. Then she added, "My father's done enough secret-keeping to last ten generations."

"I didn't want to keep it a secret, especially not from you. It was eating me up inside, but you seemed so fragile when you first came here and then you got the concussion. And after that, I couldn't tell you because you were so moved by the notes your father had written to your mother—"

"I shouldn't have been," Emily said bitterly. "They weren't love notes. He was drafting an apology."

"Yeah, I figured that out as soon as I read the line, 'I need you to know.' Of course, I'd already gotten my test results, so my perspective was biased. Anyway, that's why I was so concerned about whether you'd found anything else in the desk, something that troubled you. If you had, I wanted to be able to help you to process it," Wilson explained. "It's going to take time. I'm still getting used to the idea myself."

"I don't know if I'll ever get used to the idea of dad cheating on my mom."

"Imagine how I feel, knowing *both* of my parents betrayed your mom. She was like a second mother—a third mother, after my grandma—to me. I hate to think of how hurt she must have been." Wilson sniffed and he looked down the beach, toward the east.

Suddenly, Emily understood why he had refused to accept the chess set; it was because he felt guilty taking something that had belonged to Janice's side of the family.

"What they did isn't your fault, Wilson. I hate thinking about how hurt my mother must have been, too. But I'd hate thinking about what my life would be like without you in it even more." Emily quelled a sob. "Besides, maybe my mom never found out. I'm not sure my father ever actually gave her the note. Or a version of it."

"I think he probably did, Emily."

"Why do you say that?"

"Your father loved and respected your mother too much to keep a secret like that from her throughout their marriage. Their relationship was too strong, too honest."

"I thought he loved and respected her too much to have an affair, but that wasn't true, either."

"He was a lot younger then. I'm sure it took time for him to mature into the man he was when you were born. And I'm relatively certain that when he told your mom about the affair, she eventually forgave him. That's what she was like."

"But what if she was oblivious? Remember how we used to jump out of the tree at the sanctuary to scare her? She never saw it coming."

"I'd forgotten about that," Wilson said with a chuckle. "But she was never fooled by us. She just acted surprised so we could feel good about ourselves. Or maybe so she could spend a few minutes alone with your dad. It was all harmless fun, a children's game. For the things that mattered, nothing got past your mom."

Emily shrugged, unconvinced. "I want to believe my dad told her, but I feel like...like everything about my parents' marriage was a lie. And that makes me doubt other things I used to think were true, too."

"Hold on there. Not *everything* about their marriage was a lie. One tiny part of it was a *secret*, a secret about something that happened thirty-five years ago and had absolutely nothing to do with you. Their love for each other and their children was the truest reality in the world. Why else do you think I always wanted to be with your family?"

"Oh, Wilson," Emily whispered. "You *are* my family."

And then she leaned into his shoulder and cried as hard as she'd cried at the memorial services, but for the opposite reason.

CHAPTER THIRTEEN

Since she needed time alone to come to terms with what she'd learned about her father's secret, Emily didn't see Lucas all week. And instead of going into the hospital to work on the murals, in the mornings she secreted herself away in the nursery, painting the silhouette she'd chosen as a surprise for Wilson and Collette.

Every day until Wilson left Dune Island to meet up with Collette in Connecticut, he and Emily spent the afternoons walking the beach together so they could talk and process their emotions, which included confusion, disappointment and anger, among others. Although Wilson regretted not knowing he was related to the Vandemarks earlier, he was much more forgiving than Emily was, primarily because he was confident his parents weren't aware he was Frederick's son. He also firmly believed Frederick had either given Janice a copy of the letter or had told her in person about the affair.

"How can you be so sure?" she asked him.

"Because that's the kind of man he was."

But Emily had given her father the benefit of the doubt before, when she'd insisted he never would have cheated on her mother, and she'd been wrong. *If he can't be trusted not to have an affair, he can't be trusted to tell the truth about it when he did have one*, she'd think.

But the next moment, she'd doubt herself for doubting *him*. Around and around her thoughts went, until Emily got sick of her own obsessive rumination and decided for now she'd just have to live with unresolved emotions and unanswered questions. Besides, she missed Lucas like crazy.

He must have missed her like crazy, too, because he showed up half an hour early for breakfast. Emily was washing blueberries to serve on top of the waffles she was making with the waffle iron she had borrowed from Collette's pantry when she heard him knocking at the front door, which was unusual, since he usually came in through the back sliders.

Glancing down, she took a quick inventory. Her short, white, spaghetti-strap eyelet nightgown could have passed for a sundress, but there was a yellow stain where she'd spilled a blob of batter and she hadn't showered or brushed her teeth yet.

Lucas knocked again, louder. *Oh well.* She pulled the door open and swept her arms in front of her body with a flourish.

"Voila! My grand unveiling," she quipped.

There on the front step stood Devon Richards.

"Hello, Emily."

She caught her breath as if she'd been socked in the gut and dropped her arms.

"Wh-what are you doing here?"

"Like I told you on the phone, there's something I want to talk to you about, but can it wait a minute? Between the plane, the ferry and trying to find my way around this island in a rental car, it's been a long trip. Can I come in and use the restroom and get something to drink, first?"

She let him pass and while he was in the bathroom, she filled a glass with cranberry juice, thinking, *What does he mean, "like he told me on the phone"?*

"What a quaint place," he said when he came out, looking around.

Still too stunned to speak, Emily watched his Adam's apple bob as he downed the cranberry juice. He set it in the sink and turned his attention on her.

"You look good."

Emily crossed her arms over her chest. *You look the same*, she thought. *The same thick dirty-blond hair, the same even white teeth, the same wrinkle-free khakis and golf shirt—even after a red-eye flight across the country. Perfectly the same.* And yet, she couldn't recall why she'd ever been attracted to him.

"How did you know where to find me?"

"I stopped by your apartment. I told the students staying there I needed to talk to you about something important but I couldn't get through to you on the phone or by text. They said you'd be gone until September, but they gave me your mailing address."

What could be so important he'd travel across the country to discuss? "What is it you wanted to talk about?"

He hesitated. "I don't know how to say this . . ."

Just spit it out—Lucas will be here any second and I need to change my clothes and start the waffles.

"I'm here because I'd like the engagement ring back."

Emily was so shocked that she made a grunting sound.

"You came all the way here to ask me for the ring back? What makes you think I have it with me?"

"Are you kidding me?" A panicked look crossed Devon's face. "I told you I was stopping in today because I have a consultation with a client in New York on Monday. You said it was fine, that I could come anytime and you'd be home."

"When? When did I say that?"

Devon threw his hands in the air. "When I called you. Don't tell me you can't remember. We've only talked once since you've been gone."

Oh. That was the day she was in a hurry because she was going with Collette to her dress fitting. "I remember your call, but to be honest, Devon, I couldn't hear half of what you were saying. The reception is lousy."

Emily could practically hear Devon's blood pressure going up. "You mean to say you don't have the ring?"

"Oh, I have the ring. And yes, you can have it back. But I don't understand. Why didn't you just wait until I got back to Seattle? What's the big hurry?"

"I, um, well, I . . ." Devon seemed unable to tell her the reason aloud.

"You got fired?" Emily didn't have time to mince words. "You're having financial problems?"

"No, nothing like that," Devon scoffed. Then he softened his tone. "I'm getting engaged."

Emily's stomach flipped. She gripped the edge of the counter. "Engaged? When?"

"Soon. That's why I need to get the ring."

"You're giving her a *used* engagement ring?" Emily was appalled.

"No, of course not. But if I'm going to be able to afford the ring she wants, I'm going to have to sell the one I gave to you when I pro— Well, you know. I have a jeweler who is interested in buying it, but I have to sell it to him before the end of the month."

Emily was silent as she allowed herself to process what Devon was saying. Rationally, she recognized that her relationship with him ended long ago, months before they'd officially broken up. But the fact that he was already planning to marry someone else served as a painful reminder that it was her fault their relationship ended. She'd come to understand that it didn't end because of her grief. It ended because of her inability—perhaps even her unwillingness—to communicate with him. She'd driven him away. What if she did the same thing to Lucas, despite her best efforts not to?

"I'll get it for you." She retrieved the ring box from her bedroom and placed it in his palm. She knew this would be the last time she spoke to him. She needed to take responsibility for her shortcomings if she didn't want to repeat them in her relationship with Lucas.

"There's something I've been thinking about, Devon. I'm aware I shut you out all those months. I see now that I was—and am—handling my losses as well as I could, so I'm not apologizing for that. I'm saying I recognize that it must have been painful and frustrating for you to be with someone who was hurting so much but who couldn't—or wouldn't—let you into that pain. I don't blame you for breaking up with me and I wish you all the best in your new relationship."

Devon looked down at his shoes. "I didn't break up with you because you withdrew while you were grieving, Emily. I broke up with you because I knew that eventually, I would have added to your grief."

"That's not true. You were very loving and patient. I was the one who couldn't be joyful and loving back. What makes you think that you would have added to my grief?"

"Trust me. I would have."

Modesty was never one of Devon's predominant character traits and Emily didn't understand how he could have been so sure he would have disappointed her or caused her sorrow.

"You've been seeing this other woman for what, five or six months and you're already going to ask her to marry you? How is it you're so sure you'll make *her* happy? Why aren't you worried you'll cause *her* grief?"

"I haven't been seeing her for six months, Emily. I've been seeing her for nine."

When she finally absorbed the meaning behind Devon's words, Emily quietly and calmly asked him to leave. She felt like she was sleepwalking as she stepped outside onto the deck. She sat down and buried her head in her arms on her lap.

"Oh, Mom," she moaned, wishing more than ever that the two of them could talk.

When Lucas arrived half an hour later, he found her in that same position.

"Emily?" His hand was warm on her bare skin.

"Devon was here," she said, lifting her head. Her lips were dry and her nose was stuffy from crying.

"He came here from Seattle? Why?"

"He wanted his ring back. He's getting engaged." Emily's head dropped and her shoulders heaved. She felt so humiliated she couldn't bring herself to tell Lucas the rest of what she'd discovered.

Lucas lifted his hand from her shoulder and stated evenly, "You're upset. You probably want to be alone."

She shook her head into her arms. "No, I don't."

"Yeah, well, I do." Lucas's van pulled out of the driveway before Emily even realized he wasn't still sitting there beside her.

She knew this would happen. Eventually, Lucas would get sick of her tears. *She* was sick of her tears.

Emily went up the hill and tried to call him to apologize, but he didn't pick up, so she decided she'd call again after he'd had a chance to catch some sleep. After taking a shower, Emily cleaned up the waffle mess in her kitchen and then she swept the floors. *Too bad I didn't get around to whitewashing these*, she thought. But the project would have kicked up too much dust for her to sleep in the cottage and she hadn't wanted to impose upon Collette and Wilson, especially not when she'd been at odds with him.

Still, I've made a lot of progress. She had, in fact, completely transformed the cottage by painting its walls, installing beadboard and a new backsplash in the bathroom and fixtures on the sinks, as well as replacing all the cabinet knobs in the kitchen. She'd even whitewashed the ghastly fireplace. Outside, she'd repainted the doors and the exterior trim. *Mom would have been tickled to see this place now.* Replacing the chandelier was the last improvement Emily hoped to make before she left Dune Island.

Having failed to reach Lucas and needing a distraction, she carried her phone up to Collette and Wilson's deck to research lighting options online. While she was there, they drove up the lane. Collette pulled herself from the car and waved a handful of shopping bags.

"Wait till you see what we got for the baby's room!"

Wilson followed with an oversized box. "I'll be assembling this stuff until the kid's twenty," he complained good-naturedly.

"Do you think this color will go with the walls?" Collette asked when they were all inside and she showed Emily the blue and white geometric patterned curtains she'd bought.

Emily knew they'd perfectly complement the silhouette she'd painted, but she said, "Hmm, I'm not sure. Let's go upstairs and hold it near the window." She winked at Wilson, who knew about Emily's surprise, but hadn't been allowed to see it yet.

"What is this?" Collette marveled when she saw the bow hanging on the door. She pushed it open and gasped. Then she spun around and hugged Emily so tightly that Emily could feel the baby kicking between them.

"What do you think, Wilson?" she asked.

Wilson stared at the wall, examining the navy blue life-sized silhouette of a man and a woman. The figures, whose profiles were unmistakably Collette and Wilson's, both held on to a little boy's hands as they lovingly gazed down at him.

Wilson pulled a tissue out of his pocket. He blew his nose loudly before speaking. "If my son's childhood can be even a fraction as happy as mine..." was all he could manage.

Tears beaded on Emily's lashes as she crossed the room to embrace him.

"That's enough, you two." Collette sniffed. "I won't be able to stop the fire hydrant once I loosen the valve, so break it up. Let's go have a snack, huh? I'm famished."

*

By the time she returned to her cottage for the evening, Emily still hadn't received a call back from Lucas. After that, her phone wouldn't pick up the signal, so she couldn't check her messages anyway. Disappointed she'd gone another full day without spending any time with him, she got up early on Sunday to invite him over for breakfast again, since he had the entire day off. To her surprise, as she crossed the lawn to call him, she spotted him loading his surfboard into his van.

"Hi, Lucas, how's the surf?"

He hardly glanced at her. "Not bad."

"You hungry? I'm making waffles for breakfast and I've heard the place next door serves free coffee," she said.

"No, thanks." He walked past her and opened the driver's side door.

Emily was taken aback by his dismissive tone. "Lucas, wait, please? I have something to say to you."

He paused but didn't release his grip on the handle.

"I'm sorry I was out of sorts yesterday. I didn't mean to ruin our breakfast plans."

"Don't worry about it." Lucas shrugged. "It was a perfectly normal reaction. First your fiancé broke your heart by calling off the wedding and then he broke it a second time by coming here to ask for the ring back because he's getting engaged. Believe me, I know what it feels like to have your hopes dashed when the person you care about is interested in someone else."

He climbed into his van and slammed the door in one swift motion, driving off before Emily had a chance to react.

Her eyes smarting, she raced back to the cottage and grabbed her purse and keys. She still had the invitation list somewhere in the stack of papers and envelopes on the antique desk. She rummaged through them until she found Lucas's home address. Once she got closer to Rockfield, she pulled over and entered his street into her phone. *Two miles from here!* She drove off the main road onto an isolated dirt road that was bumpy with potholes. Thinking she'd made a mistake, she was about to reverse her direction when she spotted Lucas's van parked in front of a lone, tiny house on a sandy plot scattered with scrub oak.

"I wasn't crying about the ring," she said when he opened the door.

"You don't owe me an explanation." Lucas didn't invite her in. "I knew you weren't over him. I shouldn't have gotten involved with you."

It almost sounds as if he's breaking up with me! "I told you before I don't feel anything for Devon. It hurts that you don't believe me."

"Well, Emily, I guess you're not the only one who sometimes has a difficult time trusting people. But in my case, I have reason not to."

Emily shoved her hands on her hips. "What reason is that?"

"Someone who is over her fiancé doesn't keep his engagement ring under her pillow."

"I only did that for safekeeping—"

"So you've told me. And I believed you. I convinced myself you were just hanging on to it because you'd already lost so much you couldn't stand to let that go, too. I wanted to believe the ring was only symbolic of a dream you had for your life, that it wasn't an indication of how you felt about *him.*"

As upset as she was, Emily realized Lucas had hit the nail on the head; bringing the ring to Dune Island had less to do with keeping it safe than it had to do with holding on to a dream. Lucas's insightfulness was one of the many things she loved about him.

Before she could tell him that, he added, "But I was wrong, wasn't I? The ring wasn't a symbol—it was a *lure.* You were using it to reel him back to you, except it didn't work. He didn't bite. *I* was the one who fell for it, hook, line and sinker."

Emily didn't know quite what to make of his fishing metaphor. "You fell for *what*, hook line and sinker?"

"For *you.* What was I to you anyway? Was I someone to entertain you? Someone to *console* you until he came back?"

Emily inhaled sharply. "That's not how it is. That's not how I feel about you. How could you even think something like that?"

"Gee, Emily, I don't know. Could it be that you've kept me at arm's length all week, the very same week your ex fiancé *happens* to be here on Dune Island? Or maybe it's that yesterday after he asked for his ring back, I found you half-dressed, crying your eyes out?"

His insinuation hit a nerve and Emily's temper flared. "Watch what you're saying, Lucas. I wasn't half-dressed. I was wearing a nightgown because I'd just gotten up. And for your information, I had no idea Devon was coming to Dune Island."

"The fact remains, you were devastated. Absolutely devastated. Admit it."

"I do admit it! I was devastated, but not for the reason you think!"

"Then why?"

Emily hesitated. Could she really tell him? It was so humiliating. She shook her head.

"That's what I thought," Lucas said and started to close the door.

Emily used her foot as a wedge. "I was devastated because I found out he'd been cheating on me while I was going through the worst experience of my life."

Lucas's expression softened but kept his arms crossed against his chest. "If you're really over him, why is that so upsetting now? I'd think you'd be relieved you dodged a bullet."

As indignant as she was that he still seemed skeptical, Emily knew if she wanted Lucas to trust her, she was going to have to trust him. She took a deep breath and tugged at his arm. "Come here," she said and he allowed her to lead him to where her car was parked in the shade.

They leaned side by side against the hood as she told him about her father's infidelity and about Wilson being her half-brother. She told him how disillusioned and angry she felt. And that she still had so many unanswered questions, especially about whether her mother knew or not.

"So when you saw me on the deck, I wasn't crying because Devon betrayed my trust. I was crying because my father betrayed my mother's trust," Emily explained, embarrassed to look at Lucas, who'd been uncharacteristically silent the entire time she was talking. Too late, she worried, *What if I just told him my most intimate family secret and he still decides he's not interested in a relationship with me?*

Finally, he said, "I'm sorry. I should have heard you out before I jumped to conclusions."

"Yeah, that hurt. But now I know how you must have felt when I got so angry at you after you found the ring box under my pillow." Emily gave him a sidelong look. "Want to guess what's under my pillow now?"

"What?"

"The piece of beach glass you said reminded you of my eyes."

"Really?"

Emily turned so she could look directly at him. "Really."

Lucas took a step closer. Wrapping his arms around her waist, he pressed his forehead to hers. They both stood like that a long while, their eyes closed, before he said, "C'mon. I'll give you a tour of the palace."

Lucas's cottage was about half of the size of Emily's, with a tiny galley kitchen and an even tinier bathroom, which had a shower but no tub. It was sparsely furnished with a small loveseat and a large leather recliner positioned across from a big screen TV mounted on the wall. There was a desk with a laptop in the corner of the room, and the kitchen contained two chairs and a small round table. Emily was inwardly pleased to see the card she'd made him was displayed in the center, next to the invitation to Collette's shower. Except for a tide chart and the TV, the other walls were completely bare.

"You're probably thinking, 'Is this the best Lucas can afford on a doctor's salary? He must be putting all of his money toward paying off that fancy yellow bus he drives,'" Lucas joked. "The fact is, I'm rarely here. Any time off I have I spend fishing or surfing or hanging out with people somewhere else. Although, as you can

tell, when I am here, I like to sit in that thing to take in a game."
He pointed toward the recliner.

"When you're on your feet as much as you are at work, a decent
chair is a necessity at home. That's what Collette says, anyway,"
Emily said. "You remind me of my brother, Peter. His place was
small like this, too—by choice. He had a studio apartment in inner
city Chicago. He saw a lot of poverty in his line of work and it really
shaped his priorities."

"Yeah, for me it was my residence in Portugal that did it. I often
visited families in houses that weren't any bigger than this. There'd
be eight or nine people from three generations living together under
one roof. Completely opposite from how I grew up."

Lucas explained that he came from an affluent family in New
York. Because he was such a warm person, it surprised her to hear
his family had never been very close. He said he was sent to board-
ing school from the time he was twelve until he graduated. Prior
to this, Emily had only known his parents were retired and they
lived in the south of France and that he had one sister, a CEO of a
technology firm in Boston.

"Sometimes when I hear you talking about your parents and
brother, I wonder what it would be like to miss my family that
much," he confided. "I spent so much time away from them at such
an early age that being apart felt more normal than being together."

Emily listened quietly. She couldn't imagine what it would've
been like to grow up the way Lucas did. She supposed she'd rather
choose to lose her family as an adult than to grow up apart from
them as a child and teenager. But of course, she didn't get to choose
and neither did Lucas.

"Thank you for telling me more about your family. Maybe some day, you'll tell me about the woman you had a difficult time getting over, too."

"What?"

"You said you knew what it was like to care about someone and have your hopes dashed."

"Emily," Lucas said, putting his hands on her shoulders. "I was referring to *you*."

Emily felt a rush of warmth and she wanted to tell him that she had no intention of dashing his hopes, but it was as if there was a knot in her throat rendering her speechless. Lucas smoothed back a wisp of her hair to kiss her cheek. Then, her mouth.

"I appreciate your telling me about why you were so upset yesterday. That couldn't have been easy."

"No, but it was easier than losing my relationship with you."

Lucas narrowed his eyes and shook his head. "Not going to happen, Em," he promised somberly, before kissing her again.

*

When she woke early on the morning of August 22, instead of taking her routine morning beach walk, Emily traipsed next door to see if Collette was up, since she figured she'd be too excited about the shower to sleep. Collette was still in bed but Wilson had already showered and shaved and he served Emily a bowl of granola and yogurt. They sat on the same side of the table and stared out the window toward the ocean as they ate. Emily could feel the significance of the date hanging over them like the oppressive clouds that threatened to erupt at any moment.

"I expected you'd sleep in later today," she finally said, an indirect reference to Wilson's earlier confession he wished he could sleep through the anniversary. "How are you doing?"

He paused with his spoon midway to his mouth. "So far, so good," he said and took a bite. It was good to see his appetite had returned. "How about you?"

"I'm okay. It helps not to be alone." Emily didn't just mean it helped that she and Wilson were together; she meant it helped that she and Wilson were related. Her family wasn't completely gone.

Wilson nodded. "Yeah, it helps me, too."

Emily gestured to the photos on the bookshelf. "Peter had that same photo of your graduation in his place."

"It's actually his. I took it when I went to, uh, clean out his apartment. I hope you don't mind that I kept it."

Emily shook her head, remembering how grateful she'd been when Wilson had flown to Chicago to take care of Peter's personal effects. Having given most of his income to support various charities, Peter didn't own anything of significant monetary value, but Emily was still relieved that Wilson had been the one to sort through his belongings. Afterward, he'd sent Emily her favorite photo, the one she now displayed on the antique desk.

"Those two photos were the only things he had on his walls," Wilson said. "Peter and your parents were so proud of you for becoming an artist."

"It's not exactly life-saving work. I've always felt kind of guilty about not pursuing the kind of careers you and Peter chose."

"Who says art doesn't save lives? I don't think we can measure the effect of it on our well-being the way we can measure the effect of medication on our blood pressure. But that doesn't mean that art doesn't serve a vital purpose. Besides, I'm the one who feels guilty. I've got this big house and comfy life—"

"Wilson, don't give me that," Emily interrupted. "I happen to know you and Collette are major donors for the children's wing. Besides, you can't put a price tag on how—"

Collette suddenly appeared at the bottom of the stairs, disheveled and grimacing. "I hate to interrupt, but I'm having contractions."

Wilson leaped up and began asking her a barrage of questions. Collette was pretty sure she was having Braxton-Hicks contractions, but, true to his character, Wilson insisted they call her doctor, who suggested she should go to the hospital to check it out.

Emily scampered upstairs and collected toiletries and night clothes to put in an overnight bag. When she came down, Collette was sitting on the edge of a recliner, rubbing her lower belly. "It's too early for me to be in labor and I am *not* missing the baby shower or my massage. I'm warning you, Wilson, they'd better not admit me."

"They won't. Not unless it's necessary."

Because the baby shower was scheduled for late afternoon, one of Collette's friends had given her a gift certificate for a massage in the morning. The plan was for Wilson to take Collette to the spa and then they'd swing by the boutique so Brandi could make one last alteration to her dress. Meanwhile, Emily and Sara, as well as Liz and Gail and their husbands, would be preparing the house for the party.

Standing to leave, Collette promised Emily, "I'll be back, with the baby still inside me, and I'll be wearing my new dress. Don't you dare cancel a thing."

As Wilson whisked Collette to the car, Emily got to work clean-ing the breakfast dishes. Collette was such a neat freak there wasn't much to do in the rest of the house, so Emily just touched up the bathrooms and she was running a vacuum cleaner across the floor when the others arrived.

The forecast predicted isolated thundershowers, but sunshine was breaking through the hazy sky. Gail and Liz debated with the men about whether they should set up the tables for serving food and drinks buffet-style indoors or out. They finally decided to compromise and set up half of them indoors and half outdoors. Around the deck and throughout the house, they strategically placed the bouquets of lilies, hydrangeas, roses and wildflowers Gail had clipped from her garden.

They were tying helium balloons to the railings when Wilson called to report that Collette was right, she'd only been having Braxton-Hicks contractions, and they were now on their way to the spa. He relayed Collette's message that she'd wanted to show the guests the mural and asked if Emily would mind tidying the nursery since Collette hadn't gotten a chance to do it that morning.

Emily lugged the vacuum cleaner upstairs and tapped the nursery door open with her foot. Inside, Sara was bent forward in the rocker, with her elbows on her knees and her face in her hands.

"Sara?" Emily hesitated to enter.

"It's beautiful," Sara said, motioning toward the walls without looking up. "But it hurts to look at it."

Emily closed the door behind her and put down the vacuum. She crouched beside Sara, one hand on the arm of the rocker.

"I don't know why a baby shower would hit me so hard, of all things. It's not as if I had even started trying to get pregnant. We just assumed we had plenty of time," Sara confided. "Collette and Wilson were so good to me when Craig died, I don't know what I would've done without them. I've wanted to give them a terrific party, but I don't know if I can pull it off."

"You don't have to show up this afternoon. Collette and Wilson will understand."

Sara shook her head slowly. "Nah, I'll be okay."

How many times have I said that to myself this past year? Emily wondered. "I'm glad you want to be there, because you've put so much work into this already and it wouldn't be the same without you there. But if you feel overwhelmed, my cottage will be open so guests have an extra restroom to use. Feel free to make yourself at home in my bedroom. There's a lock on the door if you need to cry in peace."

"'Cry in peace.' There's an oxymoron that only makes sense if you've lost someone you love," Sara responded and they both laughed.

The set-up process took longer than expected and as everyone returned home to shower and change, Emily darted across the lawn. She had to give her cottage a quick scrub, too, since guests might be using the bathroom. Afterward, she took a fast, indoor shower, knowing she'd have to scramble if she wanted to get up to the house before the first guests arrived. She quickly dried her hair into soft waves and then slipped her dress over her head.

It wasn't as loose as she thought it would have been. Had her body changed that much since she tried it on at the boutique or was it only her perception that had changed? Either way, Emily would have sworn she actually had cleavage again.

Crossing the lawn beneath an ominous sky, Emily noticed several cars in the driveway already and as she got closer she heard voices drifting down from the house. Sixty of the seventy-two guests were expected. *I can do this*, Emily said and pulled open the door. Standing immediately inside the threshold, Collette was dazzling in her dress, with her silky hair swept into an elaborate half-do and Wilson beaming beside her as laughter rose and fell around them.

No sooner had Emily greeted them than a tremor of thunder rattled the house. The guests hurried to move the chairs, dishes and flowers indoors before the sky let loose a torrential downpour and people started cracking jokes about the "baby shower." Fortunately, the rain cooled the air so the temperature was bearable. As more guests arrived, everyone shifted to accommodate each other on the chairs and couches or milled in the hallways, up the stairs and in Wilson's study. Emily paired up with Sara to take Collette's place, welcoming guests at the door.

"How are you doing?" Emily whispered from the corner of her mouth. She'd always thought when people had asked her that same question in a hushed tone, it was because they pitied her. Now she wondered if they were trying to be discreet, the way she was trying to be with Sara.

"I'm fine now, really. Nothing a hot shower and a cold drink didn't cure. But thanks for checking in. How are you doing?"

"I'm good." Emily almost felt guilty for admitting it, considering what today's date was. Almost, but not quite. "Really good."

When Lucas finally arrived, he was carrying a gift box in one hand and a platter of ice-packed fish fillets in the other. Beads of water were dripping from the tips of his curls, like on the day she first met him. Emily's mouth turned to cotton and she licked her lips, suddenly shy. Wilson greeted her and Sara and joked that he should have paddled over on his surfboard because there were so many cars in the lane he'd had to park down the road. Sara laughed and offered to place his gift with the others in Wilson's study.

"Hello, again," he said quietly to Emily once they were alone.

"Hello, Lucas. Here, let me take that for you." She reached for the platter.

He wouldn't let go. They stood opposite each other in a tug-of-war stalemate, their gazes locked until he lowered his eye to take in her outfit. "You've really blossomed," he whispered.

A gust of wind slammed the screen door behind two other guests and Lucas jumped back with a start.

"Way to make an entrance, Joe," he said.

"Wait till you see my exit."

"Hi," the woman said to Emily. "I'm Donna."

"Sorry. Donna, Joe, this is my, ah— Emily," Lucas said. "Emily Vandemark, meet Donna and Joe Bergeron."

What was that all about? Doesn't he want his colleagues to know he's seeing me? Emily wondered while shaking their hands. When she returned from putting the Bergerons' gift in the study, Lucas cornered her in the pantry, frowning.

"Em, I never got a chance to ask if it's okay with you if people know we're a couple?"

"A couple of what?" she asked coyly. "Of course it is."

She gently nudged him toward the living room and resumed her hosting duties. Despite the rain, the party was festive and rowdy, if a little cramped. Emily was so busy tending to the guests' needs that she never had time to enter into the kind of discussions she feared might lead to them asking questions she didn't want to answer. When they chatted with her, it was mostly to answer questions *she* asked or to compliment her on the invitations and the nursery mural, or on her dress.

After a while, Lucas beckoned her to come try the flounder he'd just finished grilling beneath one of the golf umbrellas the men rigged up on the deck. She told him she'd meet him in the living room when she was done refilling bowls with ice.

As she entered, she noticed him claiming two spots that had just opened up on the couch, but by the time Emily squeezed past the other guests, Barbara had seated herself so close to Lucas, she might as well have been eating from his plate. She was wearing a skimpy mesh slip dress with blue topaz dangle earrings, which caught the light when she flipped her hair over her shoulder, laughing at something Lucas was saying.

"Over here, Em." Lucas waved. "If Barbara will scoot down a bit, you'll fit right here beside me."

Barbara begrudgingly inched in the opposite direction. Eyeing the plate Lucas handed to Emily, she said, "I see Lucas is trying to load you up with fish."

"You want some, Barbara?" Lucas asked. "There's plenty more on the grill."

Lucas, does she look like a girl you can tempt with brain food? The words were on the tip of Emily's tongue, but she bit them back.

"This fish melts in my mouth," she said instead, tapping Lucas's knee with hers.

Just then lightning brightened the room, causing Emily to start. Lucas instinctively wrapped his arm around her shoulders. Barbara left in a huff, clearing a space for Gail, who said she was thrilled with how everything was turning out, despite the rain.

As they were finishing eating, Sara came to tell Emily she'd set up the "pickles 'n' ice cream craving bar" for dessert, but she was concerned they might run out of spoons and bowls. By then the lightning had stopped, so Emily said she'd go grab some from her cottage. She was nearly at the door when she spotted Collette, whose back was turned as she spoke to a guest.

"Excuse me." Emily spoke softly so she could squeeze past her friend without interrupting her conversation.

Collette shifted and when she saw it was Emily behind her, she said, "Look who's here, Emily."

Although she had allowed her hair to go white and she was thinner now, with her fuchsia dress and deeply tanned skin, Wilson's Aunt Julia was no less glamourous now than when Emily was a girl. Emily had completely forgotten she was coming to the shower, so she was surprised to see her, but would have recognized her even if Julia hadn't been wearing her trademark gold and silver bangles.

"Hi, Julia. It's so good to see you again. I've thought about you often over the years."

"Emily, dear, what a beautiful woman you've become," Julia exclaimed at the same time, pulling Emily into her arms.

Other than Collette, Wilson, and Devon, Julia was the first person Emily had seen since the funerals who had personally known her parents and Peter, and the realization unexpectedly made her eyes water. It was as if Julia's presence emphasized *their* absence. Embarrassed, she told Collette and Julia she was on her way next door to get more spoons and bowls.

"I'll come, too. It will give us a chance to chat in private."

Until that moment, Emily had completely forgotten that Wilson must have spoken to Julia about Frederick being his father and she sensed that's what Julia wanted to talk about. *I've made it this far without crying today, I hope whatever she tells me doesn't make me lose it now.*

"Oh, this place looks darling!" Julia exclaimed when they went inside. "The cottage my parents owned was so gloomy compared to this."

"*Our* cottage was gloomy compared to this, too," Emily admitted. "I've been working on it all summer."

"It shows." Julia perched on a stool at the breakfast bar. "Renovating was probably a good distraction for you, wasn't it?"

Emily knew what she meant and she nodded. "Yes. Being with Wilson during all of this has been good for me, too."

"Mm. He feels the same way about having you here. Is it all right if we talk about what you two recently learned about your dad?"

Emily said it was but first she excused herself for a second. She thought she heard something down the hall so she went to check the bathroom to be sure none of the guests was using it before Julia continued.

"I know this might not be the best time or place, but I've wanted to share something with you in person. Something I think might help you accept things a little better."

Emily reached to hold on to the edge of the stove for balance, again nodding to indicate Julia should continue.

"Firstly, I genuinely don't believe your father knew Wilson was his son. As I've told Wilson, my sister Michelle insisted her Italian boyfriend was his father and I think she truly believed that herself. In fact—" Julia stopped speaking and looked down at her long, manicured nails. "In fact, I was the first one to get to the hospital after her accident. I knew how dire her situation was, so before she went into surgery I asked her—I *begged* her to tell me who..."

Julia glanced up again and her dark eyes were swimming with tears. Emily knew she was reliving the moment and she didn't want her to have to go through that kind of agony again, not even in her mind.

"It's okay. I understand what you're saying."

But Julia blinked a few times and completed her sentence. "I begged her to tell me the full name of Wilson's father but all she said was, 'Marco.'"

Emily nodded, appreciating what Julia had sacrificed emotionally in order to convince her that her dad didn't know about Wilson. "Thank you for sharing that. It does help. It helps a lot."

But Julia wasn't finished speaking. "I imagine you might feel angry at my sister for having an affair with your dad. You might have wondered what kind of woman would have a fling with a married man she hardly knew."

Emily couldn't look Julia in the eye because at times, that was exactly how she felt. But it wasn't something she felt she could have discussed with Wilson. Julia seemed to read her mind.

"There's no need to feel guilty, Emily. It's a natural reaction. But if you're open to hearing it, I'd like to tell you some of the same things I told Wilson about his mother?" When Emily nodded, Julia explained, "My sister was one of the brightest, most accomplished and bighearted people I've ever known—when she wasn't drinking. But when she was drinking, she became a different person. She was angry and resentful. Sometimes, she could be cruel. But mostly she was self-destructive."

Julia went on to tell Emily that Michelle had grown to hate her high-powered position but felt pressured by her employer, as well as by her dad, to keep moving up the ladder. She was lonely and stressed and had turned to alcohol for comfort.

"The summer before Wilson was born, Michelle was so distraught she came all the way home from Italy to New York for a long weekend to tell my parents she intended to quit her job. My father lived vicariously through Michelle so he was furious and they had such a big argument she took off for the cottage, where she undoubtedly spent the rest of her vacation drinking. So, I think that was her state of mind when she slept with your father. Which isn't to say that excuses her behavior, but I hope it helps you understand it a little better."

Emily shifted her weight to her other foot. *That explains* her *state of mind, but why did my father sleep with her? Was it really just that he'd been drinking, too?*

Julia kept talking. "Michelle was so thrilled to be pregnant I don't think she even cared that much when her boyfriend in Italy broke up with her. She stopped drinking and moved back to New York—to the suburbs, not the city. She took a part-time job and bought a condo. My father practically cut her off from the family, but she was so calm, so blissful. As I've told Wilson, he may not have been planned, but he was a godsend. I think it's fair to say his life saved hers. And once he was born, he was her world. She couldn't have loved him more."

Emily's eyes brimmed. She felt conflicted between being overjoyed to hear how much Michelle wanted Wilson and resenting it that Michelle's happiness had come at her own mother's expense. *If Mom actually knew...*

But now wasn't the moment to be dwelling on this. And there was no use going over questions that she'd never be able to ask her mother. "Everyone's probably waiting for us up at the house," Emily suggested as she pulled open the cutlery drawer.

Julia walked around the breakfast bar to join her in the kitchen. "Wait. There's one more thing I think you should know. It's something your mother told me in the strictest confidence. I've never shared it with anyone but under the circumstances—"

Emily dropped the spoons back into their compartment. "Did she know about the affair?"

Julia pressed her lips together and nodded definitively. "Yes."

"How can you be sure?"

"She told me about it the summer after Michelle died, the first year my parents brought Wilson to the cottage. My husband and I had come for our annual August visit and my mother told me how generous both of your parents were to Wilson. How they'd been including him in their family activities, which must have been a real effort for your mom, since she was pregnant with you at the time and the boys were so active.

"One day, I happened to see Janice down at the inlet and I thanked her for her kindness toward Wilson. That's when she opened up about the affair. I think she may have thought Michelle had already told me—which she hadn't—and she wanted me to know that she'd forgiven her. That she wasn't holding anything against my departed sister."

"How did she find out about the affair?"

"She said your father had told her about it shortly after it happened."

Mom knew. At once Emily felt relieved and remorseful. *Dad must not have mailed the letter—he must have told her in person. But either way, she knew.* "Did she say anything else?"

"She told me the summer it happened, Frederick had come to Dune Island alone to open the cottage for the season. Your mother was in Maryland helping out her mom—your grandma, because your grandfather had been hospitalized with pneumonia. According to Janice, she and your dad had been struggling with fertility issues and they'd hit a rough patch in their marriage. She said she was livid at Frederick after the affair and she considered leaving him. It took a long time for her to trust him again but ultimately, she forgave him and she forgave Michelle, too."

Emily exhaled heavily. "Is that all she said?

"Yes. After that, we never spoke about it again . . . Although later, shortly after you were born, she sent me a Christmas card. It was the only card I'd ever received from her and inside was a photo of Peter holding you."

Emily remembered. She was chubby and bald and wearing a red and white striped onesie that reminded her of a candy cane.

"On the back of the photo she'd written, 'My best gifts ever.'"

Emily sucked in a sharp breath as the realization struck her: if her mother hadn't forgiven her dad, then Emily and Peter wouldn't have been born. *If mom forgave dad, who am I not to forgive him, too?* As a few tears sprinkled down Emily's cheeks, Julia enveloped her in a maternal embrace.

"If you have any more questions, give me a call," she told her. "And rest assured I won't tell anyone else about this."

"Thank you," Emily said. "Thank you for telling me all of that and thank you for your discretion. I hope you know that I couldn't be happier that Wilson and I are half-siblings, but..."

"No need to explain," Julia assured her.

They loaded up their arms with extra spoons and bowls and carried them back to the house, where everyone was oh-ing and ah-ing over the gifts Collette and Wilson had begun to open, at the guests' urging.

The next morning, Collette came over with a platter of treats. "Leftovers from the party. I tried to choose the things I knew you'd like best."

As Emily unwrapped the tinfoil and peeked inside, Collette thanked her again for the shower. She gushed about the flowers, food and gifts and said she received a ton of compliments on her dress.

"I'm fortunate to have such good friends, a wonderful husband and you as my fantastic sister-in-law. My son will be very fortunate, too," she said. "I especially appreciate what you and Wilson did, considering the date. I hope it wasn't too upsetting for you?"

Emily realized that the events of the day had kept her so preoccupied that she couldn't think about anything other than what was happening from one minute to the next. Preparing to say hello to a new life was a beautiful way to honor the anniversary of when she'd had to bid such painful goodbyes—and so was forgiving her father.

"I honestly can't think of a better way to have spent the day."

CHAPTER FOURTEEN

On the evening of the day she finished her mural at the hospital, Emily and Lucas celebrated with takeout Thai food for dinner on the beach. Emily's excitement about finishing the art project was mingled with the sadness of knowing she would soon have to return to Seattle.

"I can't believe this is how you wanted to celebrate," Lucas griped. "I wanted to take you someplace more romantic."

"What could be more romantic than this view? Plus it's so intimate, having the beach all to ourselves," Emily pointed out. "Wait, I spoke too soon—I think I see a seal out there!"

"That's a bird," Lucas said, squinting toward the water. Then he asked if she thought the Thai food on Dune Island was as good as in Seattle.

"When you visit me in October, you can be the judge of that."

"Do you really have to go back? Why don't you stay here?" Lucas asked. "Your cottage is winterized, isn't it?"

"Yeah, but what would I do for a living?"

"Paint more murals? Do interior design? My place could use some redecorating. Heck, my place could use some *decorating*. Any decorating."

"Or Collette and Wilson could hire me as an au pair."

Luke gave her a smug look.

"What's with the smirk?" Emily asked. "You're not the only one who relates well to kids, Dr. Luke."

"I know I'm not. I was just wondering if your nephew is going to call you Auntie Em."

"If he does, that's fine with me." She tilted her head to the side. "You know, I think that's the first time anyone has referred to the baby as my nephew."

"Sorry. You said Wilson already knows I know you're related and no one else is around to hear me say it, so I thought it was all right to mention your nephew."

"Even if anyone does hear you, who cares? It's better than all right to talk about my nephew. After Peter died, I never dreamed I'd get to be an auntie unless I married someone with siblings, so I'm thrilled."

"Talk about thrilling, when are you going to let me take you out on my surfboard? You can enjoy the seals up close and personal out there."

"Not if I'm drowning, I can't. There are rip currents near these sandbars and I've told you I'm not a good swimmer."

"But I'm a doctor, remember? I know CPR." To prove his point, Lucas tipped her backward in the sand and covered her mouth with his.

Laughing, she squirmed away and propped herself up on her elbows next to him, watching the surf and listening to its familiar refrain. She lifted a handful of sand and slowly let it drizzle out of her fist onto his forearm.

"The sands of time," she said wistfully.

Lucas kissed her until dusk waned to dark and then he kissed her some more. The moonlight cut a path of light across the ocean and illuminated the white spray of waves along the shoreline. A breeze rustled Emily's hair and she shivered, so Lucas enveloped her tighter.

"I don't want this to end," he moaned.

"But you'll be late for your shift, I know," Emily replied and moved to gather their things.

Lucas pulled her back down next to him. "No, I mean this. Us."

"Neither do I," she murmured into his neck. "Let's not talk about that now. Let's not talk about anything."

She held a finger to his lips and then slowly took it away so she could place her mouth there instead. He responded with such intense passion that her head buzzed. He caressed her shoulders as they kissed and under the spell of his touch, she felt like she'd promise anything he asked; to try surfing, to stay through the winter, to love him for the rest of her life... When his fingers moved across her neck to trace her clavicle, she broke away.

"It's getting late."

She picked up the tote bag and tiptoed across the cool sand in the moonlight. When Lucas caught up to her near the van, he asked if something was wrong.

"No, not at all. I just think if you're going to get to work on time, we'd probably better end tonight with a handshake, don't you think?"

Lucas's smile reflected the moonlight as he heartily pumped her hand up and down. "Congratulations on finishing the art project, Ms. Vandemark. The Board, the public and the patients are looking forward to the ribbon-cutting ceremony."

"Thank you, Dr. Socorro. I hope you like my work."

Lucas pulled her closer. His voice was a low growl. "I like everything about you, Em."

"I like almost everything about you, too, Lucas," she joked, to break the tension. Then she wiggled her hand free and kissed him goodbye on the cheek.

I wonder how he would have replied if I had said I hoped he loved *my work*, she mused as she watched him drive away.

*

Although she was glad she finished the art project on time, Emily ironically missed the slow morning commute and the familiar views that it afforded her, so she made a point of driving to the various hamlets during the final days of August. School had already begun so the crowds were thinning in the market and at the cove and Emily noticed the light on the beach was changing, too. She remembered hating the end of summer so much as a kid that when school started she'd wear her swimsuit beneath her clothes until her mother caught her and made her change.

"I'm going to have to wear my sunny, happy dress every day when I get back," she told Collette. "Otherwise I'll be too sad about leaving."

"I have a better idea. You could stay here on the island. At least until your nephew is born."

"You sound like Lucas."

"See? We all love you and want you to stay."

But did Lucas love her? And did she love him? Every evening the two of them would eat dinner and then stretch out together on the beach beneath the stars, delaying his departure for as long as possible. Yet no matter how romantic their time, neither ever claimed, "I love you."

The closest Emily thought Lucas came to uttering the phrase was a couple days before the ribbon-cutting ceremony when he left a message saying, "Hi, Em. Wanted you to know I was interviewed by a journalist about the auction next week and he asked a few questions about you and your work on the murals. I'm afraid I may have revealed too much but I figured you'd want me to be truthful. Love you. Bye."

Or did he say, "I figured you'd want me to be truthful *of* you?"

It wouldn't have made much sense if he did, but Emily replayed the message seven times, and she still couldn't distinguish what he said. Then her battery died so she plugged the phone into her charger and took a nap.

Some forty minutes later, a clap of thunder woke Emily from a deep sleep and she dashed up the hill so she wouldn't have to sit out the storm alone.

"I'm here to organize your pantry," she announced to Collette, who looked very confused.

Wilson must have remembered her fear from when they were kids because he knowingly explained, "The pantry is the only room that doesn't have any windows, so Emily can't see the lightning from in there. She's always been a chicken about thunderstorms. When she was little, she used to hide behind the knee wall. Which was pretty stupid, considering if lightning struck the roof, she was a lot more likely to get hit there than if she was standing in the middle of the room."

"At least I wasn't afraid of the spiders in the knee wall the way Wilson was. Peter dared him to crawl from one end of it in his room to the other end of my room and he wouldn't," Emily shouted from where she was grouping boxes of pasta according to their shape.

"I wasn't afraid of spiders," Wilson scoffed.

"No? Then why wouldn't you do it? Were you afraid of the dark?" Emily taunted.

"Wilson and Emily, do I have to separate you two? It's bad enough it's raining, and we're cooped up inside. I don't need to hear you bickering."

"It's his fault. He started it," Emily accused, but it was all in good fun. After the shower, the two of them had had several more conversations about Michelle, Janice and Frederick. And now that Emily had forgiven her father and she and Wilson didn't have any more secrets between them, they were able to enjoy the best parts of being siblings—just like they used to—including teasing each other.

"I don't care *who* started it. If I hear one more word—"

"That's exactly the kind of thing my mother would have said," Emily shouted from inside the pantry. "See, Collette, you're going to make a great mom!"

*

Lucas insisted on taking Emily out for a special, non-beach date the Thursday before the ribbon-cutting ceremony. Since she was saving her gray sheath dress to wear to that event and she didn't want to wear her floral print dress again so soon after the shower, she slipped on her plain navy sundress and spent a long time styling her hair and applying makeup before she went next door to ask Collette if she could borrow a colorful scarf.

Reclining on the sofa, Collette looked ready to burst. "You're welcome to wear any of my accessories, but you have to go look through them yourself. Because once I go up those stairs tonight, I'm not coming down again until morning."

Instead of a scarf, Emily selected a gorgeous white silver statement necklace she'd never seen Collette wear and hustled back downstairs to show her what she'd chosen. After saying thanks, Emily rushed out the door.

Wilson was standing on the deck with a young man who looked to be the same age as Emily's undergraduate students. According to Wilson, his name was Alex Larkin and he'd wandered over from the cottage, looking for Emily.

"I'm a reporter from the *Gazette* and I have a few questions for you about the mural in the children's wing at Hope Haven Hospital," he said. "Do you mind if I record our conversation?"

"Sure," Emily agreed, glancing toward the driveway for Lucas's van. "But it will have to be quick. I'm going out."

"It won't take more than a few minutes. Dr. Laurent, you're welcome to join in on the interview."

"I'm not involved in the art project," Wilson objected.

"That's okay. My editor wants this to be more of a personal interest story than an event listing and since you know Emily best, it would be great if you could give me a few quotes about her as a person, not necessarily as an artist."

Addressing Emily, Alex explained, "See, the angle I'm going for is that you escaped to Dune Island because you were so raw with grief after losing your family in the helicopter crash. So you came here to focus on something else—the children's wing project—and through your work on the murals, you found healing from your pain. In turn, your art will help the kiddos at the hospital recover from their pain, too, that kind of thing."

Emily was so astounded to hear the journalist sum up her life—her bereavement—like that, she couldn't speak. Wilson appeared as shocked as she was. Oblivious, the journalist pushed his glasses farther up on his nose and continued his spiel.

"So, that's the overall gist. But if it's not too personal, what would really tug at our reader's heartstrings is if we could include a few details about your fiancé breaking up with you and how you found out your childhood friend was really your brother and—"

"Stop recording!" Wilson abruptly thundered.

The young man tapped at his phone screen and then slid it into his back pocket. He scratched the back of his neck. "Uh, like I said, if any of those details are too personal, we don't have to print them."

Emily felt as if she were watching everything unfold in slow motion. Collette came out onto the deck just as Wilson stuck his nose inches from the journalist's face and yelled, "Where did you come up with that stuff?"

Alex inched backward. "It's-it's what that other doctor at the hospital told me."

"What doctor?"

"I-uh-I can't reveal my sources. But I'm sorry if I got it wrong. That's why I-I was fact checking." He looked ready to make a break for it and Wilson looked ready to chase him.

Collette stepped forward and slipped her hand around Wilson's arm, pulling him toward her. "If you print anything about Emily or my husband, we'll sue the newspaper for invasion of privacy and then I'll sue you personally for causing a pregnant woman emotional distress," she threatened, shaking a finger at Alex.

"I'm really sorry," the young guy mumbled as he charged off the deck. He didn't even take time to turn his car around; he just put it into reverse and backed down the long driveway.

Once he was gone, the three of them went back inside the house. Collette dropped onto the sofa in the living room and Emily took the armchair but Wilson paced from one end of the room to the other.

"Emily, I swear I never said anything to anyone except Collette and my aunt," he promised.

"*I* certainly didn't tell anyone," Collette assured them both. "Not a soul."

"It had to be Lucas," Emily concluded in shock. "He's the only one I told those things to. The reporter even quoted verbatim a phrase I'd used when I talked to Lucas about how sad I'd been."

As if on cue, Lucas's van drove up the driveway. Emily popped up from her chair. "Once he realizes I'm not at the cottage, he's going to come looking for me here. Please tell him I don't want to see him," she called as she headed toward the staircase so she could hide out in the spare room upstairs. "Not ever again!"

*

Emily appreciated it that whatever Wilson said to Lucas, he said it outside. She didn't want to be able to overhear him apologize because his words would be meaningless to her.

As it turned out, she needn't have worried; Collette later told her Wilson said Lucas denied doing anything wrong.

"You have got to be kidding me! How can anyone be such a liar?" Emily raged.

"The only explanation I can offer is generally the more someone has to lose, the bigger the lies they tell to keep it."

Collette invited Emily downstairs for a late supper, but Emily was too upset to eat. She was too upset to do anything except stare out the window and seethe. How could Lucas possibly deny telling the reporter her secrets? His own voicemail testified against him. "I'm afraid I may have revealed too much, but I figured you'd want me to be truthful," he'd said.

He probably wasn't expecting I'd get so angry—and that Wilson would get so angry, too. So now he's trying to take it back instead of owning up to it.

But why would he ever give a reporter all that information about her deepest personal struggles and most private family secrets—Wilson's too—in the first place? Emily couldn't believe Lucas didn't know her better than that by now.

Did he think it was okay to mention my broken engagement because I said I was over Devon? Did he take it to mean he could tell the journalist about Wilson being my brother because I said I was thrilled to have a nephew and I didn't care who heard us talking about it? she wondered. *Or was it that the journalist kept digging for information and Lucas let it slip?*

Emily finally decided it didn't matter *why* Lucas had told the reporter what he'd told him; it just mattered that he had. There was no taking it back. There was no making it right. What he'd done this time had crossed the line; it was unforgiveable.

"Do you mind if I spend the night here?" she asked when Collette came upstairs at around nine o'clock. "I'm afraid Lucas might return to the cottage to try to talk to me and I just can't handle it if he does."

"I wouldn't worry about that. As inflamed as Wilson was by that pipsqueak reporter, he was even more appalled that a grown man like Lucas didn't have the common sense—the common *decency*—to realize it was completely unacceptable for him to reveal what he did. If you can believe it, he actually tried to claim he thought he was being helpful by giving the reporter his personal take on you and your art. Wilson was so enraged he told him—well, let's just say Lucas won't be coming back anytime soon," Collette assured her. "But you're more than welcome to sleep here."

So Emily stayed the night, although she hardly slept a wink. Her mind kept churning and when it finally quieted enough for her to drift off, she dreamed Lucas was kissing her. The kiss was lingering and sweet but suddenly he had a five o'clock shadow and his stubble dug into her flesh, at first like a hog's hair bristle brush and then like barbed wire. She woke with a jolt, her hand touching where the wound on her chin used to be. The dream was so disturbingly symbolic she wouldn't let herself close her eyes again after that.

*

"I'm officially taking my maternity leave early," Collette announced the next morning when Emily came downstairs. "I had more Braxton-Hicks contractions last night and my feet are killing me."

Wilson was on his way out the door but he stopped and gave his wife a kiss on the cheek. "You two take care of each other today, okay? I'll call you at lunchtime but if you need me before then, promise you'll page me."

Emily regretted it that Wilson was worried about her; he had enough on his mind worrying about Collette, who looked even worse than Emily felt. Because she needed to diffuse her wrath and beating eggs seemed like a good outlet, Emily said she'd make breakfast. Meanwhile, Collette pushed herself back in the recliner, elevating her feet and snoozing off and on.

"Wow. This looks fantastic," she said when Emily brought her a plate of fruit and half of a veggie omelet.

"I don't think I can eat mine after all." Emily set her plate on the coffee table. "I need to pace. And vent again. Okay? Just whatever you do, please don't defend Lucas."

"Defend him? I'd still like to wring his neck. So you go right ahead and vent about him all you want. He has it coming."

Emily told her how furious, disappointed, hurt and exposed she felt. After she expressed everything she had to express, she rehashed it two or three more times. As Emily spoke, Collette made ardent declarations of anger. And when Emily was finally spent, Collette took over with a tirade of her own.

"I think you might be even angrier than I am," Emily said after Collette used a few choice words to describe Lucas.

"That's because the big, fat blabbermouth hurt *two* people I love. And that rag of a newspaper isn't any better. Wilson called them and lit into the editor. The journalist was just a kid, but they should have trained him better before they let him loose in public."

Emily giggled. "Yeah, otherwise some pregnant woman might sue him for causing her emotional distress."

"Did I really say that? I thought I did but I was so angry I couldn't remember and I didn't want to ask Wilson. But hey, it worked, didn't it?"

"That's because you, Collette, are one fierce mama bear."

As Emily reached to collect Collette's plate, the landline rang. Wilson was calling, exactly at noon. Collette asked if Emily would answer it, because she urgently had to go to the bathroom, but when she tried to push herself forward in the recliner, she couldn't budge.

"A little help here," she called.

Emily grabbed the phone with one hand and shoved the back of the recliner with the other, but only Collette's head jolted forward. She tried again and the same thing happened.

"I'm stranded!" Collette shouted. "I can't believe I'm actually stranded in a recliner!"

Their peals of laughter filled the room and—as it had done countless times this summer—made their difficult situation a little easier to endure.

If there was one thing Emily had learned about grief, it was that it came in waves. And, as in the ocean, sometimes the waves were billowing and foaming, sometimes they were uniform and constant and other times they were only an occasional blue curl. They were unpredictable, but they were always there.

Likewise, Emily's anguish over Lucas's betrayal ebbed and surged throughout the day as she helped Collette launder and fold the baby clothes she'd received at her shower and prepare lemon chicken for dinner. When Wilson returned from work, Emily excused herself to go to her cottage where she could be utterly alone with her thoughts.

After taking a shower, Emily pulled her suitcase from the closet so she could pack, since her flight left on Sunday. But the thought of leaving Dune Island—leaving the ocean and the cottage and Wilson and Collette and even the baby she had yet to meet—made her so sad that she yanked a brush through her wet, tangled hair and pulled on a pair of capris. She needed air, but before she scurried down the beach stairs, she dialed her voicemail to make sure the international students hadn't tried to get in touch with her before they departed, too. Emily had nine messages. The first was from Lucas the previous evening; she deleted it without listening. The same for the next three. The fifth was from the art department chair at the university.

"Emily, this is Nate Bosworth. Wanted to say how sorry we are you're not coming back this semester. But we wish you the best of luck. Take care."

Emily couldn't have heard him correctly. She sat down on the top of the staircase and listened to the message three more times. *Why in the world would he think I'm not coming back? I never told him that! I teach the same three courses every year.*

Emily had a horrible thought; they'd given her courses to another adjunct because of her subpar student evaluations last semester. *They should have at least had the decency to discuss it with me!* Her heart racing, she logged into her university email account to look up the number so she could call the dean of faculty.

Scrolling through her inbox, she saw she had twenty-eight messages from the human resources department with subject lines reading: ADJUNCT FACULTY COURSE SELECTION—DEADLINE AUGUST 21. If Emily hadn't already been sitting, she would have fallen down. She didn't have to open one of the auto-generated messages to know what it said.

At the end of the spring semester, the university had informed the faculty they were streamlining their scheduling process; going forward, adjuncts were required to register their intentions to teach and indicate their preferred courses in the new online system. It was the first time Emily hadn't signed a contract at the end of May for the fall semester and she'd totally forgotten about the change.

After all of my devotion for such a crummy salary and no benefits, I would have thought someone in HR would have given me a personal heads-up, she thought. But simultaneously, she acknowledged she couldn't fairly pin the blame on them. It wasn't the university's fault she hadn't checked her email all summer. How could she have been so careless? This was one hardship she was solely responsible for bringing upon herself. *Stupid, stupid, stupid.*

She logged out of her email and listened to another voicemail message but as soon as she heard Lucas's voice, she deleted it. She walked down the stairs and marched toward the west. The water was clear and the sky bright, but there was an early chill in the air that smacked of autumn. For as long as she could remember, September had signaled the start of the academic year for her, first as a student and then as an instructor. *What will I do now?* Emily wondered. She had absolutely no idea.

Yet somehow, she felt—not calm, by any stretch, but relieved. She recognized that by neglecting to return the contract on time, she—not the university—had made the decision that she wouldn't be teaching there that fall. It was a passive decision, but it was her decision all the same, one she'd made over the course of the summer without fully realizing she was making it.

It occurred to her that that's what had happened with Devon, too. He had been the one to call the wedding off. He had been the one to say the words, *Emily, it's time for us to let go and move on.* Words she'd translated to mean, *Emily, it's time for you to let go of your family, and for me to move on from you.* Regardless, she had passively opted out of marrying him long before then, just as she'd passively agreed to marry him when he first proposed.

Now she'd have to deal with the consequences of being unemployed, just like she'd had to face the truth about her relationship with Devon. It bothered her to realize that she hadn't been more direct about pursuing what she wanted. Or about saying no to what she didn't want. But in the end, she'd gotten what she subconsciously desired in both situations: a way out.

For the briefest second, she wondered if that was why Lucas had disclosed all of her private information to the reporter. Could *he* have subconsciously been looking for a way to sever their relationship? After all, given his family background, maybe a close, committed relationship was more intimacy than he was prepared to handle?

No. The idea was laughable—Lucas was too forthright for that. She knew she was clutching at straws, trying to understand why he'd betrayed her confidence in such a public way. It didn't make sense. There was just no accounting for why he'd done it. But neither was there any denying *that* he'd done it. She stopped and picked up a stone and flung it into the water, and then another and another. Emily screamed into the wind, imagining the sound traveling all the way to the horizon, which was where she wished she could run to at that moment.

When she turned to go back to the cottage, Emily was panicked to see Lucas on the beach at that hour, hurrying in her direction. There was nowhere to run and nowhere to hide, so she stood where she was, immovable. He kept coming, closer and closer until he was within arm's length.

"Emily, I—" he started to say but she shoved him away with her palms.

"How could you?" she screeched. "How could you do that to me?"

"I didn't, Emily. I swear, I didn't. Wilson told me what the journalist knew, but the kid didn't hear any of that from me."

"Don't lie, Lucas. You already confessed on my voicemail. Don't take it back now."

"What are you talking about?"

Emily imitated his voice, "I'm afraid I may have revealed too much, but I figured you'd want me to be truthful."

"You have got to be kidding me," Lucas intoned. "You honestly believe I would tell a reporter—tell *anyone*—such private things about you? And about Wilson? For your information, I told him I thought your work was breathtaking—and that I wasn't just saying that because we're seeing each other. *That's* what I meant when I said I was being truthful. When I said I may have revealed too much."

"The journalist told us his source was a doctor at the hospital. He quoted the exact phrase I used to tell you how horrible I felt. He used the phrase 'raw with grief.'" Emily was sobbing by then. "Lucas, please don't do this. If you started talking and got carried away, if you thought it was okay to say something about Wilson and me being siblings because I said I'm thrilled to have a nephew and don't care who knows—"

"Emily, I would never do that," Lucas promised, taking her hand. She wrenched it away. "You *did* do it!"

Lucas looked as if he'd been assaulted. "I am not the man you think I am," he said before stalking off.

CHAPTER FIFTEEN

"I can't believe you're really going tomorrow!" Collette was nearly on the brink of tears. "Are you positive you can't extend your stay a few days? I'd really like you to see the baby before you leave, and my female intuition tells me he's coming on Monday. It is Labor Day, after all."

Emily felt guilty when she stretched the truth, claiming she had some job-related things she was just notified about that she needed to address immediately. But she didn't want Wilson to worry about her being unemployed, nor did she want her situation to diminish Collette's anticipation about the impending birth. And, unless Lucas were to suddenly get a job off-island, she definitely didn't want either of them to try to convince her she could stay at the cottage permanently now that she wasn't teaching.

As Emily cleaned the cottage and continued packing, she thought about how adamantly Lucas had insisted he wasn't the one who told the journalist all those things about her. How he'd said, "I'm not the man you think I am." *Meaning what? That he's not like Devon? Or like Dad?* Or was he pointing out that because of them, Emily had a problem with trust?

That's not what this is about. It's that all the facts point to Lucas.

Emily picked the framed photo of her family off her nightstand and cushioned it in bubble packing. Then she wrapped her quahog shells in tissue paper as if they were fine china and rinsed the sand out of her swimsuit one last time before hanging it outside to dry.

She was just about to take a shower when Wilson came over, saying Tim had called their landline because he couldn't reach her and he needed to talk. Apparently, one of the technicians had scraped a long line of paint off the rainforest mural when he was moving a piece of equipment. Emily said she'd go right over to the hospital to take a look at it.

It turned out to be such a thin line it hardly showed. Emily decided it was better to leave it as it was than to risk the guests being exposed to fumes or brushing up against wet paint. *I guess I made a trip here for nothing*, she thought. Then she remembered she hadn't seen any of the paintings for the silent auction yet, so she ducked into the conference room being used as a makeshift gallery.

Hung from the walls were gorgeous watercolors and still-lifes, with a few abstract paintings mixed in. But Emily was most interested in seeing the one donated by Clive McGrath, the mysterious artist from New York, whose circumstances in many ways mirrored her own. She scanned the walls until she found it. Titled *Facing the Storm*, it was an oil painting of portentous clouds billowing over the ocean, which roiled tumultuously across the canvas toward the viewer.

Emily felt a pang of fear, knowing that the lightning a storm like this produced would terrify her in real life. The painting was so emotionally compelling and hauntingly familiar that she almost felt as if she recognized its physical location, too. She studied it further and noticed a small figure with her hands on her hips, facing the horizon. She was wearing a long black dress and her blonde hair danced frantically in the wind.

Emily tottered backward: *she* was the figure in the painting. But how could that have been? Then she remembered the artist on the cliff. Emily had seen the person's long, salt-and-pepper hair and assumed it was a woman, but people weren't always as they appeared. *Wow. Clive McGrath painted a portrait of me and he called it* Facing the Storm. The woman in the painting emanated such determination that Emily stood a little taller just by association.

With that in mind, she rushed home to change one of the lines in her remarks for the ribbon-cutting ceremony. After she'd showered and done her hair and makeup, Emily went next door. Collette was sitting on the couch, dressed in her baby shower dress and rubbing her stomach clockwise as she always did.

Wilson came into the room with the keys in his hand, ready to chauffeur them to the hospital. When he saw Emily, he remarked, "You look exactly like your mother."

"Thank you. I can't think of a better compliment."

"Are you nervous about your speech?"

"It's not really a speech, it's just a brief intro to the paintings. But yes, I'm so nervous I had to write it down. Will you take a look at it first, to make sure it sounds okay to you?"

While he was reading it, Collette comforted Emily, saying, "Don't worry, if you draw a blank, I'll pretend to go into labor to distract everyone."

*

The gala was held in the hospital's stately event room and when Wilson, Collette and Emily arrived, an attendant ushered them to their designated table near the podium. Tim and his wife, Caroline, were already seated and so was Lucas. He gave Wilson, Collette and Emily a terse hello before returning to a conversation with Tim. Since Emily and Lucas were each permitted to bring a guest, there were two empty seats between them, which still wasn't enough distance for Emily's comfort. She leaned forward so she could converse across the table with Caroline.

"When do you have to leave the island, Emily?"

"Tomorrow morning."

"You're aware a tropical storm is supposed to pass by the island overnight, aren't you? It's pretty far off-shore, but you'd better check the ferry service before you leave or you'll be stuck at the dock."

As Caroline was talking, a short brunette in a skirt and suit jacket made her way toward Lucas, who stood to embrace her. She kissed him on the cheek and then apologized for being late. Before Lucas could introduce her, the string quartet that had been performing in the back of the room stopped playing—Tim's cue to take the microphone.

Throughout dinner and the speeches, Emily experienced the same underwater sensation she felt when she first arrived on the island. All around her, people were clinking silverware against their dishes and laughing or applauding for the various speakers, doctors and donors, but she just wanted to vanish. If ever she thought about forgiving Lucas, that thought had passed. She couldn't believe he had the nerve to show up with a new woman on his arm, adding insult to injury.

Then she wondered if it wasn't a "new" woman, but the co-worker Collette once mentioned he used to date. Mid-meal, Emily slinked off to the restroom, where she stayed as long as she could before she knew Collette would come looking for her.

When she returned, dessert was being served and Tim asked Emily if she'd join him, Lucas and the other Board members for photographs. Emily reluctantly agreed. The newspaper photographer situated her next to Lucas and remarked, "Squeeze in, people—act like you actually enjoy each other's company."

Her arm scalded where it bumped against Lucas's skin and Emily slipped into the hallway after the first round of photos was snapped. Lucas followed her.

"Really, Emily?" he asked. "I'm so repulsive to you that you won't even stand next to me for a few photos?"

She opened her mouth to speak, when Lucas's date came around the corner. "Lu," the woman addressed him, "everybody's going to the children's wing now."

Emily took a sip of water from the nearby fountain and then trailed after them at a distance. She comforted herself with the thought, *Within twenty-four hours from now, I'll be three thousand miles away from him.* The time couldn't come quickly enough.

"Earlier this evening, we heard from our dedicated Board members, innovative doctors and generous donors who made this addition possible," Tim announced to the crowd of people gathered near the entrance to the wing. "Now it's my privilege to introduce you to the talented artist who transformed a sterile, clinical environment into one of beauty and peace. Please welcome Emily Vandemark."

After the applause died down, Emily began speaking, her voice aquiver. "Tim asked me to tell you a little bit about the source of inspiration for my murals. First and foremost, I was inspired by my parents, whose life work was teaching, helping and loving children all over the world, especially me and my two brothers, one of whom also chose a career working with kids and the other who is a doctor here at Hope Haven."

Emily felt a catch in her breath and she wasn't sure she could go on but she glimpsed Wilson standing on the left side of the corridor. For the first time, Emily noticed how much his smile resembled their father's smile. Or maybe it was the look of pride on his face that was so similar to their dad's. In either case, it heartened her. It made her feel as if her dad and mom and Peter were all there, too; as if they were all as proud of her as she was of them.

Her voice steadier now, she continued. "Their example inspired me to volunteer for the project in the first place and their travels, as well as my own, inspired several of the murals you'll see tonight.

"Of course, I was also inspired by the incredible beauty of Dune Island and I was encouraged by the people I've met here, especially those at Hope Haven Hospital. No one likes to be ill or in pain, but I can't think of a better place to recover. It's my hope that these murals will comfort, distract, amuse and engage Hope Haven's pediatric patients and their families and friends."

Emily stepped away from the mic but Tim led her back and vigorously shook her hand as the audience clapped and someone near the back whistled loudly. Before he handed the scissors to the donor who had been selected to do the honors, Tim reminded everyone that they had until midnight to bid—in person or online—on the paintings in the hospital gallery.

After the donor clipped the ribbon, the automatic doors flew open and everyone streamed past. Lucas's date tried to catch Emily's eye as she and Lucas entered, but Emily pretended not to notice. She stood to the side, waiting for Collette and Wilson. Some of the guests had brought their children, who flitted from room to room, beckoning, "Aw, cool, come see this," or "Look what's in this room!" After the last guest trickled in, Emily walked down the hall toward the main wing, wondering where Collette and Wilson were. Sara scuttled toward her.

"Am I glad to see you! Collette said to tell you your speech was perfect. But she's been admitted—she's having close contractions. She was just glad her water didn't break because she said she would've been mad at her son for ruining her favorite dress."

"Oh! I have to go see her!"

"You can't right now—she just kicked me out. Except for her labor and delivery team, Wilson is the only one she's allowing in until after the baby is born. Besides, she'll be upset if you miss the open house in the children's wing. Wilson gave me the keys to his car. I'm on a break right now, but after my shift ends, I'm supposed to drop you off at your cottage and pick up their overnight bags and the baby's car seat, bring them back here and then I'll drive home in my own car."

"Listen, you'll be too tired after working to drive back and forth between here and there. My part's done for the children's wing. Give me the keys and I'll go gather Collette and Wilson's things and bring their car back. When your shift ends, you can drop me off at the cottage on your way home. They never need to know—they've got bigger things on their minds right now."

On the way back to the house, Emily turned on the wipers to clear the windshield of a fine mist. A thick fog had rolled in, making it difficult to navigate the roads. She found it eerie being in Collette and Wilson's house without them. Fortunately, Collette was so organized that it was a cinch for Emily to locate the car seat and overnight bags.

When she delivered the items to the nurses' station, the nurse informed her Collette and Wilson were resting. "They've got a long night ahead of them."

"Could you please tell them I'll be back in the morning?" Emily planned to get up early enough so she could make it to the hospital and back before her taxi arrived.

Since she wasn't meeting Sara until eleven and it was only a little after ten o'clock now, Emily decided to browse through the gallery again. Most of the auction sheets had several bids in the $3,000 to $5,000 range, but when Emily read the sheet for Clive McGrath's painting, she noticed there was only a single bid for $5,000.

She was surprised no one had outbid that amount until she read the bid sheet again—it was actually for $15,000, made by an anonymous bidder. She examined the painting further, wondering if she was being narcissistic to imagine she was the figure represented in the foreground. It wasn't an exact likeness of her or of the landscape, so she still couldn't be absolutely positive; regardless, it made her happy the painting had brought in so much money for such a good cause.

When they pulled into the driveway, Emily emphasized to Sara how much she'd enjoyed getting to know her. In the foreground, a finger of lightning touched the ocean so Emily cut their conversation short and after a quick hug goodbye, she sprinted to the cottage, changed into her nightgown and dove beneath the covers.

Even if she hadn't been so wound up, Emily would have had a difficult time getting to sleep. The wind was howling and branches kept knocking against the roof. Rain bulleted the windows and lightning blazed so many times that she pulled her pillow over her head, too. When she did, something poked her cheek; Emily had forgotten she'd put it there for safekeeping. It was the piece of sea glass Lucas had given her.

She got up and switched on every lamp in the cottage in order to diminish the contrast between the darkness and the lightning and then she curled on the couch in the living room and tucked her knees to her chest. She buried her head in her arms, rocking ever so slightly until she fell asleep.

*

Woken by a choir of birds, Emily brushed her teeth, threw on her clothes and grabbed her purse and keys. She had planned to give the cottage a final cleaning before the taxi arrived to take her to the ferry, but her only priority right now was getting to the hospital.

It was still windy and mizzling but the air was nearly as hot and humid as it had been in late July. On the way to the car, Emily thought she heard thunder again until she realized it was the ocean, more turbulent than it had been all summer, pounding the shore.

She was already at the nurses' station when she realized she probably should have checked her messages before coming—it was possible Collette was still in labor and if not, she and Wilson might be resting. Even so, Emily wasn't about to leave the island without seeing them in person and she'd put up a fight if she had to. But the nurse told her they were in room 236 and after washing her hands, she could go ahead in to see them.

Emily rapped the door lightly before slowly pushing it ajar. Wilson was perched on the edge of the bed, his profile expressing admiration as he watched Collette, who adoringly coddled the baby to her breast. Emily paused to memorize the moment—she wanted it to be the next painting she created.

Collette lit up when she noticed Emily, and Wilson glanced over his shoulder, smiling. "Look who's here," Collette cooed. "It's your Aunt Emily."

Emily came closer, bending to admire the baby's brown peach fuzz head and his pink fingers like tiny earthworms. "And what should I call you, little one?"

"His first name is Michael, after my mother." Wilson cleared his throat. "And we'd like his middle name to be Peter, if that's okay with you."

"His namesake would be honored," Emily responded.

*

When the doctor came in to examine Collette, Emily walked to the lobby and listened to her voicemail. There was a message from Wilson at 2:30 a.m. announcing that the baby had arrived and he and Collette were doing well.

Then Collette came on the line saying, "So much for women's intuition—he came a day earlier than I thought he would. Now that I've seen him, I'm so glad I didn't have to wait another minute. I can't wait for you to see him, too."

Emily inhaled deeply, her eyes clouding at the thought of how much Michael Peter Laurent would change and grow before the next time she saw him. Her phone vibrated in her hand and she answered it without looking at the display screen.

A male's voice asked, "Emily?"

She had a momentary notion that it was Lucas, calling to say goodbye. Or calling to apologize and to try to convince her to stay. "Yes, this is Emily speaking," she replied expectantly.

"This is Island Cab. I'm sorry to say that due to the off-shore tropical storm, ferry service is suspended until further notice. Judging from the surf, I'd guess that won't be for another twelve hours."

Dazed, Emily wasn't sure if she wanted to yelp for joy or if this only prolonged the inevitable. She called the airline and rebooked her flight for Tuesday, since classes would have begun on Wednesday and she didn't want Collette and Wilson to be suspicious if she stayed longer than that. Then she went to tell them about the change in her departure date.

"Now you can show Michael his nursery on Monday!" Collette exclaimed, trying to stifle a yawn. Thirty seconds later, she was softly snoring.

"I'll let you two boys rest, too," Emily said to Wilson, who was cupping Michael's head with his hand. "Call me if you need me to bring anything else, okay?"

As Emily was leaving the maternity ward, Gail passed her in the main corridor and said she'd heard the great news about Collette and Wilson's baby, as well as how successful the auction and ribbon-cutting ceremony were. She handed Emily a newspaper so she could see the coverage for herself and then, like Sara had done, gave her a hug goodbye.

Hoping that whatever journalist wrote the article wasn't anything like the one from the *Gazette*, Emily sat on a bench and began reading:

On Saturday night, guests at the ribbon-cutting ceremony for Hope Haven Hospital's new children's wing enjoyed a feast for their eyes as well as their palates. After a dinner of steak, seafood and cranberry cobbler, the attendees moved down the corridor to view the creative touches Seattle artist Emily Vandemark brought to the walls of the children's wing.

The family room welcomes patients and visitors with an assortment of painted details hinting at what can be found when guests follow the illustrated footprints through the corridor.

Each of the patient rooms displays a full wall mural featuring the scenery and plant and animal life of a different ecosystem; for example, there's an ocean room, a rainforest room and a desert room, among others.

In the girls' bathroom, mermaids dive behind the mirrors or swim side by side with seals across the walls. The boys' bathroom is painted with bold pirates who surf oversized waves and reel in flounder and toothless sharks on their fishing lines.

Compliments from spectators ranged from, "She has a botanist's eye" to "This is absolutely magical."

Perhaps the best compliment came from the young girl who was overheard asking her parents, "When do I get to stay at the hospital?"

Emily was delighted by the write-up. She turned the page to a centerfold photo spread of the evening's events. The first one she noticed was a darling picture of Caroline and Collette, whose head was thrown back in laughter—that must have been before her contractions came on full force. There were several photos of donors and guests, a group shot of the Board and a picture of the ribbon being cut.

There was a variety of pictures of the children's wing, too, with onlookers gazing and smiling. Her favorite was of a small girl standing with her mouth agape in front of a detail of a butterfly. She was reaching one finger toward it, as if she believed it might actually alight on her hand.

In the bottom left-hand corner of the page, Emily spotted a photo of herself with Lucas and Tim. Wearing the same dress she'd worn the first day she'd met them at the hospital, she was grimacing, one arm bent across her stomach as she leaned away from Lucas, who looked at her instead of the camera.

Ever since the day she'd asked him to stop visiting her in the children's wing, Emily had fantasized about how proud of her Lucas would be when he saw the final murals. She imagined his bright eyes and animated smile when he recognized he'd been the inspiration behind the pirate and flounder and shark illustrations. But in the photo, a crushed expression shadowed his face. Emily only wavered a moment before she closed the paper and chucked it into the recycling bin.

On her way to the cottage, Emily stopped for groceries so she could make meals for Wilson and Collette and stock their fridge before they returned home. Because of the holiday weekend, traffic was slower than usual and by the time she arrived at the cottage, it was after noon. Realizing she'd have more room to cook at Wilson and Collette's, Emily brought all the bags into their kitchen. After putting the food away, she walked over and lifted Wilson's medical school graduation photo from the bookshelf.

"The baby came today. His name is Michael Peter Laurent and he's the most beautiful creature I've ever seen," she said aloud conversationally, as if her family was waiting to hear this news.

On the shelf above the photos, she noticed Wilson's binoculars and suddenly she had an irrepressible impulse: the cliff-side artist usually painted on drizzly days like this. She was going to try to find out for certain whether he was Clive McGrath. Emily clumped down the beach to the west, realizing that she, of all people, shouldn't stalk another artist, but her curiosity got the best of her. The wind was so strong it whipped the sand like a hundred little needles into her calves and her hair blew in spikes across her face.

When she was close enough to the cottage to focus the binoculars without being too obvious, she sat down in the sand casually, just in case the artist could see her, too. She made a visual sweep of the cliff. Although the binoculars were so powerful she could actually make out the lines between the bricks on the cottage chimney, she didn't see anyone on the dunes.

Disappointed, she was about to rise when there was a flash of white within the beach grass. She zoomed in on the figure, who appeared to be shaking a rug over the dune. The person was turned and Emily could only see a mop of white hair; she couldn't discern any features from that angle. When a gust of wind ripped the rug away and the person stooped to grab it, Emily saw without a doubt that a long, unkempt beard sprouted from his chin. *People aren't always who they seem to be on the surface*, she reminded herself.

As Clive McGrath straightened his posture, he looked straight in Emily's direction, so she quickly pretended to search the water to the east instead. As she was peering through the binoculars, she noticed something in the water—was it a small seal, a pup? A wave crashed over its dark torso and she realized it was too slender to be a seal. It was a surfer. Lucas. It was Lucas. Emily lowered the binoculars.

She couldn't imagine swimming in those waters; that particular sandbar was rough enough on an ordinary day, but how many times had Lucas described how much he loved surfing in post-storm waves? *He has some nerve coming here after both Wilson and I made it clear he wasn't welcome*, she thought. Then she wondered if she assumed she'd left for Seattle already and he knew Collette and

Wilson weren't home, either. To be sure it was him, she looked through the binoculars again.

It was definitely Lucas; who else could it be on this private land? Besides, just like his van, his bright yellow surfboard gave him away. He'd let the kids from the city camp emblazon their handprints on it in a rainbow of hues. "They're hang tens," he'd explained. "They're like high fives or fist bumps for surfers."

Terrific. Now how was Emily going to sneak past him to the beach stairs without being seen? She decided she'd just have to wait until he left. She covered her ears against the wind and dug her toes into the sand. Although Lucas never wore a full wetsuit, he didn't get cold easily and with the air being so balmy, Emily figured it would be a long time before he got out of the water and went home.

She honed in on him with the binoculars once again, just as a huge wave pummeled him from behind. Lucas sailed off his board and was buried by the froth. His board rocketed to the surface a few seconds later, but Emily didn't see him anywhere. She dropped the binoculars, which hung from a cord and they banged against her chest. She stood, ran a few steps, then stopped and raised them to her eyes again.

Where was he? Should she get help? Would Clive McGrath have a telephone? Paralyzed, Emily froze in place. This was where the rip currents were. Lucas knew that; like Collette and Wilson, he had warned her about this area. He'd even instructed her what to do if she was ever caught in a rip current. Emily scanned the deeper water in both directions. No Lucas. She broke out in a cold sweat. The clouds were white, the surf was white, there was too much white. And then, there was a dot of dark; Lucas's head popped above the surface. A few seconds later, he was standing, shaking water from his ear. Then he dove forward and swam several yards to retrieve his surfboard before staggering toward shore.

Emily collapsed onto the sand as if she were the one who'd just been thrashed by the sea. She covered her face with her arm and when she wept, she wept from pure gratitude and joy. By the time she caught her breath and sat up again, Lucas was gone.

If I don't forgive him, then I'm not my mother's daughter, she thought.

She didn't remember running down the beach and getting into her car, nor did she remember exactly how she traversed the unpaved roads leading to Lucas's house. She only knew that she was there and she was banging on his door. His hair was still wet and matted when he opened it. If he was surprised to see her, he didn't say it. He didn't say anything.

"I've already lost three of the people I love most in this world—I don't want to lose you, too," Emily rasped. "I'm sorry for being so unforgiving."

"I don't need your forgiveness I need your trust," Lucas replied, his voice gravelly. "Because I didn't tell your secrets to that journalist or to anyone else."

As Emily peered into Lucas's eyes, which were the same brooding blue of the storm in Clive McGrath's painting, she saw him for the man he was. The patient, understanding, trustworthy man he'd been since the first day she met him. And despite all the outward evidence—all outward *appearances*—to the contrary, she was inexplicably certain he was telling the truth.

"I know you didn't, Lucas."

Lucas pulled his head back as if he hadn't heard right. "Why? Why do you suddenly believe me now?"

"Because I know what kind of man you are," she said. "And you're absolutely right—you don't need my forgiveness. I need yours. I'm so sorry for losing sight of who you are. No matter how long or what it takes, I'll do anything to make things right between us again. Will you give me another chance? Please?"

Lucas answered by drawing her to his chest. "You're trembling," he murmured.

They embraced each other so fiercely that Lucas said he could feel Emily's heart beating against his chest. He stroked her hair until her pulse stopped racing and her muscles relaxed against his.

"I'm thirsty," she said. "Can I come in and have a drink of water?"

"Yeah, well," Lucas hesitated. "There's something in there that I'm kind of concerned about you seeing. I don't want you to take it the wrong way or to think I'm creepy or to get angry at me."

At first she thought he was kidding. She couldn't imagine what he'd have to hide. Then she remembered. "Is it your date from last night?"

"My date?" Lucas repeated. "Emily, you nut, that was my sister. She was visiting from Boston. In fact, you're the reason I invited her to come to the ceremony. I realized I've always taken it for granted that I had a sister. We're not that close, but seeing how much you miss your brother and your parents...I figured maybe it was time to work on my relationship with my family. I also wanted her to meet you."

"So she's inside?"

Lucas screwed up his face and pinched the top of his nose as if he had a headache. "No. She only came for the evening. But

I might as well let you see what's in here now, since you'll see it eventually anyway."

Lucas opened the door and Emily looked in. Leaning against the wall was the Clive McGrath painting, *Facing the Storm*.

Emily clapped her hand to her mouth. "You were the highest bidder?"

Lucas nodded.

"Lucas, that's amazingly generous of you. I'm absolutely floored." Emily paused before she spoke again, in awe of this man she was growing to love more and more each moment. "I know how humble you are, so I can understand why you'd bid on this anonymously, but why were you concerned I'd see this and think you're a creep?"

"Not a creep, but creepy. Voyeuristic or something," he abashedly suggested. "Don't you see it? The figure is turned. She's mysterious. She isn't going to let you into all of her secrets at once, but you can tell just by looking at her how strong she is. It's all right there in her stance, in the way she's facing the storm. It's why I fell in love with you. It *is* you. I'd recognize you anywhere."

Once again, Lucas proved to be so perceptive that Emily melted with attraction for him. She had never felt so intimately known by any man she ever dated, and instead of causing her to retreat, it made her want to draw even closer.

"Did you just say you fell in love with me?" she marveled.

Lucas nodded, his cheeks going red. "Is that, uh, is that okay with you?"

"Okay? No. It's *wonderful*. Especially since I'm in love with you, too, Lucas."

*

"I can hardly tear my eyes away from him," Collette said the next morning as she gazed at her son breastfeeding. "He was worth every second of the agony he put me through during delivery. I'm telling you, Emily, I didn't know I had it in me to be that strong. I will never criticize this incredible body of mine again."

"Can I quote you on that?" Emily joked as Wilson came back into Collette's hospital room with a cup of coffee in hand. "Oh, I'm glad you're here, Wilson. There's something I want to talk to both of you about. I've changed my travel plans."

"You're not leaving tomorrow, are you?" Collette whined.

"No, I'm not leaving…at all. I've decided to stay on the island for the year."

Collette gave the baby a start when she squealed. She soothed him until he latched on again. "That's great," she whispered.

"It sure is." Wilson touched a fingertip to his son's soft hair and his expression made Emily think of the photo of Michelle holding *him* when he was a baby.

She told them about what happened with her adjunct position at the university in Seattle. She added that Lucas had told her Tim said after the ribbon-cutting ceremony one of the guests was so impressed she asked if Emily would consider teaching art to children. Apparently, the man who had accepted the position as artist-in-residence in the public schools relocated off-island at the last minute to care for an ailing parent. The position was Emily's, if she wanted it.

"I can't wait to show Lucas I have just as good rapport with kids as he does," she joked.

"So you've...spoken to Lucas recently?" Collette asked and Emily noticed Wilson's jaw tense.

"Yeah. He forgave me, so we're seeing each other again."

"*He* forgave *you*? For what?"

"Essentially, for calling him a liar," Emily replied.

Wilson cleared his throat. "If it wasn't him, then who was the doctor who told the journalist—"

"I don't know. But I know it wasn't Lucas."

"How can you be so sure?"

"The same way you were so sure Dad didn't know you were his son," Emily insisted. "I know because I know Lucas, and he's not that kind of man."

Wilson and Collette exchanged a look, but Emily figured in time, they'd forgive him, too, because that's the kind of people *they* were.

"Your mother is still welcome to stay with me at the cottage when she comes to help out with the baby," Emily offered Collette. "I can get beds for the rooms upstairs and she can choose which one she wants. It has always sort of depressed me to see the bedrooms so bare anyway."

"That's really generous of you, but I think it may have hurt her feelings when we suggested she stay in the cottage. I think she felt like she was being banished or something."

"Yeah, but that was before I renovated the dungeon. When she sees it now, she might reconsider. Especially if Michael's voice is as loud as his mother's," Emily teased.

*

The Saturday after Labor Day, Emily hosted a small gathering for lunch at the cottage. She dubbed it a homecoming, in reference both to Michael's birth and to her returning to Dune Island for good, but mostly it was just an excuse to show her family and friends she appreciated them.

As she was vacuuming in preparation for her guests' arrival, she noticed something shiny beneath the bed near the nightstand. It was a blue topaz earring and it looked familiar but it wasn't hers, as she hadn't brought any jewelry to the island.

Assuming it must have been Collette's, she set it aside to give to her later but suddenly it struck her where she'd seen it: the earring was Barbara Reed's. *When was she ever in my cottage?* Then Emily remembered she'd allowed guests to use her bathroom the day of the shower. Barbara must have come into her room, the little snoop. Emily's stomach dropped as she realized, *She must have been there the whole time I was talking to Julia—she probably overheard every word we said!* She *was the doctor who told the journalist about Wilson and me!*

But that didn't make sense because the journalist also knew about Devon breaking up with her, and Emily hadn't mentioned a word about him to Julia. Nor had she used the phrase, "raw with grief," like she had when she and Lucas were arguing in the hospital parking lot.

Oh! Emily covered her mouth with both hands as she recalled nearly hitting Barbara with her car afterward. *I'd been shouting so loud, she must have heard every word I said.*

Incensed, Emily pinched the earring from the floor, clenching it so tightly in her fist the earring dug into her palm as she charged out the door and over the dunes to the staircase. She strode down the beach to the east, mulling over the significance of what she'd discovered.

Mortified to realize she initially blamed Lucas for something Barbs had done, Emily imagined dangling the earring in front of Barbara's nose and saying, *I believe this belongs to you*, just to watch her squirm. But Barbara had already left the island. Besides, as livid as she was, deep down Emily recognized that she would have had no one to blame but herself if she had walked away from her relationship with Lucas. It would have been her own fault if she had allowed distrust to ruin one of the best things that had happened to her since the accident. No; one of the best things that had happened to her, *period*.

Approaching the inlet, she pulled the hood of her sweatshirt tight around her ears. The air was cooler and the September light turned the water a darker shade of blue than when she first arrived on the island, but the beauty of the seascape continued to inspire emotional clarity. Walking along the curve of the shoreline, she resolved not to waste even another minute of her life with any ill-will toward Barbara. She cast the earring as far into the depths as she could.

Then Emily rushed back to tell Collette and Wilson, who were as outraged as she had been.

"Didn't I tell you she was a hurricane waiting to happen?" Collette asked.

"Cardiology made the right decision when we chose the other resident," Wilson remarked. "But I've made a huge mistake about Lucas."

"Me, too," Collette chimed in.

"He's coming early to help me set up for the party if you want to talk to him then. I think he'll understand. He's very forgiving."

In addition to Lucas, Wilson, Collette, and baby Michael, Emily had invited Sara, Liz and Gail and their husbands, and

Tim and his wife Caroline to the party. It was a breezy day, but warm, so between the cottage and the deck, there was room for everyone.

"That is gorgeous," Gail said, pointing to the round, eight-light brushed nickel chandelier hanging above the dining-room table. It had green and blue beach glass adorning its rim and even though it was daytime, Emily had switched it on so the glass would sparkle in the light.

"Thank you. I just got it this week and Lucas hung it for me."

Sara came down from checking out the color of paint Emily had used in the upstairs bedrooms. "I love the antique cradle you have up there."

"It's the one I used to play with when I was a girl. I figure now it will make a cozy bed for Michael to sleep in if I'm babysitting," Emily said just to get a reaction from Wilson.

"I doubt that cradle meets safety standards," he predictably objected and Collette and Emily immediately burst into laughter.

"I was kidding, Wilson. I'm using it to put my art books in."

"I wonder if Michael will take after his auntie and become an artist or be like his parents and go into medicine," Sara said.

Between Emily's remarks at the ribbon-cutting ceremony and individual conversations with their friends, all of the guests knew that Emily and Wilson were siblings. Everyone had either expressed excitement about Wilson and Emily's discovery or they'd simply taken the information in stride. Their reactions—or lack of reactions—made Emily realize she'd worried unnecessarily about having to field meddlesome questions.

"Maybe he'll go into an entirely different field," Lucas suggested. "You never know. He might want to become a professional surfer. I could help him get an early start."

"Don't you dare joke about bringing my baby out on your board," Collette warned Lucas.

"Which baby? Michael or Wilson?" Lucas countered.

Hearing their cheeky but affectionate banter made Emily smile, because she knew it meant Lucas had been as gracious about accepting Collette and Wilson's apologies as he'd been about accepting Emily's, and everything was back to normal between them again.

Emily went into the kitchen to take out the cake, as well as sparkling cider or champagne for those who wanted it.

"This is a great cottage. I heard you might be interested in selling it at some point?" Liz's husband remarked as he helped Emily by pouring the drinks.

"I'm afraid that's not true. I could never sell this place. It's my home. It's my *family's* home." *My past, present and future family's home—from Grandma and Grandpa all the way to Michael. Maybe even to my own children, one day.*

"I understand. It must contain a lot of memories."

"Some of the best," she acknowledged. *And now it contains a lot of hope, too.*

Once everyone had been served, Emily announced she had something to say. Suddenly, she felt even more nervous than she'd felt before the ribbon-cutting ceremony, but when Lucas winked at her, she stood taller and began by telling everyone there how much she appreciated having them in her life.

"As many of you know by now, about a year ago I lost my father, my mother and my brother. I lost my fiancé, too, but that turned out to be for the better." Emily chuckled nervously along with the others before turning serious again.

"When I came back to Dune Island for the summer, I was a broken shell of a person. I didn't think I'd ever—I didn't think I'd ever feel whole again."

Emily had to stop to modulate her voice and when she glanced at Collette, she noticed she'd tucked her chin to her chest and Emily couldn't tell if she was gazing at Michael in her arms or trying to hide her expression or both.

"There are moments and hours and even days when I still feel completely fragmented, but there aren't as many of them in a row as there used to be. Now I'm able to experience moments and hours and days of joy, too. Plus, I can paint again—and I can socialize and I'm sleeping and eating a lot better, too. In part, that's because being here in this cottage, and walking on the beach my family relished so much, brings them back to me. And although the three family members I've lost are irreplaceable, I've found three others—my brother and sister-in-law and nephew—to love and to be loved by."

"Do you mean the same sister-in-law who is raining on her son?" Wilson cut in, referring to Collette, who was definitely weeping as she bent over Michael.

"Shush, Wilson, or *you'll* be raining," Collette threatened, waving her hand at him and providing a moment of levity.

When the guests stopped laughing, Emily said, "I'm so grateful to my newfound family and to you, my newfound friends, for sharing your humor, as well as your pain with me. For being so open and encouraging and kind. Especially you, Lucas, for demonstrating more patience than I deserved."

"You're worth it," he replied, meeting her eyes.

Emily was feeling weepy again so she looked away. Addressing everyone, she ended by saying, "So thank you—*all* of you—for helping me find my way back from grief."

Ironically, when Emily finished speaking, the baby was the only one in the room without tears in his eyes.

"To family and friends, old and new," Liz toasted.

"To finding our way back," Sara added.

"And to coming home," someone else chimed in.

"Hear, hear!"

After they'd emptied their glasses and eaten their cake, Lucas pulled Emily into the downstairs bedroom and closed the door.

"What you said out there was beautiful," he told her. "But I'm surprised you shared it. You're a real mystery, you know it?"

"Mm, you may have mentioned that before." Emily interlaced her fingers behind his neck and stood on tiptoe to give him a long, warm kiss. "But I like hearing it again and I hope you never stop thinking of me that way."

Lucas's wide grin lit his face. "Not going to happen, Em," he said.

A Letter from Kristin

I can't tell you how much I appreciate it that you read *Summer at Hope Haven*—thank you! Emily's story was a pleasure to write and I hope it was a pleasure for you to read.

One of the reasons I enjoyed writing this book so much is because even though the setting is fictitious, it reminds me of one of my favorite places in the world. As I was writing, I could imagine myself sitting on the deck of Emily's cottage and I hope as you read the book you felt transported to Dune Island, too.

Do you have a special place you visit when you need to contemplate or nurture your creativity or simply relax? Like Emily, I'm inspired by beautiful seascapes and long walks on the beach, which always encourage me as a writer. The other thing that always encourages me is when a reader loves my book and takes the time to tell me and to tell others about it.

If you loved *Summer at Hope Haven*, it would mean the world to me if you'd write a review. I'd value hearing your thoughts, and you'd be helping new readers to discover one of my books for the first time.

It delights me to hear from readers, so please feel free to get in touch on Twitter, Goodreads or my website.

Thanks,
Kristin Harper

@KHarperAuthor

www.kristinharperauthor.com

Acknowledgments

It's a privilege to thank my publisher for its innovation, expertise, and uniqueness. I can't express enough how amazing it is to have the Bookouture team behind me. I particularly appreciate Ellen Gleeson for seeing the potential in my manuscript and helping shape it into the novel it is now. Also, a huge thank-you to the team at Forever.

I'm forever grateful to my family, who has supported my creative pursuits in countless ways and for many years; I especially owe a world of gratitude to my parents and my sisters. But thank you *all* for understanding, encouraging and inspiring me.

My thanks to JA for the opportunity to stay on Martha's Vineyard, which helped spark my imagination for this novel, and to those kindred spirits who enjoy two of my favorite passions—writing and Cape Cod.

Finally, thank you to LC for spurring me on to finish this book.